Park Lane South, Queens

Park Lane South, Queens

Mary Anne Kelly

ST. MARTIN'S PRESS NEW YORK

M

2-90BT 1700

 For information, address St. Martin's Press, 175 Fifth Avenue, New York, N.Y. 10010.

Design by Judy C. Dannecker

Library of Congress Cataloging-in-Publication Data

Kelly, Mary Anne.
Park Lane South, Queens.
p. cm.
"A Thomas Dunne book."
ISBN 0-312-03907-7
I. Title.
PS3561.E3946P37 1990 813'.54—dc20 89-24094

First Edition

10 9 8 7 6 5 4 3 2 1

For Tommy

CHAPTER

There were no stars as thick as bedbugs over Richmond Hill. There was only a moon. All you could hear were the faraway clunks of the avenue el, the spurt of the radio squad car parked halfway up Bessemer, and the dark, runny lull of the woods still alive with raccoon.

Eleven miles and ten thousand light years from Manhattan, elderly front porches throned inbred and bigboned cats who looked up nervously, then yawned with affectation when an ugly black runt-legged dog made his rounds industriously through the backyards and the tilted streets.

Dubbed by all as the Mayor, the dog patrolled the trestle tracks for female scent, investigated any unlocked garbage pails along his way, enjoyed a clandestine and cooling drink from Mrs. Dixon's controversial Roman birdbath, and then headed north along old Park Lane South, going no farther in than the rim of the woods (there were things going on in there even he didn't want to know about). Finally, back he waddled to his own front porch, job done, neighborhood checked, home just in time for the blue-bellied dawn climbing over the pin oak.

Claire Breslinsky, slender and still beautiful at thirty, slept soundly in the hammock on the porch. The Mayor padded over, cocked his head, and watched, deliberating whether or not to jump right up and nestle in. Claire's hair, loosened in sleep, was dark as chestnut and the briney bitches of his youth. He sighed. That was years ago. He'd put on quite a bit of weight since then and doubtless he would wake up Claire. That wouldn't do. Although she'd just returned to Queens from ten years overseas and he had only known her briefly as a pup, he felt a fond attachment to her. Claire's accent didn't bother him. He was English bulldog–blooded himself. At least a good part of him was. He liked her foreign ways. And at meals she fed him every bit of her meat beneath the table. Mother and Pop Breslinsky (or Mary and Stan, as he chose to think of them, with all due respect) said she had spent some years in India to boot. That would explain it.

Claire stirred. The first shaft of light had hit her on the face. She looked right at him with those eyes queerly bright and blue as the Lanergan's Siberian husky.

"Ah," her deep voice cracked, "good morning, your honor."

The Mayor joggled his tail to and fro. He bolted directly onto her breast and slurped her broad mouth with his tongue. Claire pushed him firmly off her face but let him stay right there, her soft hand buried in the bristly fur of his fighter's broad back. She put her leg out onto the porch railing and rocked the two of them back and forth, back and forth. There was no wind today. It would be hot.

They looked up and watched the garbage truck come lumbering up the block. Mrs. Dixon next door stretched her terry bathrobe around herself one extra time, slammed down the can lid, and waddled briskly back inside her house. No garbagemen were going to see *her* front without a sturdy brassiere. Of that they could be sure. Some things, Claire smiled, never changed. Then a decrepit Plymouth rattled down the broken street from Park Lane South and turned left onto Myrtle. And back they fell to sleep.

The old house was still for just a little while. Mary Breslinsky, up with the birds, was quick in and out of the shower and down to squeeze oranges, poach eggs, pop the toast in. News radio accompanied her as she went about with her transistor in one apron pocket, rosary in the other, eyes wide for any international catastrophe (Claire was finally safe at home, thank God, but still she liked to be the first to hear of any tragedy). The white braids curled around her neat head would quiver with excitement at just any break in a major criminal event. She'd clear her throat and store this or that away for announcement at the table. She was Irish, was Mary.

Before you knew it, she had the marmalades lined up like soldiers: blueberry for her husband Stan, apricot for raven-haired Carmela (her eldest and her fashion columnist), orange for Claire (her long-lost wandering photographer come home at last), grape for Zinnie (her good humoured, blond policewoman) and mint (again) for Michaelaen (Zinnie's son and his grandma's own miracle, just four years old and russet-haired like Claire used to be). Her husband Stan referred to them as his Clairol Group, and so they did look when you got them all together around the table.

Stan Breslinsky, hardware store proprietor (semiretired), weapons enthusiast, and passionate lover of opera, shaved to the strains of *Rigoletto*. He hummed along. He took his time. He warbled and lingered until the last pretty notes of "La Donna E Mobile" came to a halt. Reverently, he put away his Sony tape recorder and descended the stairs for the kitchen. A spider as big as your thumb scooted down the bannister behind him.

Mary was at the *Daily News*, checking off her Wingo numbers. She played all the Zingos, Wingos, and Lottos. Each morning brought another chance to win a million. Her corner of the table by the stove was cluttered with all kinds of tickets, bingo circulars, crossword puzzles, coupons, and contests for prizes like a fun-filled trip to Atlantic City. Stan waited for her to be finished with the *News* and move on to the *Post*. Then he could have all his favorite funnies. The *Times* was lying there unopened (nobody read that thing but Carmela) and so was *Newsday*, the one they all read while waiting for the *News* or the *Post* to be free.

"Good morning, dear." He kissed her on the cheek.

"They caught that fellow who was robbing all the 7-Elevens," Mary said. "About time, too. He's been busy as a widow at the fair."

Stan reached into Mary's apron pocket and switched the news channel of the radio over to WQXR, the classical station, then took his seat.

"Is today league day?" They bowled together on Tuesdays and Wednesdays, then again with the league every Friday.

"Sure." She looked at him over the tops of her reading glasses. "You might want to put your bermudas on. News says it's going to be a scorcher."

"Claire's bed is empty. She sleep out on the porch again all night?"

"Mmm."

Stan shook his head. He sipped his juice and Mary handed him the *News*.

"You give it back before Carmela gets it. She'll do the crossword out from under me."

In marched Michaelaen, stark naked and transporting a truck in one downy arm.

"Back in your room and don't come out without your shorts." Mary reached for the scissors and began her coupon clipping. Michaelaen returned in a moment wearing nice plaid bathing trunks. He went out the screen door and into the yard to go check on his rabbits. Zinnie came in, her short blond curls spilling this way and that, and kissed her parents good morning, all the while busily at work with a nail file.

Mary put a glass of juice down in front of her. "No guns at the table, officer."

Zinnie removed her pistol and stuck it on top of the refrigerator. She yawned and eyed the *News* in her father's hands.

Michaelaen, satisfied that his rabbits had lived through the night (no small feat with all the raccoon about), returned and climbed onto Zinnie's lap. She spread his green mint jelly onto a piece of white bread, folded it over, and pushed it into his little mouth. He cradled his truck and chewed.

Carmela entered crisply, her usual forboding self without her coffee, so no one greeted her yet. Neat as a pin, her black hair coiled in a knot at the nape of her neck, Carmela buried herself behind the *Times*. She swallowed a series of pills: lecithin, rose hips, brewer's yeast, and silica, a round of B's, a multi, an E, and an unscented garlic. (In the winter she included cod liver oil.) She sloshed this parade down with one long gulp of black coffee.

A sirening cop car raced down Eighty-fourth Avenue and up to the woods.

"Gee, that's close," said Mary. "I hate sirens." She loved them, really, but she didn't think she should.

"Anybody got 'Dear Abby'?" asked Zinnie.

A resounding belch from the *Times* alerted them that Carmela was now awake, aware, and prepared for verbal exchange. "Jesus," she swore at a picture of a rather mannish-looking female politician. "Who the hell does this friggin upstart think she is."

"She needs a good slam bam in the thank you, ma'am," Zinnie agreed. "Is Claire out on the porch? What does she think, she's still in the Himalayas? You'd better tell her, Mom. She can't sleep out there."

"Why not?" Carmela arched one well-plucked brow. "I'm sure she's only levitating."

"Better," Stan said, "she sleeps on the porch than over there in God knows where with God knows whom."

"Hear that?" said Zinnie. "Another siren."

"They both seem to have stopped by the monument," Stan lifted an ear and strained to look outside.

"It's probably crack smokers, again," Mary decided.

"Too early in the morning for crack smokers," Zinnie

said knowingly. "And anyway, no one wastes sirens on crack smokers." She took a bottle of clear nail polish out of her trousers pocket and repaired a chip. "What's Claire doing wandering around the woods by herself? Mrs. Dixon says she's always in the woods."

"Taking pictures," Mary sighed. "What else?"

"Well, tell her she can't just sashay through the woods around here anymore. This neighborhood isn't what it used to be."

"You tell her," Stan said. "She listens to you."

"I already told her not to sleep in the hammock. So where is she? Sleeping in the hammock."

"She does have the dog out there," Mary pointed out.

"Hah," Carmela snorted. "A lot of good he'll do her. He's off half the night looking for girls."

"He sure is," reflected Stan with a touch of pride.

"You wouldn't think he could still get it up at his age," Carmela mused out loud.

"Carmela!" Mary waggled her head. "Such thoughts!"

Zinnie looked up from her manicure. "Aw, c'mon ma. We're grown-up, divorced women."

"Well, I'm not divorced. Neither is your father and neither is Michaelaen. Majority rules."

"I am too divorced," insisted Michaelean.

"Oh, yeah?" Zinnie shook him around on her lap. "Where's ya papers, huh?"

"Claire's not divorced, either," Carmela added, somewhat viciously, for they all knew that Claire had been "involved" with two different men, neither of whom she'd told them much about.

"The last one was a duke, you know," Zinnie, still impressed, reminded them.

"That and a token will get you on the subway," Carmela said.

Zinnie helped herself to another poached egg. "A hell of a lot more interesting than that dip shit accountant you were married to."

"At least Arnold didn't live off my money, like hers did."

"Right. He left you so well off. That's why he's got a house in Bayside and you're back in Richmond Hill with us."

"Arnold might be tight," Carmela smiled, "but he never took it in the kicker."

"Now, girls."

"That's ok, Mom," Zinnie shrugged. "It wasn't Freddy's fault he turned out gay. And it wasn't mine, either."

Mary frowned. "Well, then, at least not in front of Michaelaen."

"I don't know why the hell not," Zinnie buttered her English muffin. "At least when he grows up he'll know enough to marry someone who knows what they're there for."

"It says here," Stan interjected, "that they're thinking of making the old Valencia Theatre into a landmark."

Mary's coffee pot suspended in midair. "I remember going there with my cousin Nancy as a girl. She took the trolley in from Brooklyn and we packed a lunch and went to the Valencia. This was the country to her, can you imagine?"

"Really, Zinnie," Carmela snorted. "You talk as though you'd never heard of homosexuality when you married Freddy."

"That's just what I mean. I knew it existed in Greenwich Village, but no one ever spoke of it in normal terms. Everyone around here whispered about things like that while we were growing up. I never imagined it happened in normal people, too. What I say is, the more matter of fact you are about something, the less it can hurt you."

Mary Breslinsky cupped her face and shook her head. "Well, if anything, this family has become more matter of fact. More coffee, Stan? Stan? Arsenic in your coffee?"

"Hmmm? Uh. Uh huh." Stan was lost in Jimmy Breslin's column.

"See what I mean?" She filled his cup.

"Who does this Breslin think he is?" shouted Stan. "He's got it in for the entire NYPD!"

"Just the corrupt ones, Dad," Carmela spoke with elaborate patience, "and there are enough of them." Carmela had exchanged three words with Jimmy Breslin at a press party. Now she was keeper of his every motive and intention.

"No," Stan grew agitated. "He accuses the whole force!"

"He's practically right," Carmela said.

"Oh, no he's not. You're not, Zinnie. And Michael sure as hell wasn't."

Mary Breslinsky didn't look up then, because Michael was dead and had been for ten years, and it hurt just as much now as it had then. He was Claire's twin and he had died at the hands of a young killer he'd tried to talk into surrendering. He'd looked at the thirteen-year-old, tear-stained kid huddling in the stairwell and he'd taken off his gun and walked right into the arms of death. Rookie good-hearted, valiant, stupid Michael.

The Mayor walked into the kitchen.

"I gotta go to work," Carmela stood.

"Me too," said Zinnie, but she didn't move, she sat there, because she knew that if the Mayor was here, Claire was coming in, and she loved Claire, loved to look at her face. Claire had Michael's clear blue eyes, pure as sea glass, and Zinnie hadn't had them to look into since she was fifteen. Zinnie had thought she'd lost the both of them back then, because Claire hadn't been able to stay home after Michael died.

"If you're going to put on something cooler," Mary told Stan, "you'd better get cracking."

The Mayor, glad to see breakfast coming to such an abrupt halt—there would be that much more leftovers for the picking—jumped into Stan's chair to oversee what Mary might unthinkingly discard. There was no sense in being wasteful. He whimpered at the sight of Carmela's three quarters of a piece of buttered toast heading for the bin.

"What, you want that, too?" Mary looked at him skeptically. "I don't know how you can enjoy it in all this heat. All right. Take it." She finished up most of the dishes (Mary had a dishwasher but was rarely known to use it), left the coffee on for Claire, took her apron off irritably, and went out into the yard with Michaelaen. He'd help her water the strawberries. He was the only one who could do it without wetting the leaves.

Mary was annoyed at Stan for bringing up Michael. She knew she shouldn't be, but she was. She didn't want them upsetting Claire so soon after she'd come home and she might very well have been listening. That was the type she was. Michael had been the talker and she the listener. Gravy and bread. Claire had all but died herself when Michael was killed, and Mary knew inside herself what kind of suffocating pain Claire felt when she bumped into some old thing of Michael's that they still had lying about. A picture. Or Michael's old copies of *Motor Trend* that no one had seen fit to throw away. What if Claire took off again? What then? A nervous breeze unsettled the trees. Mary looked up and narrowed her eyes. The white sky glared. With any luck they'd have a thunder storm.

"Gram?" Michaelaen wrapped his hand around her thumb.

"Mmm?"

"What's a kicker?"

Claire, in her father's knee-length undershirt, bleary-eyed and mouth still parted from her dreams, came into the kitchen, tripped quietly over the vacuum cleaner, and dunked her whole face under the faucet. Was the cloth she dried off with the same as one she remembered from years ago? It smelled the same. Ivory Snow and Cheerios.

"We have bathrooms here in America for that sort of thing," Zinnie said.

Claire turned and looked at Zinnie, all grown up and sharp as a tack. When Claire had left New York, Zinnie had still been wearing braces. Now here she was: married, a mother, divorced. There and back and no scars on the outside to show for it. But then Zinnie had been the kind of kid who would take a tumble off her bike and laugh out loud. Hard. Zinnie used to tag along with Claire and Michael all the time back then. She'd been their favorite. Claire suddenly felt too old for so early in the morning. She poured a cereal bowl half up with coffee and the other half with milk. Then she lit a cigarette.

Zinnie watched the cool blue smoke surround Claire's tousled head. "Whadda ya takin' pictures in the woods for?"

"Oh. It's the people."

"What people?"

"The old people who promenade up there. Half the survivors of Dachau and Auschwitz seem to be living right up here in the apartments at the end of Park Lane South."

"And you like that, eh?"

"I like them," Claire admitted, enjoying her coffee. No one who'd lived in India could ever take a luxurious cup of well-brewed coffee for granted. "They fascinate me because they survived what was impossible. They're very sad and matter of fact and somehow not bitter at all. Numbers tattooed on their arms as though they were cattle. They have faces that shrug."

"So you photograph them."

"Well, I'm starting to. They're opening up a little more now that they think I understand Yiddish."

"Now you speak Yiddish. My sister the Jew."

"I don't understand it, really. But it's not too different from Schweitze-Deutsch—Swiss-German. Between High German and Swiss, you can pretty much understand."

"High German, Low German—it's all Greek to me."

"Anyway, they have extraordinary faces for black and white."

Zinnie rolled her eyes. "If you think they're good, I

oughta take you with me on my four to midnights. You want characters, I'll give you characters."

Claire looked stung. "I couldn't do that."

"Why not?"

"I'm having a hard enough time getting used to the idea of you being a cop . . . let alone drive around with you in uniform . . . and you deliberately conjuring up all sorts of dangerous possibilities just to make my day . . . even though I would give anything to photograph the authentic types you must meet up with."

"I don't get it. I mean, how can you get so excited about these normal creeps when you've been all over the world? You've seen just about everything, and you act all hepped-up and goggly-eyed to photograph the local riffraff."

"You'd be enthused, too, if you'd been gone for ten years."

"I doubt it."

"Ah, but you would, Zinnie. You'd come back with new eyes. You only can't see what you're so used to you can't see it."

"I dunno. You're the artist in the family. I'll let you 'capture' the neighborhood while I go capture the mutts."

"The who?"

"The mutts . . . perps. The inmates from our very own concentration camp: Ye Olde Ghetto." She stood up and retrieved her gun from the fridge, slipped it into her arm holster, and covered it with her very best seersucker jacket.

The Mayor was rummaging through his toy box. He had a worn out grocery carton that housed his decade of a lifetime's accumulation of bones and doggy toys, silly things that people give to animals to chew on: plastic frogs and purple pussy cats and, in the Mayor's case, a fine figure of a gnawed up Barbie doll. The Mayor never gave up on a toy. He might stick it away in the box and forget about it for a year or two, but he was a sentimental old sod, and out he'd haul the smelly thing, sooner or later, give it a friendly chomp, and rest his snout on it for old times' sake. Then he'd fall asleep, its reminiscent odors transcending him to dreams of long ago and far away. This morning it was a little french fries container, shredded and almost colorless, but a favorite just the same at times like these, when no one paid him any mind.

Claire leaned back in her chair and watched him. How easy it was, she thought, to love someone or something that could never hurt you. How wonderful it would be not to know that—to be innocent and still think that the world offered nothing more than what you wanted to take. She longed, for a moment, for the innocence she'd lost. Growing up hadn't solved all of the mysteries. It just pushed them to the back shelf.

Out the window and across the street, an elderly figure in red tottered across her backyard lawn. Even at that distance, her gash of lipstick was visible.

Claire sat up straight. "Is that Iris von Lillienfeld?"

"Huh? Oh, sure, that's her. Who else wears Japanese kimonos and emeralds at seven o'clock in the morning?"

"I can't believe she's still alive!"

"Oh, she's alive all right. To the great dissatisfaction of every real estate agent in town."

"I'll bet. That house looks like Rhett Butler will be home any minute. I wonder if she'd let me photograph her?"

"Not likely. That old broad is a recluse from the get go. She thinks she's Garbo. Ooo, this was funny. Her dog—she's got this really themey poodle—well, this dog was in heat and you know how uh . . . virile the Mayor here is—"

"Ha."

"Yeah, he practically lived over there. Wild. She won't be bothered with people, but the dog didn't seem to put her back up too much. At least she didn't complain. Although how is she gonna complain, when all she bothers to speak in is German? Hey! You speak Kraut. Naw, she'd never let you in. She wouldn't even let the city tree pruners in—"

"Do you remember, Zinnie," Claire interrupted, "how Michael used to love that woman? He used to tell me she could read the future. Remember how he was the only one not afraid to go into her backyard? We all used to call her the old witch and throw stones and run away, and Michael used to crawl through the hedge and visit her? Remember?"

"I don't know," Zinnie turned her head away moodily. "I was too young, I guess. No, wait. I do remember him going over there. There was a nest of baby robins knocked out of the maple in a storm and everyone said that the cats were sure to get them and that it was too bad because you couldn't put them in a cage or they would die in captivity. Michael went over there—I remember he did, because I was scared to death she'd put a spell on him. Yeah, and then he came back . . . went into the garage, put the ladder smack in the middle of the backyard, in the shade but not too close to the trees, made a nest at the top, and popped them in, and he covered, I mean completely covered, the ladder steps with thorny rose branches so the cats couldn't climb up."

"And Mom was furious that half of her rose bushes were destroyed."

"Right. But those robins, they lived. Remember they lived? He left his little nest open at the top so the parent robins could go on feeding them from above, and they all lived. Every one of them. And Iris von Lillienfeld gave Michael that idea."

They shook their heads fondly at the memory. Claire bubbled with laughter. "I can still see Pop putting bacon bits on a pole with scotch tape and hoisting it up to them."

"They ate it, too, the carnivorous little devils. I wonder where Mom and Michaelaen went," Zinnie bolted back to the present. "Probably up to the woods to see what all the sirens were about." She put the ceiling fan on low. They could hear the strains of *Pagliacci* from upstairs.

"Zinnie, I wanted to speak to you about Carmela."

"Oh, yeah? How come?"

"I don't know. Is she all right?"

"Whadda ya mean? Carmela hasn't been all right since I've known her."

"Yes, but besides that. She seems so sour."

"Yeah, well, her divorce was pretty bloody. And he took the house 'cause he supported her while she was getting her masters."

"But why did they break up?"

"They fought all the time."

"So does everyone."

Zinnie looked left and right. "Promise you won't tell anyone? Especially not Mom?"

"Certainly I promise," Claire crossed her heart. She liked the idea of a secret with Zinnie. Particularly since Zinnie had come across her twice talking to herself since she'd come home.

Zinnie lowered her voice. "Right when Carmela was working on her finals, she got pregnant. And she got an abortion. Without telling Arnold."

"What?"

"Sure. You know nothin's-gonna-stand-in-my-way Carmela. The only reason I found out was because she started hemorrhaging afterward and she called me up to take her back to the clinic. He wound up finding out about it anyway. She hit him with it during one of their famous shouting matches. You know, top of the ninth and the bases are empty? She just laced it into him 'cause she had nothing else left to hit him with, I guess. Anyhow, that was the beginning of the end. Now she's all wrapped up in this therapy shit. Even the people she hangs out with are these intellectual, overanalytical uptown types."

"Too much Freud, not enough roast beef?"

"Yup. Exactly. Now she writes about 'winter- or summer-palette people' and 'hemline psychosyndromes' and she calls herself a columnist. She makes me sick. I mean, she has such a good mind and it's all off in the wrong direction. The divorce just sent her off the deep end, Claire, I swear it did."

"You and Freddy went through it. And you had Michaelaen. You seem all right."

"Do I? I was pretty shaken up at the time. But with Freddy and me it was different. We were friends growing up. I still love him, you know it? I always will, the sap. I mean, behind all the fresh-out-of-the-closet fruitcake, Freddy's a stand-up guy . . . and he pays all of Michaelaen's bills, without being asked to. He's got a steady boyfriend already, can you imagine? They're opening a restaurant on Queens Boulevard." She laughed ironically. "May they live happily ever after."

Zinnie stretched as though she didn't give a hoot. "God, I'm tired," she moaned. "I just get used to one shift and they put me on another. Say, Claire? Whatever did happen with that duke guy?"

"Wolfgang? The last time I saw him he was leading some Brahmanic heiress around by the nose."

"You still hurting?"

Claire's eyes went out the window and all the way up Park Lane South. "It's difficult to describe. I feel lighter. After I left Wolfgang in Delhi, I spent six months on my own in the Himalayas. In a place called Dharam Sala. McLeod Gange, Dharam Sala. It's a sort of refugee camp for Tibetans. Anyway, after one sort of difficult but illuminating month, I couldn't figure out why I'd stayed with him as long as I had. In Dharam Sala, I started looking at things in a different way, you know?"

"Yeah, I know what you mean. Those Himalayas'll clean your eyes right out."

"Aw, c'mon Zinnie. Not you, too."

"All right, go on. The Himalayas cut your cataracts. And then?"

"And then I decided that as long as I was changing half of my life, I might as well change the rest of it. No more working for travel brochures or fashion magazines. I didn't have too much money left over so I sold my pearls—"

"Those luscious pearls from the German doctor? How could you?!"

"They didn't exactly go with my life-style anymore," Claire laughed. "They hadn't for a long time." (No sense mentioning all the other things she'd had to sell.) "Anyway, to make a long story short, without Wolfgang's expensive tastes to support, I figured I could do what *I* wanted for a while. You know, the 'virtue of selfishness' and all that."

"That doesn't sound like you. You usually bolshevize everything."

"Not anymore I don't. Not after Wolfgang."

"Tell me something. Did he do coke?"

"Sure he did coke. That's why his allowance from home was never enough."

"Did you?"

"Oh, God no. I got high on my mantras."

"Huh?"

"Meditation."

"Oh. Well, just don't go doin' none a that stuff around here," Zinnie warned. "Bad enough Mom's got Michaelaen going to church with her."

Claire stood up and paced to and fro. "I don't pray anymore," she scowled. "I'm so full of self-congratulation when I do that I disgust myself. It's like, I've done this, so now I deserve a reward . . . or . . . or progress, at least. My motives are all egotistical and self-serving, which is not the point at all, or it shouldn't be." She threw her arms up in a hopeless, almost comical gesture. "I'm much better when I'm not so good."

They looked at each other.

"And," she added, "I did used to smoke hashish occasionally. Does that make you feel better?"

"Not really. So then what happened with Wolfgang?"

"I guess I started seeing him for what he was."

"Yeah, a pimp."

"I wouldn't call him a pimp."

"I would. He sent you out to work and he collected, right?"

"He helped me, Zinnie. I have to say that. He got me lots of clients and he can be very charming. He kept things running smoothly on the shoots."

"Like I said. A pimp. What are you defending him for, huh? So you wised up and got him out of your life. Next?"

"You're funny. You really are a cop, aren't you? Okay. I thought I'd start all over, you know? Back to go. I've been trying to get a book together for years. Only my best stuff. When I came home I started looking around me. Zinnie, the Himalayas are magical, but this is real life. This place is a photographer's dream."

"I get the idea. Real life is what you photograph after you've photographed all the dreams. But you don't wanna go along even on a day tour with me. And how are you going to support yourself while you're being artsy-craftsy?"

"I've got enough money saved to pay Mom and Pop rent, and I thought I'd ask Mom if I could make a small darkroom down in the cellar."

"In all that junk?"

"I only need a sink and darkness, Zinnie, not atmosphere."

"So make a darkroom. Maybe you'll meet some nice guy in Manhattan when you try and sell your pictures."

Vexed, Claire rummaged through a little bin of blueberries. "I don't want to meet anybody," she said. "I want to stay around here and shoot pictures that tell stories without words. I want to shoot anything I well please and not what some art director thinks will sell."

"And the first time you hear someone mention they're going to clean up Michael's grave . . . you'll hightail it off to some ashram and not come back for another ten years."

Claire shook her head slowly. "No, Zin. I came to terms with Michael's death a long time ago. I carry it always, in my heart, like you do. New York doesn't bring me any closer to it."

Zinnie, angry and embarrassed by her own emotion, blurted, "It's New Yawk, jerk! This ain't no David Niven film."

They laughed together at themselves, relieved not to speak about Michael. Zinnie sighed. "I don't know. Maybe this *is* a David Niven film and I'm the one going off the deep end."

Impulsively, Claire threw her arms around Zinnie and held her. "Of all of us, I think you're the one who's the most together."

"That's not saying a hell of a lot," Zinnie smiled.

"You'll be just fine," Claire said. "Although I'll never understand how you can be a cop. You're so beautiful and smart. You did so well in college. Why don't you go to law school?"

"I don't want to, Claire," Zinnie pulled away. "You're not the only one who loves what she's doing, you know."

"I know. Those aren't the reasons why I don't want you to be a cop, anyhow."

They watched each other carefully, each checking the other one out for emotional scars from Michael's death. Claire knew that a good part of Zinnie's joining the force had been because of him. She hoped there had not been too much revenge in her reasoning. Zinnie, on the other hand, remembered just how devastated Claire had been at the time. She wondered how difficult it was for Claire to watch her go out the door with a gun. Whatever she felt, that pain would always be there between them as a bond, and there was nothing either of them could, or wanted, to do about it.

Zinnie touched Claire's hair. "What about you? You wanna come out with me tonight? Do a little trip the light fandango up at Regents Row?"

"Me? Oh, no, thanks. I've had it with men."

"Is that right? And how do you expect to hold them off, eh?"

"Don't you worry about me. I've got castration toxins leaking out of my eyeballs."

"I'll bet," Zinnie sneered.

"Anyway, I've got no time. I want to finish my black-and-white series as soon as possible. The colors around here are just too tempting in this season. Look at the dog! He's playing catch all by himself! Look!"

"Oh, he's just showing off. So. You think this neighborhood is great, eh? Let me see. You've got the old Jews and the young Israelis north of the park. You've got your mafia fledglings along Lefferts. And you've got your Puerto Ricans, Colombians, and Indians down on Jamaica. You've got some taste, kid."

Claire didn't say anything then, because she couldn't describe what she felt when she saw an Indian woman in a shocking-pink sari gliding past an el train covered with graffiti. She'd have to shoot the scene and show it to her. Claire's heart swelled when she thought of all the ideas she had for portraying the neighborhood. She'd show the standing-stillness in all the flurry of transition. She'd achieve something true. And then maybe Zinnie wouldn't look at her with that suspicious, worried face. "Look, Zinnie," she said, "I want to get one thing straight. No, listen to me. Don't look off as if you weren't listening. I just want to tell you that I'm not running off again. Not anywhere. And I won't have you and Mom and the rest of them pussy-footing around me as if I were a ghost. When I said I was over Michael's death, I meant it. Will you tell them that? Will you help me try and make them understand?"

Zinnie pried a perfectly good cuticle up with her teeth and bit it off. "Sure," she said. She would have said more, but then Stan came back into the kitchen, lilly-legged in his bermuda shorts, and announced that he was heading on up to the woods to see what all the commotion was about.

"Wanna come?" he asked.

Claire shook her head no.

"I was looking out the bathroom window. They've got the brass up there," he tempted Zinnie.

"Okey-doke," Zinnie agreed.

I'll not be left out of this, the Mayor thought, and he hoisted his broad beam up on all fours.

Claire wandered around the old house while they were gone, sipping her bowl of coffee, enjoying the dark rooms and the full sun blasting against the screens. She sat up in the dining room window seat, always her favorite place, and felt the house—just her and the house. This was where she'd curled up as a child and pored through each new issue of *National Geographic,* struck with wonder at the glossy, important-looking pages alive with color and exotic cultures. This was where it had all begun for her. The tall-ceilinged rooms were littered with dusty books and her father's homemade cannons. All of these things, she thought, so long in their same old spots that you forgot they were there. She bet nobody in the family ever saw the stained glass window over the pantry anymore. Well, maybe Michaelaen did.

Michaelaen saw a lot of things the others didn't. He was an intense child, very involved in his four-year-old world of animals and mechanics. Michaelaen seemed to have inherited his grandpa's love of junkyards. That's what the two of them would do for fun: visit junkyards and collect "treasure," odd bits of copper and brass and all sorts of rubble that could only attract little boys and old men. It was a good education for the boy, Stan swore. He was learning the value of real resources, he said. There was some question as to who enjoyed these jaunts to the junkies more, Stan or Michaelaen.

The cellar was so full of their accumulations that a ragged path was all you got when you had to make your way through. Stan and Michaelaen found enough place to do things down there. They would hammer and fiddle and come up the stairs all covered with dirt. Stan would dust his knees off proudly and say, "He's all boy, that kid."

The only trouble was, he'd say it over and over again, as if he were trying to reassure himself.

"Shut up, Pop, willya?" Zinnie would finally look up from the TV and snap at him. And Michaelaen would busy himself with some toy car, pretending not to understand for fear their feelings would be hurt.

Claire smiled to herself. Six days home and already she knew their ways. Any minute now they'd all be back and full of the news from the park, bubbling and scandalized, each with his or her own private theory, clattering in and out and filling up the now-still rooms.

White sheets hung on the line in the yard. A small breeze rippled, and the spaces revealed the distant figure of Iris von Lillienfeld, ruby red across the street in her own very green backyard. Claire froze. Then, like a huntress stalking her prey, she crept across the room to her camera bag, whispering to herself, "Please, God, don't let her move"; and hurriedly, trembling, she attached a zoom lens to her camera, expertly and swiftly loaded a thousand ASA color film, and turned to wait. "Come on, God, now give me back that little breeze. Oh, come on, don't let me down." And framed by a sudden ripple of the weightless white and sturdy clothespins was Miss von Lillienfeld, now close through the magic of zoom, standing still with brittle grace and contemplation and a pigeon on her pillbox hat.

All the mantras and the prayers and even the gange Claire had smoked trying to lose herself, and always her consciousness had been there, a leering monkey on her back, an ever-present watching, observing her efforts and plaguing her sincerity. Now here she was doing what she loved, and this was what she couldn't feel because she wasn't there. She was lost in what she was doing, looking out instead of in and only coming to herself when she was through—when all the frames were full.

Claire was just putting away her camera bag when they came back. Anticipating their excited chatter, she was surprised when her mother came speedily in gripping Michaelaen, her lips pressed into a hard, drawn line, her face white as chalk, the Mayor trotting busily behind.

"What's going on?" asked Claire.

Mary, making a sign that consisted of nothing more than a nod of the head but that meant, "Not now, Claire," and "Not in front of Michaelaen," and "What in God's name is the world coming to" all in one movement, marched through the rooms with a determined gait and left her standing open-mouthed and alone once again in the kitchen. A moment later Stan came in solemnly, shaking his head as he sat down at the table.

"Gee, Pop . . . what's—"

"It was murder, Claire. Up in the woods. Jeez . . ." He covered his face with a great freckled paw.

"Who—" she whispered. "Who was murdered?" Claire remembered with fresh, cold pain the moment they'd told her that Michael was dead.

"A boy," Zinnie answered dully from the doorway. "A little boy. It was really bad, Claire." Zinnie looked as though she were going to be ill.

"Sit down, Zin," Claire's heart beat with morbid curiosity. "Did you see?"

"Yeah, I saw. The rest of them had to stay down by the monument, but they heard enough. It was up in the pine forest. An old man found the body. One of your old Jews, Claire. Taking his morning stroll. He was wailing like a banshee when we got there. They had to take him to the hospital for shock. Christ, that kid was really messed up."

"Nothing like this ever happened before in this neighborhood," Stan murmured. "I've never heard of anything like that around here."

Mary came in swiftly. "Michaelaen's in his room watching 'Woody Woodpecker,'" she said to Zinnie. "I don't want anybody talking about it in front of him. You got that?"

"Sure, Mom," "Of course, dear," they all nodded in

agreement. You didn't argue with Mary when she meant business, and she meant it now. She took a frozen fruit bar from the freezer and started to leave, then stopped in her tracks.

"It was drugs, wasn't it, Stan? Only Colombians murder children for vendettas."

"It looks like it, Mary," Stan agreed.

Mary swept out of the room to try to further distract her grandson. They waited until the sound of her footsteps reached the top of the stairs.

"Not for nothing, Dad," Zinnie locked eyes with her father, "but that was no Colombian's revenge."

"Those Latinos have pretty short fuses, honey."

"Cut the crap, Pop. I'm on the job, remember? I saw him."

"I know. I know. Only not in front of your mom. Not one word."

"That bad?" Claire caught her breath.

"The killer was a maniac."

"Anybody who would kill a little boy is a maniac," Stan fumed.

"Yeah, but Pop, this was as sick as they come. It was . . . evil."

Claire shuddered.

Zinnie's upper lip was beaded with sweat. "And he was . . . uh . . . abused, you know? Just a little kid. Maybe seven or eight. I used to see him up in the playground. He was a real good-looking little kid, you know? I think it was him. It was hard to tell." Zinnie's voice caught in her throat. "He was lying there in a clearing of pine needles . . . he had this *look* on his face, his . . . his eyes were open . . ."

"All right, Zinnie," Stan patted her on the shoulder.

"I'm okay." Zinnie brushed his hand away, the way she would when she was truly upset. "The press didn't get it. Not yet. They got him out of there and into the body bag quick. You never saw those Queens boys work so fast."

"But they'll get the story from the old man," said Claire.

"Sure they will. But they'll keep him sedated so long, he won't be giving interviews till later. They've got to do a positive ID on the body. At least the press won't have pictures. They'd have a panic out there."

"A panic is better than another murder," Claire said.

"Not until they notify the parents, it ain't," Zinnie snapped. "And I don't want Michaelaen riding his bike up there with this going on."

"He'll come bowling with your mother and me. And we'll just have to take shifts keeping an eye on him."

"Listen, Claire," Zinnie pointed a finger at her, "You're another one I don't want up in the park. Not for a minute, you hear me?"

"Oh, Lord, Zinnie, I wouldn't even think of going in deep—"

"Not even on the rim, dammit! Don't you hear what I'm saying?!"

"Okay, okay. I won't go into the woods till all this blows over, all right, sheriff?"

"Promise!"

"I promise."

Zinnie stood. "Now I really gotta go."

"You going to stop in at the one-o-two?" Stan asked her.

"I can't do that, Pop. You know that. My precinct's in the city."

"I know. I know. Just unofficially, I mean."

"No. They've got a whole new staff over there. I don't know anybody in there anymore, except Furgueson. It's all new. And look. You keep Carmela's nose out of this. You know, 'Miss Reporter.' That's all we need is her poking her nose around up there and getting into trouble."

"God forbid," agreed Stan.

"So just don't tell her about it. Let her hear Mom's version."

"Fine," said Claire, feeling all at once as though Zinnie were the elder and she the younger.

Zinnie went to say goodbye to Michaelaen. Then she climbed into her gray Datsun. Claire and Stan sat silently and watched her drive away. The ceiling fan went slowly round and the sink faucet dripped.

"Pop?"

"Yeah?"

"I'm sure it's nothing, but early this morning, when I was out in the hammock, I saw this car drive by."

"So?"

"No, I mean very early. Before the sun was quite up. An old Plymouth came down from the park."

Stan's eyes focused on her own. "You see the driver?"

"No, but I remember part of the license. I remember because it had three numbers from . . . well, three numbers or three other numbers. They were either Buddha's estimated year of ascension or the year of his birth. I don't know which of the two it was, now, because I went right back to sleep, but it was definitely either one or the other."

"Jesus, Claire, which numbers??!"

"Well, it was either 563 or 473."

"You're sure?"

"I don't remember which, but it was definitely one of those. I'm sure of that."

"We'd better go over to the precinct."

"Oh no, Dad, not me. I don't want any part of detectives. You go. You tell them, all right? Don't get me involved."

"I understand." He put his big hand on top of her small one. "I'll go. And not a word to your mother. Tell her I just ran over to the store. Tell her I went to look in on how the new kid is doing and I'll be back in half an hour. She'll fall for it."

"Pop?"

"Yuh?"

"Don't bring any cops home, all right? I don't want to go through it." She stood on the back stoop and watched him until he was out of sight. When she turned to go back in the kitchen she could have sworn she saw Iris von

Lillienfeld looking dead at her from a half-closed window across the street.

Michaelaen sat quietly on his bed. He listened. Grandma was down in the cellar putting in the laundry. Aunt Claire would not come walking in without knocking. He shook his head to himself. She acted like he was a grown-up. Michaelaen went into his closet bottom, carefully moved his folder of Spider Man stickers, and pulled out the tackle box Grandpa had given him for his very own. He carried the box back to the bed. For a moment he just sat there and held the box fondly. Then he blew on it. A nice powder of dust made a storm in the sunshine. He watched it settle on the wooden floor and then opened the box. There was Daddy's fine school ring, safe and sound. There was the ivory elephant Aunt Claire had sent from India, the insect corpses he loved best, a magic blue jay feather, an abacus from Chinatown, and a cat's eye marble. It was the best cat's eye marble he had ever seen. Probably worth a lot of money. Ah, there it was. The cufflink. A genuine roulette wheel. He gave it a good spin and his eyes lit up to follow the golden ball round and around. Eleven. Red. He laughed out loud. It was a shame he couldn't show it off. But he had sworn he'd never tell, right before Miguel had pressed it into his hand. That was the deal. He wouldn't tell what they were up to, looking at those pictures and all, and Miguel would let him keep the cufflink. Only he must never tell. No matter what.

Johnny Benedetto parked the silver Triumph Stag on the hill behind the pizza place. It was still broiling at three PM. He loosened his tie and removed his jacket. A large big-jointed man, he never felt comfortable in a suit and there were days he forgot he wasn't still wearing a uniform. Johnny took off his shoulder strap and slipped his gun into the Velcro holder in his sock. He needed a shave. His thick black hair curled onto his collar. The sharp hazel green eyes caught sight of himself in the rearview mirror. That was another thing. A haircut.

Swiftly and with a thin-waisted grace for one so broad and hulkish as himself, Johnny sprang from the car and headed for the Row. He hadn't eaten since yesterday and this wasn't the kind of man who took his appetite lightly. There came a point when he had to eat.

Regents Row was dark and cool, was reasonably priced, served magnificent steaks, and catered to the force. Not that you were treated special in there, mind you. You waited your turn for a table no matter who you were. Hizzy ran that place the same way Captain Furgueson ran the station house: no favors for no one, no freebies. And Hizzy never forgot your name. Johnny respected that, too. It showed control.

He slung his jacket over one shoulder and crossed the street, oblivious to the admiring glances of the housewives coming and going from the supermarket and the Homestead Deli. His shin was throbbing like a bastard but he hardly noticed. One more medal from Nam that congratulated him every time rain was expected.

Johnny opened the door and his heart sank. The bar was filled with women, church social women, waiting to be seated for their Rosary Society lunch. Hizzy came right over and extended his plump hand. "How ya been, Johnny?"

Johnny gave him one of his rare, disarming smiles. "Yourself?"

"Hey, I'm fine," Hizzy pumped his hand, then waved in a broad, all-encompassing sweep. "Sorry about all this. Every month, like a clock. You can't get 'em seated and then you can't get 'em to leave." He squinted at Johnny. "Bad doings up in the park, huh?"

Johnny looked at his feet and said nothing. Hizzy knew better than that. "I gotta go, Hizzy. Good to see ya an all but I gotta get something to eat real quick and then get some sleep."

"Why doncha come back in the kitchen and I'll have Irwin fix you up a couple a sandwiches to go . . . how bout it?"

"That's okay, Hizzy. Next time. I'll get something at the pizza place. Short and sweet." He knew Hizzy was dying to get some inside dope on the murder. So it had spread this far that quick, eh? Terrific. Nice can a worms this was gonna be. He left as fast as he'd come in and walked across the hot white boulevard. Johnny slapped himself in the head. He must be punchy. He'd told Furgueson he'd try and check out that crackpot license number story. Furgueson had said it was probably a waste of time but Johnny had said he'd look into it anyway. It could wait until he'd had some sleep. It was gonna have to.

The pizza place was pretty empty; at least it was cool and shaded under the canopy on the street. He ordered three slices and a large Coke and sat down at one of the little tables outside. Johnny rubbed his eyes with both hands and looked down the street. He wished the weather would make up its mind. One minute dark clouds threatened and the next you thought you should be at the beach. He was tired. Real tired. He'd just been going off duty when this whole mess had started, and this was the first moment he'd had to sit down and think.

A group of young paisan, the criminal sort with nothing much to do with their daylight hours, cavorted like Gay Parisians at the next two tables. Coke spoons dangled from 18 karat gold chains and silk shirts were opened the obligatory four buttons.

Each passing female was graded with uproarious detail. Plans were made for Saturday night's rent-a-limo. A blond flight attendant's phone number changed hands.

They didn't know who Johnny was (what cop drove a 1972 Triumph Stag?) and so they spoke openly, sometimes in Sicilian, among themselves. He understood most of what they said and on another day would have been remarking every word. As it was, he had other things on his mind, some sort of psychopathic, child-molesting monster whose evil he could still see in his mind's eye and probably always would, and he wasn't paying them much mind.

The boy came out with his pizza and Johnny inhaled two of them, swallowed his entire Coke, ordered another, then sat back and enjoyed the third slice. God, he loved good pizza. In all his thirty-three years he must have consumed seven thousand pizzas. Nobody cooked for him, that was for sure. Nobody ever had.

Johnny Benedetto had no family to speak of, unless you counted his old friend Red Torneo. He'd had a wife for about four months. She was lucky she was still alive. He'd found her in bed with her hairdresser. Jesus. He'd put all his clothes in one lousy suitcase while the two of them cowered in the bed like the little pieces of shit that they were, and he'd walked out and he'd never gone back. The next time he's seen her, and the last, had been at the divorce hearing six months ago. That was it.

Johnny played a hard game of handball, racquets, anything that would keep his massive frame in check and his mind from exploding. He didn't drink much—once in a while, but not too often. He knew he had to watch his temper. When he was younger, he had often found himself out of control. There were plenty of broken noses walking around New York thanks to him as it was.

What Johnny loved, what made him really tick, were cars. Or, more precisely, engines. Lately he hadn't even had time for that. Nowadays when he got home to his apartment after work he had all he could do just to climb into bed, roll over, and drift off to sleep, all-encompassing sleep, far away in the land of nod, where there were no murders, no body bags, and no ten-year-old broken bodies, no bodies at all . . . just the vapor-held swell of a fine-tuned machine doing ninety and the cut-and-dry hum of perfection.

Johnny was a born mechanic, and when he had a problem or just wanted to wind down, that's what he'd do, go down to Jojenny's Garage and work on a wreck. If he had nothing of his own to work on, he'd work on somebody else's. By the time he'd have the thing running, he'd usually have his own problem sorted out in his head.

As a matter of fact, if Johnny hadn't met Red Torneo as a kid, that's probably what he would have been, a mechanic.

Red Torneo had been a cop in Bensonhurst, where Johnny'd grown up. Red was a "big brother," a term used for men who donated their spare time to fatherless kids in the neighborhood. Although Johnny had hated Red with a passion at the beginning, Red had kept after him long after another man would have figured good riddance to bad rubbish, for that was the sort of riffraff Johnny had chosen to hang out with and emulate in his street corner days. Red had taken a real interest, bringing Johnny down to the precinct garage when he'd recognized Johnny's potential as a mechanic. Though he'd hated to admit it, Johnny was happy. Covered in grease, he'd found acceptance among the "hair bags," or old-timers, once they'd noticed that suddenly, their crummy cars were running without a hitch. For the first time in his short life, Johnny had had a family of sorts. Red had thought that Johnny was the best damn mechanic he'd ever known, and it'd knocked him for a loop when he'd found out through the desk sergeant that Johnny was taking the police academy test. The more he'd thought about it, though, the more sense it had made. Johnny was the kind of guy you might call extreme, or fanatic, depending on your point of view. Once he made a decision, it was absolute. Better he should stay on this side of the law than the other.

Red was prouder than he'd cared to admit. He liked his beer and he liked to go fishing, so when he'd retired he'd opened up a little bar by the docks down in Sheepshead Bay. Christmas and Easter, Johnny always showed up. Where else did he have to go? That little tramp Johnny had married wasn't around anymore, thank God, but he'd known from the start that that wouldn't work out. He hadn't said nothing, but he'd known. She wasn't good enough to shine Johnny's shoes. Johnny had been so broken up at the end that Red had thought he might go under. Only he hadn't. Not Johnny. He was pretty much over it already, from the scuttlebutt . . . working the graveyard shift and anything else he could get his hands on. Now that he'd made detective Johnny would be all right. Maybe. He hadn't been around to see Red in a couple of months.

Johnny Benedetto looked over at the lowlifes at the next table and thought of Red. Shit. If it hadn't a been for Red, *that* would probably be exactly where he'd be sitting. Dealing coke. Forget the mechanic idea. If it hadn't a been for Red, he wouldn't have even had the cars to work on, let alone persuade to performance, enjoy for a couple of months, and then sell for the next wreck to work on. If it hadn't been for Red, he'd more likely be stealing them. After they cleaned up this case he was gonna take a ride down to Sheepshead Bay and pay him a visit. What the hell.

Claire had to buy some film. She was reluctant to go all the way into the city to the lab. It would take too much time and she wanted to be back for Michaelaen when her parents returned from their bowling at four. She liked Michaelaen. He reminded her a little bit of . . . oh, well, he was himself. She liked him for himself. There was a camera store up on Lefferts where she could go. Twice the price, but that couldn't be helped. Tomorrow she'd take the train and pick up the chemicals she'd need for her lab. All morning she'd been clearing away years of junk from one corner of the cellar, unburying equipment that was dusty but almost certainly still good. This way her mother couldn't say, "Of course you can have a corner in the basement for your lab. One day, when we get around to clearing away all that stuff. . . ." Now it was done and there was nothing Mom could do about it. Heh heh.

Claire helped herself to a clean, fluffy towel and went into the shower. You couldn't beat hot- and cold-running water. Claire arched her brown back and met the needling shower spray head on. It was like music, strong, steady music, and she gave herself up to it, flooded in steam, pouring baby shampoo all over her body, turning this way and that till the stretching coiled backward and forth in some dance of her own graceful rhythm. No. Claire stopped herself from reaching. It would do no good. Not really. Tales of blindness hadn't sprung from vision itself but from something deeper . . . more spiritual in its sightlessness. She'd come too far to go back to that, no matter how much it seemed to want to leap out of her. Her dreams would quake inside of her and wake her up but she wouldn't return to that solitary loneliness she'd used to substitute for fulfillment all during her last relationship.

She left the shower dripping, wiped the fogged-up mirror with the heel of her hand, and looked into her eyes. Yes, it was true. There was a power there that came from overstepping weakness. She winked at her image and busied herself with the hair dryer, now wondering what sort of consciousness the murderer of that small boy must live in. Did he know what he had done? Did he remember? Did he justify his rage? What on earth had made him that way? She remembered the lumbering weight of that rusty gold Plymouth this morning. Could the murderer have been in there, sated and wary? Oh, for goodness sakes, no, she shuddered and laughed to herself. Life was good. She was home. And she mustn't let her imagination run away with her.

Claire put on a pair of her gauzy white pantaloons from Jaipur and a matching long shirt. In the fall she would have to buy herself some western clothes. The Indians had the right idea about clothes in this weather, though. Too see-through for the neighborhood, she covered herself with a brocaded ivory vest from Kashmir. Claire didn't put on any makeup, just lined her blue eyes automatically with kajal, not bothering to look in the mirror.

She put her small silk purse across her shoulder, locked the door, and walked down the steps, engulfed all at once by the hot afternoon air. Claire stopped. She had the eerie feeling of being watched. Quickly she looked toward the von Lillienfeld house but no one was there, just a heavy Siamese calmly licking his paws. The murder had her unreasonably jumpy. Halfway down the block she turned again and noticed the Mayor following her. She threw back her fine head of dark hair and laughed. "All right, your honor. I suppose you can take care of yourself in traffic if anybody can. And probably me, too, hmm? Are you coming along to look after me?"

Of course he was coming along to look after her, the Mayor snorted to himself. Why else did she think he'd hung around the house? And this the fish store's biggest day.

Together they made their long way up the hill. Claire grudgingly kept to the opposite side of the street on Park Lane South. She would have liked to take the woods path but she didn't dare. She didn't know which she feared more: the murderer (who was most likely long gone) or Zinnie's fiery wrath, should she find out, and so she stayed on the other side which was actually very pleasant, lined with mansions from another era and walled in luxurious privet hedging, thick with the unfenceable scents of late wisteria and roses.

Claire told the Mayor all about India as she walked, her memory jogged from the broad yellow heat and the smells and the comfortable shade of the trees. Her sandals made small cushy sounds on the slate and the Mayor's long nails scratched along. She told him things she'd never tell the others. They would just laugh or shake their heads or not believe her anyway.

The street was crowded up on Metropolitan; they pushed along past the piles of Korean vegetables, neat and brilliant in their tropical rows, then past the antique shops, up Lefferts, by the Jewish temple, and past the cluster of apartment houses until finally they came to the village, old-fashioned and European in style with Tudor walls and crockety red tile roofs. The Homestead Deli, with its good-looking wursts necklacing the lead-paned windows, might just as well have been a village shop in Munich or Zurich. And Regents Row resembled any pub in England. It was a potpourri and charming layout, Claire decided, delighted with the mixture of old world and new, the modern supermarket and the oriental music leaking from the Pakistani Spice Shop. One really could settle down here, so near and yet so far from anything-can-happen Manhattan. Why couldn't the murder have happened there, where it would seem to belong, instead of here, so close to her family? Hadn't they been through enough as it was? The dry dead face of Michael in his coffin came back to her in a rush and her mood was ruined. It was too hot after all, she'd just run into the camera shop and hurry back home. Now where on earth was the Mayor?

A clattering of voices and the beginnings of shouts near the corner jolted her out of her reverie.

It was . . . good God, it was the Mayor tug-of-warring a kosher chicken from a scull-capped, aproned shopkeeper! The Italian louts who held court in front of the pizzeria were howling with laughter and—what else?—rooting for the dog.

Claire, fleet-footed and all business, flew down to the hubbub and yanked the tooth-dented chicken from the fangs of the Mayor.

"Bravo!" the Italians whistled and applauded, "Bravo, bella signorina!"

The shopkeeper, highly offended, flailed his arms and whined and yelled a Yiddish tirade.

Truly sorry, embarrassed, and angry at the Mayor to boot, Claire reached into her purse and hauled out ten dollars.

"So eine scheisse!" the shopkeeper droned on and on, *"Schauen Sie mal was der verdammte Hund mit meinem Laden gemacht hat!"*

A small crowd had gathered. Claire peered into the

cool darkness of the shop and saw, indeed, that the sawdust had been strewn with torn gizzards and three or four other hens, good as new.

She reached back into her purse and pulled out the last of what she had on her, a twenty dollar bill. The shopkeeper, sweat and dandruff glistening from his voluminous neck folds, yammered on in his guttural tongue. "Tya!" he wailed. "What good is that little bit of *geld* when my entire store was *kaputt?*" He went on to inform his audience that Claire was a *"Schikse pipi mädchen"* with a "shit dog."

That was it for Claire, who'd understood each nasty word. "Is that right?!" she threw the chicken into the street and the contents of her purse right after it.

"This is what I think of your store that has been so *totally* disheveled! You're not only an exaggerator, you're . . . you're without resiliency! My dog is not a 'shit' as you so loudly proclaim, he happens to be the mayor of this town. And I am no *Schiksa* floozie but an American who finds you extremely constipated!"

Well, this was all too much for the crew of Italians. Claire's rage was just too magnificent. They collapsed into peals of laughter and a barrage of lewd Sicilian expletives.

Infuriated, Claire whirled around and yelled, *"Stati zita, imbecile!"* right in Johnny Benedetto's minding-his-own-business face.

"Listen, honey—" Johnny protested.

"Don't call me 'honey'!" hollered Claire and she snapped away, tripped, and flew over the chicken, marched past the astonished shopkeeper, and hurried down the hill, her knees still trembling with indignation and the face of that . . . that thoroughly obnoxious Italian. Mollified by all of this off-with-their-heads, the Mayor followed at a respectful distance, his tail muscled down between his legs in solemn retribution, his snout a neat mask of the called-for chagrin. But, by jove, he was pleased.

CHAPTER

2

Zinnie roared into the driveway. Wherever Zinnie went she was off to a fire. She screeched to a halt, bounded from the car, and stopped dead in her tracks. If there was one thing Zinnie couldn't take, it was crawly things, and silver-dollar-sized, dark red spiders had been spinning webs from Park Lane South to Myrtle. "Oh, Christ," she said out loud and ran into the house.

All through the woods and two blocks overflowing on the Richmond Hill side were these doilies five feet and more in diameter. It didn't help to tear them down. The spiders had their web sites obstinately chosen and, tzak-tzak, they'd only build them up again, good as new, right where you'd torn them down. No one had seen the likes of it since the caterpillar blitzkrieg back in 1957. And Zinnie, who wouldn't bat an eye over a gun-drawn gallop through a subway station at midnight after some fleeing Rastafarians, and that without a backup anywhere in sight, would whimper at the very idea of a bug near her. Once inside, she slammed the kitchen screen door and shivered, safe.

Carmela was setting the table. She was doing it pink and green, in all seriousness, to set off the fillet of sole. Michaelaen, who'd been doing his best to irritate her by driving a matchbox truck in furrows along the tablecloth, stood up on his chair and threw his arms open in mute welcome when he saw Zinnie. She scooped him up and threw him over her head. "Rrrowwll," she bit the tummied gap between shorts and T-shirt. "Where's the salt and pepper? This is my dinner right here!" Michaelaen squirmed with delighted horror and rolled his truck into her mouth.

"We're invaded," Zinnie announced. "They're taking over!"

Carmela made "Twilight Zone" noises and Michaelaen watched her with big eyes.

"The spider webs?" Mary didn't look up from her mushrooms. Peeling mushrooms was one of her peculiarities. Nobody else peeled mushroom tops, but she did.

"They're something, all right," agreed Carmela. "Revolting."

"Your father likes the spiders," Mary defended them.

"Me, too," said Michaelaen.

Stan peeked his head in (speak of the devil), wanting to know when dinner would be ready.

"Right after you go wash the sawdust off your face and hands," Mary poked him out of the doorway. "And you stay off my clean linoleum!"

"I wish he'd go back to Vivaldi," Carmela shook her head at the retreating mezzo staccato. "At least then we didn't have to listen to the words." Wherever Stan went he was locked to an opera.

"Why don't you use the frigging air conditioner?" Zinnie demanded. They'd all chipped in and bought Mary an air conditioner, but she never used it. "I stopped at Jay Dee's," Zinnie changed the subject, holding up a box of coconut custard pie.

"There goes my diet," Mary moaned.

"I get the string," Michaelaen shouted. He collected bakery string.

"Where's Claire?" asked Zinnie.

"Down in the cellar. Assembling her darkroom."

"Oh."

"Jay Dee's?" Carmela asked shrewdly. "Isn't that the one on Queens Boulevard?"

"Best coconut custard in Queens." Zinnie turned her back and removed her gun.

"I don't suppose you ran into anyone?" Carmela continued.

"As a matter of fact I *did* stop off at Freddy's, nosy."

Michaelaen's ears perked up and he regarded his mother with serpentine quiet.

"And?"

"Sweetheart, be a good boy and go get Grandma some parsley from the garden, would you?"

Michaelaen glared at his grandmother.

"Go ahead," Zinnie smiled and gave him a hug. "Then I'll tell you where your dad's taking you tomorrow. Okay?"

Michaelaen raced outside, a lit-up glider plane. Tomorrow he would see his dad.

"So what did Freddy have to say?" Mary threw nutmeg into her white sauce. "He making out all right?"

Zinnie snatched a major leaf from Carmela's strategically arranged salad and sat down. "What is this, the centerfold for *Gourmet Magazine*?" Carmela had bombarded the table with peony branches and distinguished pink roses. Zinnie frowned. "I so hate not being able to see my date."

"Your date is Michaelaen," Carmela said. "Now tell about Freddy."

Zinnie shrugged. "I just thought I'd, you know, go see how they're coming along with the restaurant."

"And how's it coming?" Mary asked.

"I'll tell ya, it looks really nice. Fancy. You'd love it, Carmela. Veddy veddy art deco."

"You sound disappointed."

"Yeah. Well . . . he's doing so damn well without me. I was kinda hoping . . . I really don't know what I was hoping."

"You tell him about the murder?" Carmela asked.

Zinnie looked from her to her mother and back. "Sure."

"Don't give us 'sure,'" Carmela sneered. "We know all

about it. The whole neighborhood knows. It's all anybody's talking about."

"Oh. To tell you the truth, I did talk about the murder with Freddy. Only it was me who did the asking. I wanted to get the gay slant on it."

"What?"

"You know what I mean. Sometimes they know about someone who's . . . uh . . . kooky in that direction. They hear things."

"And did he?"

"Naw. But he'll keep his ears open. The last thing he wants is the cops cracking down on all the gays. They've got enough trouble with the AIDS scare."

Mary and Carmela exchanged looks.

Zinnie screwed up her mouth. "Now what?"

"No, nothing," Carmela busied herself with napkin folding. "Mom was just a little worried about Michaelaen . . ."

"What, that he'd get AIDS from Freddy?!" Zinnie's face went red.

"Well, God, Zin. Children do get AIDS, you know. It's not such a farfetched concern."

"Look," Zinnie cried then lowered her voice. "Michaelaen is *my* son and I'd appreciate it if you'd let *me* worry about it, all right?"

Claire, coming up the cellar stairs, saw Michaelaen at the back door standing still with a bouquet of parsley, waiting cautiously inside his little shroud of gloom. She slipped out the door.

"Hello," she said.

He said nothing.

"I was just going to catch myself some lightning bugs."

Michaelaen regarded her suspiciously through hooded eyes.

"Just to catch. I'll let them go, of course. I like to hold them in my hand. You?"

He nodded, reluctantly, and followed her onto the darkening grass.

Johnny Benedetto tossed around in his sloppy bed. Perspiration rolled off his body and wet the sheets. He was dreaming of a little boy in holy terror. Johnny flung one fist out desperately; the woods became the streets of Brooklyn and the little boy turned into himself. He entered the crummy building with the peeling wallpaper in the hallway and took the old elevator up. It took so long, then bounced to a stop. He heard someone in the apartment. Voices. Women's voices wailing. They were in there with his mother. He stood at the open door of the apartment and the women turned to look at him. They stopped crying. "Mom?" he called, looking past their heads. "Mom?" But nobody would let him in. They pulled him down the stairs and brought him somewhere else to wait for his aunt. He didn't like his aunt, he told them. He wanted his mom. His mom had gone away, they told him, she had gone back to Jesus and he must be brave. . . . Johnny woke up with a jolt. His breath came short and fast. Trembling, he reached out and felt for the gun on the night stand. It was all right. Just a dream. He was fine.

When dinner was done, Claire hung around the kitchen and helped her mother dry the dishes. Mary was going to hymn mass with the neighbor, Mrs. Dixon. They had been walking to church together for almost twelve years now, and chatting over the hedge whenever they hung wash, and still they called each other "Mrs."

"Good Lord, it's muggy," Mary wiped her brow. "I'd better change this blouse. Smells of fish. I hate that when you stand next to someone in church who's all smelly."

"You really like to go to church, don't you, Mom?"

"I wouldn't go if I didn't like it, now, would I?"

"No. You wouldn't. But a lot of people would."

Mary slid the Mayor out from in front of the refrigerator with one foot, put the leftovers inside, closed the door, and slid him back to his spot, smack in everybody's way. It was a wonder that no one ever stepped on him, but nobody did, and he wouldn't budge on his own. He liked the ride.

"Would it be," Mary suggested casually, "that you'd like to come along?"

"Uh-uh."

"Another time, then." She surveyed the kitchen. Spic and span until the onslaught of night snacking. Claire was over at the sideboard, reaching for the tallest shelf with ease. Claire had the legs in the family. She reminded Mary of her own mother, Jenny Rose. The longest legs and most heathen ideas in all of Skibbereen. If Mary didn't know better, she'd think Claire was Jenny Rose born twice. Sometimes, when Claire looked at her . . . ah, silly notions only got you round the bend and back to where you started. You lived and died and if you'd done it well you would get your reward. There was no telling what the Holy Ghost was up to.

"Ma?" Claire steadied the plate she almost dropped, "How do you think something like that can happen? A murder like that?"

Mary closed her eyes and turned her head. Claire had always been the clumsy one. She couldn't bear to watch her with the good china.

"I mean from the murderer's side. How can someone live with such guilt?"

Guilt? Interested now, in spite of herself, Mary sat at the white pine table. "If indeed the murderer *knows* guilt," she said.

"You mean a schizophrenic?"

"Ah, these labels psychiatrists put on things! Evil was around a long time before they thought up words like that. Words that allow murderers to sit around in hospital gardens and take the sun just as nice as you please. And then back out on the street to kill again." She straightened her shoulders. "Especially in this city."

"Yeah, but there must be more to it than that, than simple good and evil."

"What's simple? We all are secrets from ourselves."

Claire sat down, too. She loved it when her mother got like this, all deep and confidential. Irish.

"We trudge along, not being especially good, hoping, anyway, for miracles. Don't we? And then there are those who, having given up, have given in, regardless of . . . *because* of the blind and total lure of evil."

"Yeah, but how does it start, the madness? When? Is it learned or inherent?"

"Or," Mary's face lit up, "is it a living force predestined and allowed to exist by some great power, planted into innocence haphazardly?"

"A plan that has no plan?"

Mary leaned across the table. "Just lessons to be learned," she whispered. "Battles to be won."

Claire lit a cigarette. Her mother would be annoyed to know that the gurus preached the same philosophy, almost word for word.

"Oh, give me one," Mary snapped.

Surprised, Claire gave her hers and lit another.

"Just don't tell your father."

The Mayor hopped up and howled. "Oh, drat," Mary put the cigarette out quickly and waved the air. "That's Mrs. Dixon. Let her in and I'll get ready."

Claire opened the door and in came Mrs. Dixon, short and plump and her hair rinsed blue.

"Now look at this!" she gushed. "The prodigal daughter returned and not a tat the worse for wear! Just as pretty as ever!"

Claire smiled. Mrs. Dixon was so nice that she made you feel not nice. "Mom'll be right down, Mrs. Dixon. Just went to change her blouse."

"Let me look at you. My, my!" Mrs. Dixon pulled her apart by the wrists. "You look like a teenager. Those lashes! And your brother's eyes!" Her own kindly, reminiscent gray orbs twinkled.

Claire's mouth went dry. She willed her mother to hurry. "Why don't you sit down, Mrs. Dixon, Mom will be—"

"I always wondered about you, Claire . . . if you were ever coming home. Your mother missed you so. And your dad—"

Mary arrived then, still buttoning up. Claire fled.

"Hello, Mrs. Dixon. Are we late?"

"Plenty of time, plenty of time."

"Oh, you've brought your umbrella! Did they say it would finally rain?"

"It's for the webs, dear. Fending off the spider webs."

Michaelaen looked out the upstairs window. He watched Grandma go. Now she was gone. Immediately, he snuck down the hallway and down the back stairs. He made himself into a tight little fellow and scooted out the doggy door. Nobody saw him. He rushed. He crossed Eighty-fifth and went straight up the block till he came to the tree. He sat down on a root two feet high. This tree was three, maybe four hundred years old. Even Grandpa said so. Michaelaen pulled one sturdy leg over and straddled the root. It was warm as himself. He dug swiftly with the shoe horn he'd brought and in a minute he had a pretty good hole. Michaelaen went into his pocket and pulled out the pictures he'd hidden there. Brian. Miguel. And a couple of the other big boys. They were a little sticky from his pocket. He folded them over and put them in the hole, then covered it up good. Just in the nick of time, too, because here came stupid Charlotte, who lived across the street. Probably on her way to the carousel, by herself. Thought she was big. Phhh. It wouldn't be too good if she saw him, so he'd better go home. She was one little freshie of a tattletale.

Johnny Benedetto lived in a three-over-three house, right on the southeast rim of Aqueduct Racetrack. The sweet smell of horse and manure and hay filled his kitchen all the time. In the summer it was worse. Johnny stood in the dark at the window, drinking Diet Coke, groggily watching through the venetian blind at the horse they'd put up in the temporary big top, a golden horse whose head was more often out than in. The horse reminded Johnny of himself. She was a real rubberneck—couldn't stay indoors without watching the street.

There were plenty of housewives on Johnny's block who'd demonstrated and fought not to have the stables extended so close to their backyards, but that was just how Johnny'd got the house, cheap, from a family whose asthmatic daughter couldn't stand it. They'd moved out to Valley Stream and Johnny had lucked out. Nobody liked the smell, but what were you gonna do? There was a feeling Johnny got from looking out and seeing that horse there with her head sticking out. He couldn't understand why his neighbors didn't feel it, too. Fury. Black Beauty. Flicker. No, there was something all right about having a frigging horse out your window.

Johnny left his Coke can on the back stairs in a pagoda of other Coke cans and locked the back door. The track was all lit up, the fourth race already underway, and the mosquitos were biting. He was very much alive and that little Hispanic boy was dead. Real dead.

"Who do you like in the ninth?" Johnny greeted the horse while he lugged out the garbage. He opened the garage and hopped into the car. The front seat was littered with old papers, outstanding bills, styrofoam cups and one change of a wrinkly wardrobe which sat there like a frazzled passenger. This was Johnny's office. The engine underneath the hood looked like a gleaming space center and fingerprints on the door were removed fastidiously almost before they got there, but the inside of the car? He wouldn't know what you were talking about. Johnny turned the key in the ignition, set the air conditioner on full speed, and snapped on the overhead light. He searched the front and back seats thoroughly and eventually came up with the address he needed. When you had nothing to go on, you went with any stupid lead before you wrote it off. The worst feeling was having nothing to do. If you thought about things too much you'd go nuts. And you usually did.

His honor, digesting, watched staunch vegetarian Claire transport shiny bologna on Wonder bread out to the porch. The crickets were singing. Claire balanced a tall glass of milk with her sandwich and a pickle rolled dangerously round the plate as she maneuvered the door with an elbow. One frozen Milky Way protruded from each under arm.

"What?" she looked at him. "You, with your Kosher chicken appetite. You've got nothing to say."

The cat can well look at the queen, thought the Mayor, miffed.

Claire climbed up into the hammock with her goods. The wobbly table was already prepared with an ashtray, a candle, and five Kodak boxes of unopened slides. These were the last days of McLeod Gange and the first color shots from her third day in Queens. Maybe one of them would be brilliant. One would be sufficient. Claire lit the candle to hold each slide in front of. This was not the way it was done, but she had sold her projector and carousel to Sami Ja back in McLeod Gange, the Tibetan village where she'd lived above the Tea Shop of the Tibetan Moon. She was used to doing it this way, now. And Sami Ja was back in the Himalayas making a living showing slides of naked Bagwanis from Poona to the wide-eyed Tibetans. His shows were a raving success. Even the sweet, aproned ladies came. The sight of those earnest, pink-faced yuppies on the road to redemption via nudity delighted them. They laughed and laughed.

Sami Ja was a Tibetan teenager who'd latched on to Claire like a suckling wolf when he'd heard where she came from. "New York?" he'd cried, ecstatic. "Want some hash?" Claire could still see him with his scant Fu Manchu and a lavender jacket that read CBS Sports, front and back. He would pay her to marry him, he'd told her on the day she'd arrived in the village, filthy dirty from the coal truck. "No? And what about a letter to sponsor? Oh, no? Well then, how would she feel about a good down sleeping bag? Brand new! Mountain climber died first day out. Good zipper!"

Claire had bought the sleeping bag. All alone, late at night when the tea shop was closed and the mice scurried joyfully over the icy rafters, she was happy to have her good zipper. Claire would miss Sami Ja. "Another day," he'd flick his prayer beads over easy, "another dollah." He would be all right, back there, taking bets from the trekkers, selling forbidden tours of the Dalai Lama's palace, playing poker with the disenchanted. One day he, too, would know these highlights of American culture that he could now only hear of and dream about: Haagen Daaz. "Dynasty." That polyester mecca of bliss: Atlantic City. Someday it would all be his.

Claire held the first slide of him up to the light.

There he was, on tiptoes, squinting at the camera from the waterfall. He was thinking maybe this photograph would be seen by some big-shot producer. Claire sighed, remembering the cool, enduring waterfall.

A car came down the block and its headlights lit up the spider web along the rail, turning it silver and exposing wriggling victims caught and now doomed. Claire groaned and looked the other way. It wasn't the spider that troubled her. Spiders were good luck. This one scrambled over to his favorite, strategic thread and waited for wind and traffic to send him his well-earned dinner. What troubled Claire were those he wouldn't eat. Grudgingly, she'd have to get up and untangle the ones she felt especially sorry for. She couldn't help it. She suspected she was only prolonging their inevitable karmic rebirths to a higher form of life, but it was a tricky problem. After all, destiny had placed her in this spot, too, complete with her sucker's instinct to save the stupid things. The spider would only catch more, so what good would it do? And what was good, anyway? What you meant well very often turned out to be a muddle. Like the time in McLeod Gange when she'd run around trying to get some help for the dying cat. Claire had barely known the cat, but Hula, the proprietress of the tea shop, had pulled the mangy thing off the street for her and her aversion to mice and so she'd felt bound to the thing.

She'd cleaned it up and fed it for a week, but the sickly thing would not get well. It lay at the top of the stairs and wouldn't move, wouldn't eat. It just stank. And Claire had picked it up and run around trying to get help for it. Everyone had laughed. Nobody cared about a damn cat. She'd carried the stinking animal into the traffic of Himalayan hubbub and she was going to find him a vet. Of course there was no vet, not even in the Hindu village down below, so she carried it to the healing lama. When she'd finally made it to the lama's cabin he wasn't there, he was up in the mountain searching for herbs to roll into pills. The narrow-eyed assistant, thinking himself helpful, had brought out a club, and he was baffled when Claire, in tears, had jogged away down the path with the now-moaning cat. In a panic, Claire had realized that she had to get the poor thing home to the Tea Shop of the Tibetan Moon. Along the way, in the middle of the village, with the prayer wheel going round and round and a session of young monks playing potsy in the road, the cat had thrown back its orange head, stretched its arms and legs in rigid agony, and died.

When things were set to die, Claire knew, one might well provide them with peaceful surroundings in which to do it and not go carting them about like a lunatic, as though it would do any good. She bit into her bologna sandwich. The bread was so fresh that it stuck to the roof of her mouth like a host at communion. And you couldn't beat sharp mustard. You really couldn't. Murmuring confusion seeped from the separate television camps the family was divided into around the house. She had the feeling, almost hope and almost fear, that nothing would ever happen again. The milk was ice cold and she drank it greedily. A burst of laughter from inside lit up her face and she smiled with them at some new antic of Michaelaen's. Or someone's. It didn't matter. She was with them, apart but close.

The car that had just passed turned around, hesitated, then stopped right in front of the house. Some sporty little car. A light went on in Iris von Lillienfeld's back porch and the Mayor crossed over the street. A big man climbed out of the car, studied something in his hand and proceeded up the front walk. Claire leaned forward. It was that—that drug dealer from this afternoon! A thrill of something went right through her.

"This 113-04?" He shielded his eyes from the lantern, then saw her shocked face. Jesus! It was that very same cuckoo from the pizza place!

"You've got a lot of nerve," she reprimanded him, her tone dating back to a decade of tight-assed, condescending grammar school nuns.

"Look, lady. Before you get all bent out of shape, I didn't come here to see you!"

Claire dropped the whole box of slides. Lady? How old did he think she was? Had he followed her home?

"Does a Mr. Stanley Breslinsky live here?" he continued, politely bending down to help her pick up the cascade of slides.

"No!" she snatched one right out of his hand. He had wrists thick with enemy black hairs. "You've put your fingerprints all over the slide." She pulled her hair out of her eyes. "Yes, he does live here," she said, annoyed, in fact, that he hadn't followed her home.

Married, concluded Johnny, hating her.

"Dad!" called Claire. Now he hated her more.

No one came and the two of them glared at each other. "Dad!" she called again, louder, refusing to get up and give those scornful eyes a good shot at her short shorts.

Stan looked through the front screen. "Oh," he said, peering out at Johnny. "I didn't hear the dog."

"He took off," Claire complained. "This man would like to speak with you."

This man, Johnny mimicked her inside his head. Like, "this creep." "Detective Benedetto," he said. "I'm with the 102nd. You stopped off there this morning?"

"Yes?" Stan looked around guiltily, then remembered Mary was off to church.

"I wonder if I could have a word with you?"

"Sure!" Stan opened the door and ushered Johnny in. What a hulk of a guy! He slapped him on the back and directed him into his "study," a room dedicated to one cannon after the next. Wherever you looked there were cannons, homemade crossbows, hunks of wood in various stages of finish. Johnny gave a low whistle. "You make this stuff?" he eyed Stan, impressed.

"What? This?" Stan waved aside the room as though he'd never seen it. "Just a hobby. Old man like me. Got to have something to do now, don't I?"

Johnny picked up a rosewood and brass miniature of exquisite proportion.

"This is beautiful."

"That's the Gustavus Adolphus," Stan glowed. "Swedish." If Michael had lived . . . Stan started to think, till he caught himself.

"God. I've never seen work like this. Look at the wheels!"

"You have a good eye. Most people don't notice detail like that. The wheels happen to have been the most difficult of all. I had to study to be a wheelwright in order to make them. Lots of time, they took, lots of time. We fired one last weekend. That's why there's still a little powder burn near the wick."

"You're kidding! You mean these things really work?"

"Indeed they do. The cannonballs are in the limber, there."

Johnny flipped open the miniature lock and opened it. It eased open like a well-oiled treasure box. Not only were there twenty little cannonballs lined up neatly on a polished shelf, but a proper bucket, a mallet, and a pickax as well, all gleaming in rosewood and brass. A delicate white cord with gold-nuggeted ends was waxed, braided, and coiled.

"But you're an armorer!" Johnny exploded.

Stan was wiping his hands on an old piece of shammy. He looked up through his bushy eyebrows and studied Johnny. "Not many people know what a small-arms expert is, either."

Fascinated, Johnny turned the smooth wheel of the Rodman. "Yeah, well, there aren't too many of them around. I got to know one of them in Nam. He was a genius with explosives."

"Really? That's what I did in World War II. Demolition. We blew up the swastika of Nürnberg." He grinned. "Among other things."

Stan and Johnny gazed at each other with final approval. The record came to an end and Stan hurried over to flip it. "Ah, Puccini," he sighed.

"Sir?"

"Puccini."

"Sounds good," Johnny scratched his forehead, embarrassed.

"So," Stan sank into his chair, "down to tacks."

Johnny reminded him of the conflicting numbers he'd reported.

"Oh, yes. You see, my daughter saw this car, and—"

Johnny looked up at Carmela pirouetting into the room. She was wearing a tuxedo and stiletto heels. Her mouth was an indignant fuschia.

"My daughter," Stan shrugged. "Carmela."

"Dad, my car won't start."

"It's just the butterfly, knucklehead. It always is."

"Yes, but I'd rather take yours, if I may." She looked Johnny over. From the lines of his car she had thought he'd be something. He had good teeth all right, but his Izod La Coste shirt was not a La Coste at all. It was a counterfeit. What's more, it looked as though it had been slept in. He was obviously ill-bred. Didn't even stand up. Stan fished in his pocket for keys and handed them over. "Be careful," he warned and she started to leave.

"You the one who saw the car?" Johnny stopped her.

Carmela gripped her chest. "Me? Of course not. That was Claire."

"That's my other daughter . . . on the porch."

"Yes, she lives on the porch," Carmela smiled.

"Oh, she doesn't live on the porch. Sometimes she sleeps out there."

"Every night since she's come home."

"You see, Claire's been living overseas—"

"Over a tea shop. In the Himalayas."

"Yes. Well. She's not used to being back in civilization yet. And she . . . she saw this car early in the morning but she thought it would be better if I went down and told about it."

Johnny's shoulder's sank. "I'm afraid I'll have to speak to her then."

"Oh, no!" they both said.

Johnny looked at them.

Carmela untangled her bow tie and pulled it up into her hair. "You see, Claire has this thing about policemen."

"She won't talk to you," Stan agreed. "I mean, she'd rather not."

A gigantic funeral arrangement came in on a pair of men's legs.

"Freddy!" Carmela cried. "Gladiola!"

Freddy struggled in and lowered the flowers onto Stan's cluttered desk. He was dressed a la Miami Vice and his hair was shaved stylishly over his ears with a brilliantined dip in the front. "From the restaurant." His lips pursed of their own accord. "I've got so many I don't know what to do with them all. I'll bring more by tomorrow when I come to pick up Michaelaen."

He's a fruit, thought Johnny.

"Daddy!" Michaelaen, so happy that he had to act mad,

marched into the room and butted his head into his father's designer-jeaned leg.

"Where's your mother?" Freddy hugged him. "Go tell her I'm here."

"This is Frederick Schmidt," Stan introduced him to Johnny. "Detective Bene . . ."

"Benedetto," Johnny finished for him, stretching out his hand, remembering AIDS. *Daddy?*

Uh-oh, thought Freddy and he put up his guard.

"Schmidt? Freddy Schmidt?" Johnny repeated out loud. "You didn't used to quarterback for Holy Cross?"

"That was me," Freddy grinned, resigned now to the look of shock, disgust, and pity that was sure to cross Johnny's face. But it didn't come. At least he has that much class, Freddy thought. "How's the writing coming, Carmela? Won any Pulitzers yet?"

Carmela threw herself across the ripped leather sofa and flung one arm behind her head. "If I don't get some dirt on someone fast, I might very well be forced to go back to writing novels." She exhaled an elaborate swoon.

"Not that you ever finished one of those," said Zinnie as she walked in and gave Freddy a kiss on the cheek. "You look good," she told him generously. "Hi," she reached over and gave a hand to Johnny.

"Detective Benedetto, meet Officer Breslinsky," Stan said proudly. He wished Freddy wouldn't sit like that, so close to the Dahlgren. You never knew when that one would fire. There were still some kinks in it that he would have to work out.

Freddy obligingly stood up and walked over to the bar. "Drink?" he asked no one in particular and helped himself to a Frangelica.

"Officer, huh? Where do you work?"

"Midtown South. Anticrime."

"Nice house. Who's your hook?"

"My brother was on the job." Zinnie suddenly began to search for fleas in Michaelaen's spanking clean mop of hair.

"No kidding? How long you been on?"

"Three years," Zinnie smiled.

Nice kid, Johnny thought.

"You want to talk to Claire?" She accepted the bourbon and water Freddy handed her.

"Seems to be a problem."

Zinnie kicked her head to one side. "Leave it to me. C'mon." She led Johnny back out to the porch where Claire was on hands and knees under the hammock, carefully retrieving the last of the slides.

"Man wants to talk to you," Zinnie took a long swig of her drink and smacked her lips.

Claire looked up at her. They traded telepathic messages, the final one being Zinnie's no-nonsense reminder that this was a murder here, not a parking ticket. Claire wobbled to her feet. Johnny just stood there, looking. And he was nice and comfortable in his own skin, a thing she rarely was. He made her feel . . . unreal. She cleared her throat.

Johnny leaned on the railing. Claire grasped his arm with both hands and transported him a few feet to the left. "You were backing into the spider's web," she mumbled.

"Thank you," he said, misunderstanding her concern for the spider as concern for him.

They were both going to be civil.

"You take pictures?"

"Mostly just old people up in the park."

"My sister shoots Jews." Zinnie curtsied and left.

"Now about this car . . ."

Claire put the slides down. "I woke up for no reason. Maybe the sun woke me up. Or the Mayor."

"The dog."

"Yes, the dog. And a big, old gold Plymouth was coming down from the park, see, right down there . . ."

Plymouth. He was writing this down. He wasn't going to let her catch him looking at those legs.

"Plymuth?" she frowned at his notes. "So you can't spell."

"No," he feigned nonchalance, "I can't spell."

"Uh . . . anyway, I wasn't thinking about anything. I didn't see who was in the car. But it was a man. A medium-build man. Not dark, really. I was looking at the license number and thinking that it was Buddha's year. It distracted me. And then I went back to sleep."

"Buddha?"

"Yes."

Johnny clicked his eyes into place. Was she kidding?

"And those are the two sets of numbers your father gave the desk clerk?"

"563 or 473. Yes."

"And you don't know which?"

"No, I really don't," she answered cooly. "The year of ascension or of birth. They're the only two I know. I tend to think it was 473. I feel more comfortable with that number."

Freddy, Zinnie, and Carmela came out the front door together, toodle-ooed and off they went in their separate directions. Johnny watched Claire distribute her good-byes. She really thought who the hell she was, didn't she? Buddha. Himalayas. Spelling.

She turned to him with puppy dog eyes. "Then you weren't with those playboys out in front of the pizza place?"

"No. Look, would you come with me down—"

"I don't date policemen," she interrupted him.

Johnny laughed. "I wasn't asking you out on a date. I was asking you to come down to the precinct and look at some mug shots."

"Mug shots?" Claire felt the blood rush to her cheeks. "But I never saw anybody!"

"Miss Breslinsky, you told me you had the impression of a man. Maybe you could look at some pictures and just eliminate . . . just give us an idea what kind of—"

"But I didn't see anybody! I have no idea who was in that car!"

He snapped his notebook shut. "Right. Thank you very much for your help, Miss Breslinsky."

"You need not use sarcasm, detective. I really can't help you."

"No," Johnny narrowed his eyes and spoke directly to her ankles. "You really can't." He started to take his dramatic leave but was stopped in his tracks by the sight of two stocky ladies trotting up the street with matching whale-sized handbags flailing. One of them, Errol Flynn, had taken the lead and was fencing the air with a turquoise umbrella.

"My mother," Claire explained.

"Whoosh," Mrs. Dixon dashed ahead of Mrs. Breslinsky up to the porch. "It's like a jungle!"

Mrs. Breslinsky, breathing swiftly, sank onto the top step.

"Aha! Another!" Mrs. Dixon broke lance with the web on the railing.

"Now why did you have to do that?" Claire asked her.

"Well, now, what do you mean, dear?" She wiped her umbrella with a hanky. "I thought you'd be pleased."

Mary's eyes blazed. "We got a good ten of them on the way home. Well, Mrs. Dixon did. Good evening, young man."

"Mother, this is Detective Benedetto. Detective, my mother, Mary Breslinsky, and Mrs. Dixon."

"Are you coming inside?" Mary smiled hopefully at him. "It's cooler in there. Didn't anyone offer you a lemonade? Or a Coke?"

"I was just taking off," Johnny thanked her.

Claire looked over at the von Lillienfeld house. Now there were no lights on.

"Isn't it a grand evening?" Mary sighed. "So tropical!"

Claire watched her Milky Ways ooze into neatly wrapped puddles. Grand evening? What was she talking about? It was so sweltering that she could feel her head begin to ache. It was awful. Why didn't he leave?

"Hello," said Michaelaen from inside.

"What? Still up? Come give your old grandma a kiss."

Michaelaen slid out the door and sidled up to his grandma. His mouth was full of cherry cough drops. Michaelaen loved those cherry cough drops.

"Who are you?" he said to Johnny.

"Just a cop," Johnny looked into Claire's blue eyes.

That did it. She got up and went inside.

The Siamese named Lü who owned Miss von Lillienfeld crept under cover of night to the spot in the pine where the murder had happened. He didn't walk right on the spot but circled, eyes capable and cunning in the dark. Nothing moved. He went with a sorcerer's stealth, watching this way and that, but the spirit was gone. Lü the cat beat a swift retreat. It was not the dead one must fear but the living.

The Mayor stood beneath the lantern on White Hill. He watched Lü leave the woods and safely cross old Park Lane South. Lü still moved well for his age. He didn't have the Mayor's paunch or grizzled knees. Lü didn't bother to glance over. He didn't have the Mayor's breeding, either, for all his certificates of parentage, and took all displays of concern as signs of weakness. A regular Frankie bachelor. On separate sides of the street, they both tobogganed home.

CHAPTER 3

A broad expanse of yellowish white spread out about her. It was some sort of desert, only vaporous. The sky was knotted into a diamond blue fist faraway. Claire turned her back on it easily, so easily, sinking to the earth in a spot that was rich and turned, like after a flood rain. She wore her aviator sunglasses. I'm tough, they told the world. But I am innocent. Notice my very best white shoes. Her feet sunk in quickly, surprised by the sudden weight of her, muck oozing up through her toes in a fertile and cool eerie depth. There were worms, dozens of worms taking off in a frantic decampment, *une échapper belle,* till the whole mudsill broke and she stood, sliding upright down the fudgy ravine, an escalator passenger in any subterranean department store. It came to a halt beside a cascade of uncovered hair, Michael's hair, from Michael's gaping grave.

"Michael," she whispered and reached out her hand, but he stayed where he was, face down in rude oblivion, preoccupied with his eternal sleep. Only his hair grew on, unstoppable, magnificent, alive with greedy, crawling maggots.

She woke up still calling his name. Her face, wet with tears, was jammed against the slanted attic wall. Claire looked at the peeling white paint for what seemed like a long time. Then, cautiously, she flipped her body over. Not too bad. On the table stood a bottle of bourbon with its own hefty dent in it. Ah, well. She got out of bed, reeled a bit, felt all right somehow, and careened down the stairs. It was barely light, but there would be no more sleeping for her. She brushed her teeth soundly, engrossed in this static melancholy, a little bit surprised and guiltily pleased to find herself alive. God, I'm famished, she said to herself. Obediently, her legs carried her straight to the kitchen.

There were four almost blue red tomatoes in the colander. She took the white bread down from the shelf. You could say what you wanted about how unhealthy it was, but when it was fresh from the grocer's like this, light as a feather, and you slathered a couple of slices with mayonnaise, carved yourself some thick slabs of those wine red tomatoes, and jiggled some black pepper onto it—it was a deeply moving thing. She poured a glass of icy milk and ate off a sheet of paper towel, still drunk. This would be the time to photograph something, feeling like this, gently woozy and still half in touch with her nightmare.

She left before the rest of the house was up, heading south toward Jamaica Avenue, excited and nervous in the already gray dawn. The veins in her ankles and hands stood out disturbingly in the heat. What could you do? If age and the humidity didn't get you, the alcohol would.

She remembered Johnny Benedetto with a sinking heart. How many attractive young women must he run into every day? On the job, at night, even in the supermarket. There was no end to the horror of possibilities.

The thing was—she strode purposefully along with her camera banging against her hip—that even if you did fall in love, you wound up eventually envying that person you were in love with. It was true. You envied him for the same silly reasons you fell in love with him.

You met him at a party, for example, where he stood against a wall eyeing you as though he could eat you up, his eyes ironic and helpless at the same time, longing for you and you knew it damn well, and then when you gave in, when you finally (after the initial mandatory and long-winded chase) let him, there you went feeling happy and safe for a perfect, incomparable, what seemed to be in hindsight ten short minutes, until you found him looking helpless with ironic longing at some stranger across another room . . . or street . . . or beach. And you envied him. You begrudged him the thrill that he was now feeling for someone else.

If she could become responsible for her own reality and keep it that way, she'd never have to feel that pain again. In went the color film. Jamaica Avenue was just what she needed, and she wanted it early, before the onslaught of heat would settle and paralyze the faces of the people. On second thought, perhaps she wanted just that. She hesitated. Up and down the broad street, shaded by the el train, nobody was out. She pointed her camera this way and that, felt nothing, put the camera down. No sense in wasting film. The Blue Swan Shoppe was on the corner and she decided to sit down in there for a bit. A cup of coffee and some air-conditioning would put her right back on the creative track.

The Blue Swan was not as she remembered it. They no longer sold penny candy at the cashier, or quarter candy for that matter. This was a place. Plastic turquoise booths and pink flamingo napkin caddies. There was no *Architectural Digest* on the magazine rack. Not even a *Better Homes and Gardens* or a humble copy of *Mademoiselle*. If you didn't feel compelled to investigate such provocative headlines as: "Siamese Twins Invent Arthritis Cure" or "Liz Moves In . . . Lock, Stock, and Jewelry Box," you were more or less out of luck.

Claire avoided the greasy-looking tables and sat down at the counter. The dark smells of last night's cold chili and salsa hung low in the air and on the counter there was a large tray of refried banana cut up into squares. The atmosphere conga'd with soft cucaracha from a younger Tito Puente. You couldn't help but mull over the gregorian orange that tapered the oilcloth in tiptoeing poodles. A throwback, no doubt, to the mystical Irish who had once lived above these stores. Different cups of tea entirely.

Now Puerto Ricans, Indians, Peruvians, and Guyanans paid rent for the privilege of dreaming in the drone of the great roaring el.

They were darker, these people. Their dreams were not as grand and so they would inevitably make out better; rent a store, work day and night, buy the store, work day and night and weekends, too, buy the building. And then rent to the next generation of foreigners who lollygagged in.

"Heezha cawfee," the kinky-haired matron clunked the cup down onto the counter.

"Thank you."

"Better tuck innat camera, honey." The waitress eye-balled right and left. "They'll grab that from ya. Don' worry!"

No, they won't, thought Claire. She gave the waitress a conspiratorial wink and made a show of settling it into her lap. The coffee was good. One thing the Latinos had brought with them into the neighborhood was good, rich coffee. There were all sorts of gooey apparitions made out of sugar, but no, thought Claire, she'd just have a cigarette instead. She was forever having something sweet or a cigarette instead. Michaelaen had told her that she smelled like an ashtray. That was nice. Don't worry, he'd patted her arm with his small hand when he'd seen her face fall, he liked a good ashtray. What generous grace from one so young.

Claire gulped down her coffee, paid, and staggered into the street. There was no reason for her to feel depressed and so she wouldn't. She'd find something to shoot, by golly. Looking at the filthy gutter, she was surprised at how improbable that prospect seemed. Nothing romantic there. Just like any other dirty place the world over. Impatiently, she walked up the avenue, past her father's still-unopened hardware store, past Gebhard's Bakery and its buttery smells, when she happened to catch her whole profile in the store window. She'd never seen anything like it. Not on her. But this was her mother's silhouette, not her own! She sucked in her gut and kneaded the inch of new blubber that encircled her waist. All these American delicacies. Claire remembered herself, not too long ago, eating everything she wanted, everything in sight, really, and never putting on a pound. Her models used to watch her enviously as she'd polish off the remains of their pasta. Well, those days were gone, it seemed. She was back in Queens with no real money, no real plan, and a very real belly. She stopped suddenly and wondered if this was it? The doubts that had haunted her throughout her life . . . was this to be the realization of them?

In Europe, during her jetsetting years, she'd always thought, oh, if only she could get away from the superficiality of her life, the whole frivolous life-style, and find a quiet place, a gentle place where she could meditate and become herself, everything would be all right. Then, when she finally had made the break and found herself in the Himalayas, there were moments when she would fathom that that was all nonsense, too, all of it, from the filthy Europeans traipsing downheartedly off to their gurus to the gurus themselves. Trying so hard not to try. And she'd thought that what she really should do was go home, back to her parents and Queens and all the things she'd tried so hard to leave behind. If she could just get back there and make an honest life for herself in the place she was put on earth to surface out of, she might put some order to the chaos. She even thought she'd get back here and all the inspiration would miraculously fall into place. Well, here she was, and what if her fears proved true afterall? What if there was only so much she had had to give and it was already gone? Perhaps she just should have moved to the city. There is a certain solid difference between Manhattan crazy people and Queens crazy people and 111th Street had a few perfect specimens of these walking up and down it. Here, if the old folks talked to themselves they would do it under their breaths, not out loud like in the city. And they didn't wear glamorous cast offs worn to shreds. These people had bought their own clothes with their very own pension checks and they wore them with a differential smugness, hunched into twelve-year-old shiny polyester shirts . . . old white people who found it cheaper to eat out (six rolls in a basket and crackers) and certainly easier than waiting on long lines at Key Food. Everybody hated Key Food—the confusion, the fluorescent lights, the unsatisfiable hunger it emptied into you, and the waxed, unbelievable fruits plump with gas that left you with nothing more than mealy tongue.

No, let's face it. You couldn't beat where you were from if you were after sorting yourself out, untangling the web of who you were, beneath the influence of all the world. Hadn't Swamiji told her just that when he'd seen her off at the bus depot? They'd sat together and scarfed down three or four *masala dosa* between them. Swami had licked his fingers and bobbed his head this way and that with pleasure and they'd both drunk still another nice black tea. It had struck her as so absurd to see him sitting there in the dusty hubbub after the tinkling quiet of his small walled garden, but then he was a very unusual swami, not megalomaniac at all like the others she'd investigated. He was a good little swami. Kind. A little bit of St. Francis what with all the broken down animals he had recovering at the ashram. Which is what might have accounted for his lack of popularity with the Western truth seekers. They tended to go more for the well-swept ashrams. No, he was not grand at all except for deep in his heart. Rather a catholic sort of swami, if one looked at it in the old Mediterranean way. Gee, she missed her dear, smelly little fellow with his magical eyes. She wondered what he'd make of the murder. "Well, well," he would say, "veddy bad. But would it be better if we did not know about it? No. Certainly not. And if we know, must we not do something about it? Certainly. If only to pray. Well, well. And so we shall pray."

Claire bent her head and repeated a couple of well-chosen mantras. When she looked up the sky was moving to the north, and so did she. It hadn't been easy to leave Swamiji. And only much later had she realized that it had not been easy for him to instruct her to go. Any Western woman was a boon to an ashram. And Claire especially had been nice for him to have around. She was tidy, for one thing. Best of all she'd shared his love of plants and helped him to categorize and bottle herbs. But it wasn't until Delhi and the outdated Western music piped into the airport lounge—" . . . you always smile but in your eyes your sorrow shows,"—that she knew he had loved her. Well. She'd loved him, too.

Claire passed the Holy Child Grammar School, where she'd gone as a child. She and Michael used to ride to school and park their bicycles right against that very chain link fence. She hung her head and crossed the road toward the church. A lovely old place it was, orange-bricked and landscaped in green, early Spanish Mission style mostly, but with Roman effects: flabbergasting stained glass and cathedral-like heights. There was a dark and hollow coolness to it, not unlike the Baths of Istanbul. She thought she might go in, just to sit down in the darkness and get out of the heat for a moment, but there seemed to be a funeral going on. Wasn't it awfully early for a funeral? She walked around the corner to the front. How horrible those black hearses were. Eerie, like that in front of the low-hanging gray sky. Claire stood stock still. She poised her camera. The doors of the church drew open and a swarm of people suddenly filled the tall steps. There were so many that they toppled onto one another. A stout young woman in black keeled over the white coffin and passed out. There was a great deal of jostling, someone was yelling, and almost all of them were in tears above the small white coffin.

Then it hit her. It was the child who had been murdered. They must have upped the hour of the mass to avoid the media. There was no shortage of cops. Twelve of them, she counted. And the captain. Very grand looking with gold braid and hair parted cleanly by a razor. Cops were used to funerals, weren't they? Claire stood there, hypnotized through the lens, but she couldn't bring herself to shoot. She had the perfect angle and the right long lens and she knew she'd make the cover of the *Post* in a minute, but there was no way she could shoot that wailing herd as they moved toward her. No way. If there was one thing that she had learned from life it was that you did not make your fortune from the private agonies of victims. You just didn't. If there was any sense to the world, to her own existence, it wasn't going to come from giving life to that picture. Some things, Claire knew, just weren't worth being paid for. She lowered the camera.

Several people, those daily churchgoers who had no relation to the funeral but who stood around caught up in the drama, watched her curiously. One nervous-looking young man with red hair made a move as though he were coming over to say something, perhaps chastise her for her camera, but he changed his mind and turned away. The cries from the murdered child's mother echoed horribly through the vestibule. Then thunder rolled not too far off. No doubt it was raining already over Manhattan.

Claire headed home. There was no traffic on Myrtle Avenue. There never was. Just the shiny trolley line still taking off in both directions. Lord, the cries of that poor woman! How did Zinnie do it? She saw pain like that all the time. And worse. No, there couldn't be much worse than that. In Richmond Hill, no less.

The nearer Claire got to her block, the more those spider webs were noticeable. The old Queen Ann houses looked, in the overcast, almost vaporous. If she shot with a breath-steamed lens it would look downright enchanted. She finished the whole roll of film standing there by the mailbox. This was what she wanted, wasn't it, the romanticism of her reality. Finding beauty right where it was. No more robbing the East . . . no more hupla onto a plane to go look for legendary sights: . . . the faceless Buddhas of Bāmiān . . . or the islands of the Maldives, sprouting up like jade mushrooms in a perfect turquoise sea. How many other photographers had shot those jewels before and after her? And what had they become, exquisite cigarette placards? No, this—this was it right here. It would have to be. It was, after all, what she wanted. Hers. No one else's. As for her blubbery middle, there were a variety of steps she could take. She could stop eating altogether. But then of course she'd smoke nonstop. No, she'd have to find a more gymnastic approach. Swimming? Swimming would be ideal except that she had no car to carry her to and from the beach. And the thought of swimming in an indoor pool left her limp with apprehension. No, swimming was out. Tennis was too expensive. What did one do without money? One jogged. Claire quickened her pace with a breast-rattling jiggle. It was not the most difficult of sports. She checked an impulse to light a cigarette as she walked along figuring all this out. It wouldn't hurt to be fit. She'd been postponing it so long now that she wondered if she was convinced she'd fail. Nonsense. She wasn't a child. Or had she turned back into one when she'd come home? She certainly had reverted to her adolescent messy self. Just look at her unmade bed and the lump of clothing she'd left on the floor.

She would change. She would change everything about herself. She wasn't doing anyone any good in this suspended state of trying not to worry about things. If one wanted to worry, one should get on with it so as to go on from there. What was it Swamiji used to say? "Curl up inside fear to find surrender. Then defend your right to overcome." Claire smiled to herself. Perhaps it would work out after all.

"Hi," she said as she came in the back door. "What's the matter?" Mrs. Dixon and her mother sat morosely at the kitchen table. Zinnie, just home from her midnight shift, hung over the counter with a tall glass of iced coffee and a case of bloodshot eyes.

"It's the Mayor," said Zinnie. "He's grounded."

Claire looked at the dog on the floor. He raised his

brown eyes to her and gave a minor salutory flick of his tail.

"He got a ticket," said Mrs. Dixon.

"For doing it on von Lillienfeld's front lawn," sighed Mary.

"A hundred bucks," said Zinnie. "Wait till Dad finds out."

"The thing was," Mary sulked, "that we were warned. I mean, that's what your father will say. Everyone knows you're not allowed out without your pooper scooper or a good brown paper bag and a leash. It's just that the Mayor is so *used* to being out on his own. Poor pooch."

"Poor Pop," Zinnie said. "A hundred clams."

"And there's nothing to be done," said Mrs. Dixon as she hurled yet another sugar rock into her coffee sludge, "It's territorial, you know. You can't stop that in dumb animals. He lusts after her poodle."

"I saw the officer out there," Mary shook her head and laid each finger on her breast. "I saw him and I thought, oh boy, somebody's going to get a ticket. But I thought it would be for parking. You know how they slink about checking for outdated registrations and too many inches from the indiscernible curb. Sure, that's their bread and butter."

"Traffic," snarled Zinnie. "Regular cops wouldn't be bothered. They'd just give you a warning."

"I was out in the yard hanging Michaelaen's clean laundry—"

"Where is Michaelaen?" asked Claire.

"Down at the store with your father. I was out in the yard watching this officer and not even thinking about the Mayor. Well, if the truth be known, I did sorta see 'im outa the corner of me eye like. But I thought he'd take off toward the trestle the way he normally does. Don't ask me why he chose to come lumbering back to me this particular mornin'. You know the way he is, he's got no use for me unless it's five and he's droolin' after his dinner. He never notices me in the mornin' as a rule. But wouldn't you know the officer comes marching over, as efficient as you please, and says, 'That your dog, ma'am?' Now what was I to say?"

"You could have said no and gone into the house," Zinnie said.

Mary shrugged helplessly. "I couldn't deny my own dog. Sure that would be denying one of your own."

They all turned silently to look at the Mayor. Clearly penitent, he sighed with them in unison.

"Anyway," Mary's tone changed, "I did try to sneak into the house, but the dog came wollypoggely up to me, happy as good-all to see me."

"I tried to help her out of it," Mrs. Dixon said. "I came running over, didn't I?"

"That you did."

"Did you tell him that Zinnie was on the job?" Claire asked.

"Sure, Mrs. Dixon told him that. He didn't care, though. Heartless man. And not at all proud of his uniform! Ice pop stains all over his front. Grape, no less. And we, law-abiding citizens in every other respect. Oh, wait till your father hears this one."

"It was von Lillienfeld who went and reported the dog, you mark my words," Mrs. Dixon scraped her chair along Mary's good linoleum. "Nobody else has that much brass. She's a bad one. Shut up in there like some old witch."

"Now," Mary wailed, "he won't be able to go out at all without his leash. Come to think of it, I don't even know where we've put the old thing, it's been so long since he's had it on. And haven't I better things to do with my day than to have to go traipsing here and there after a dog who's used to being everywhere at once?"

"Well, I'm not walkin' 'im," Zinnie said firmly. "He won't walk anyhow. He just sniffs in one spot if you've got him on a leash."

"And how would you know that?" Mary doubled her chin. "As if you've ever walked him!"

"I passed by the church," Claire changed the subject. "The funeral for that little boy was going on."

"No fooling? Already? That must have been mobbed. Did you go in?"

"Uh-uh. I just caught them coming out onto the steps. It was really awful."

Mrs. Dixon stood up heavily. She didn't want to talk about that again. "I think I'll be off," she said.

"Oh, and thank you again, Mrs. Dixon," Mary gave her her face of holy sympathy, "—thank you for helping me with the officer."

Mrs. Dixon winked and closed the door.

Mary eyed the scrape in her linoleum.

"Not that she helped you any," Zinnie said.

"Oh, hush. She means well. She hasn't much to do now, with Mr. Dixon gone."

Zinnie gnawed at her thumbnail. "I really feel like walking over there and giving von Lillienfeld a piece of my mind. The frustrated old bitch!"

"Now you don't know if it was she who called," Mary warned.

"Come on, ma. Don't be naive!"

"I'd rather be naive than judgmental and presumptuous. Conjecture is the ignorant man's tool."

"Look. He poops there every day, doesn't he? Who else would have a reason to call? And that brownie didn't show up here without somebody calling."

Claire looked up. "Does he really? Every day?"

Mary sniffed. Zinnie stuck her face in the fan.

"I'd better get Michaelaen's shirts off the line." Mary heaved herself up. "It looks like it's ready to pour."

"Want some coffee, Claire?" Zinnie asked when she had gone. "You look all done in."

"I hit the bourbon last night. And you don't look particularly fresh yourself."

"I had a collar. Nice one. Took an uzi away from a six-foot black."

"A coon?"

"What's that supposed to mean?"

"What?"

"I mean calling a guy a coon."

"Oh." Claire felt her face redden. "I just meant . . . I mean there are blacks and there are coons. I was thinking more of the apparition than of the choice of words. As a matter of fact, I thought cops talked like that."

"Maybe they do. Maybe I even used to. I mean, I did. Maybe I just grew up, you know. Like when I started living on a higher level."

"Touché."

"You're welcome. Look. My partner's black. He wouldn't let nuthin' happen to me. He's a real hot shot. You understand? When it comes to backup, he's right there. Okay?"

"Yes. And I'm sorry."

"Hey. It's all right. You saw the funeral, eh?"

"Mmm. I saw them put the coffin into the limo. It was white." She looked sadly at Zinnie. "You should have seen the poor mother."

"I wish Daddy would get back with Michaelaen. I hate to go to sleep without seeing him."

"He'll be back, don't worry. People don't die just because *you* love them, you know."

"What a strange thing to say! How the hell did you realize I felt like that?"

"I don't know. I guess because it's the way I feel and so naturally assume you'll feel that way, too. We may be very different, but I did have a hand at raising you when you were small, you know."

"You keep telling me."

"Uh-oh. Do I?"

"All the time. You make me feel like a little kid. And I'm not."

"I wish someone would make me feel like a little kid."

"That's another thing you always do. Make yourself sound like a brontosaurus."

"Hmm. The thunder lizard. Extinct American dinosaur.

You know, I'm just going to prove your point by saying this, but it reminds me so much of how you used to think big animals would come in the window and eat you while you were asleep. Remember?"

"No. But I do remember you sitting up late with me and reading me stories. Judy Bolton and Nancy Drew. You remember that? And Carmela would report us?"

They smiled at each other.

"I think I'm going to take up jogging," Claire announced. "I'm too fat."

Zinnie looked at her through half closed lids. "You can't jog, Claire. You smoke. Not for nothing, but the two don't go together. Why don't you just stop squirreling Michaelaen's stash of Ring Dings. That might help."

"Yeah. He's changed his hiding spots on me, anyhow. I thought I'd give it a go, though. Cut down the smoking at the same time."

"Give it a go, eh? Well, good luck. What brought this on?"

"Uh . . . Michaelaen, to tell you the truth. He told me I smell like an ashtray."

"My son the worrying wart."

"He wasn't worried. He was simply stating a fact."

"Yeah. Well. His little means are more devious than his ways."

"As are yours."

"What's that mean?"

"Meaning you never said a word about the murder since it happened. You just let everybody talk and you listen. Like you've got some seedy ideas of your own that you won't let on about."

"I don't. Honest. I wish I did. Look. Maybe it was one of those crimes that never gets solved. Happens all the time. I mean, if the guy had buried the kid, that's what might have happened. The way I see it, though, is this: he leaves the body in the wide open like that just so people do find it. That's what worries me."

"Because?"

"Because if no one does find him, he'll do it again. Maybe. Sometimes it's some nut job just passing through. Gets off a plane at Kennedy, kills one here, one there along the way . . . leaving a trail of bodies from here to L.A. You never know. I'll let you in on something if you promise not to tell anyone."

"Now who would I tell?"

"I dunno. Carmela. Can't you just see her doing a daily on the progress of the 102? She eats this kind of stuff up."

"You can't really blame her. It is intriguing."

"Intriguing? It's macabre."

A bolt of lightning lit up the backyard and rain came down in a sheet. Mary flew into the kitchen with a basketful of laundry. "Not that *one* of my fully grown daughters would come out and give me a hand!" she cried, but she wasn't angry, she was thrilled to feel the sudden rain. Her blood pressure was right up there and her cheeks were pink with pleasure. She pounded barefoot through the house, now dark, now bright with the powerful storm.

"Not a word?" continued Zinnie.

"Don't be silly."

"Well. Besides his little pocketful of possessions: a boy scout knife, baseball cards, and a couple of other things, the kid had a man's new cufflink on him. A roulette wheel. Like a real one. With a little bead in it. On the top was a neat little knob that you could spin the bead with."

"So?"

"'So' she says. You're right. It might mean nothing at all. But if Miguel—that was the kid's name—if Miguel knew the guy who killed him . . . if he'd met with him before, that might be just the kind of thing that would entice a little boy into the woods, wouldn't you say?"

"Yes. Except that that could have come from anywhere. His father—"

"Didn't. They checked."

"Or an uncle—"

"An uncle could have killed him, too."

"What a thought!"

"What a thought that anybody would have done it."

"I'll say one thing. Inanimate objects sometimes carry messages."

"What do you mean?"

"Like from the dead."

"Oh, please stop. You and your heebie-jeebie nonsense!"

"It's not nonsense." And why did a roulette wheel cufflink ring a bell?

"Right. Out with the Ouija board. I could clobber Daddy. He knows how worried I am to have Michaelaen out. Why doesn't he bring him back? Sometimes I think he's being purposely annoying. He is. He does it because he thinks that now that the cat is out of the bag and everyone knows that Freddy is gay, that means that Michaelaen is *his*. It's like his macho power trip. Meanwhile, he was the one who was so hot on me marrying Freddy in the first place. Sure. Cause he thought Freddy was on his way to playing pro ball."

"Wait a minute. The guy fooled you, didn't he? Why shouldn't he have fooled Daddy? You're just mad at all men because Freddy turned out gay."

"Just the opposite. I never felt more gently inclined." She made a vulgar, rhythmic movement that made Claire laugh. "Anyhow, I'm going up there tonight. To Freddy's. You wanna come with me?"

"No. I'm afraid of Freddy. He's so caustic and witty. He makes me feel vaguely stupid."

"He thinks you're beautiful. No. He says you're not *really* beautiful but you have these moments when you shine through and emote pure beauty."

"Freddy said *that*?"

"It's disturbing, he says."

"How horrible. Now I'll never know when he's watching me if he's thinking I'm having a moment or not. Not that I should care . . . but women do care even if we don't really. Something diabolical in us wants everyone we meet to fall in love with us if we think there's a possibility, however remote. It pleases our ravenous vanity. Isn't it unhealthy? How can women ever unite?"

"We can't. So why don't you come tonight?"

"Money, for one thing."

"I have money. Anyway, Freddy would never let us pay. I thought you said you had some money saved."

"Yes. For rent. For Mom and Dad so I'm not a total parasite. And to pay for film, ciggies, coffee, chemicals."

"In that order."

"That's not nothing, you know. And paper. Good-quality paper." Claire's eyes lit up when she said "good-quality paper." "Besides. Why do you always have to go to Freddy's?"

Zinnie looped Michaelaen's yo-yo around her finger and coiled it up. "I feel guilty not going. I feel like he needs my support. Only I can't pick up anybody there or I'll feel more guilty. In front of him, I mean. It's a no-win sitch. What the hell is that?"

"What?" She was trying to remember where she'd seen a roulette wheel cufflink before. Or had she never seen one?

"Those. Those muddy pots."

"They're my herbs. The one you're pointing to is borage. Or it will be. The others are basil, thyme, coriander, marjoram, chamomile, and comfrey." She didn't mention the cannabis she'd started in the yard. She'd only planted it for fun, really. To see how well it would flourish.

Zinnie looked into the pots with distaste. "Yeah. But what are they for?"

"I like them, Zin. Wait till they begin to grow. You'll like them. You will."

"You talk about them like they're new little folks who just moved into the neighborhood."

Claire opened the refrigerator and idly watched its contents. Mary had a whole boat-load of ribs going on in there, soaking up something nice. That would be for tonight. There was a bowl of rhubarb. Hmm. A couple of fat, soggy leeks. A half a cantaloupe. Oh, no. A big hunk of Tilsit. She shut the door with self-preserving swiftness.

"How 'bout a little music?" suggested Zinnie, who shared her father's passion for the stuff. Only her taste ran more to the Motown classics of the fifties and sixties. And whereas his were kept in an orderly file, hers were strewn about the house. She didn't know where anything was, but she had all of them: the Temptations, the Supremes, Little Anthony and the Imperials, the Four Tops. She picked one up from behind the Mayor's box and dusted it tenderly in a circle. "Here we go," she blew on the needle and let it drop.

"Aaaa million to wa-un," Zinnie sang along with the opening line, "—that's what our folks think about this love of ow-ers. . . ."

Claire clapped her hands with delight. "You sound just *like* him," she cried. "Really!" And it was true. Zinnie had it down. The only thing that stopped her from using her powerful, sweet voice more often at home was her own father's embarrassingly rapt attention. Wherever he was on the property, if Zinnie would start to sing he would come rushing through the house and stand harrowingly still, and the next thing you knew his eyes would fill with tears. Zinnie didn't go for that. That sort of stuff was for the birds.

"Smokey Robinson," Zinnie rolled her eyes when the song came to an end. "Vintage class, doncha think?"

"Zinnie? How did you find out about that cufflink? You saw it when you saw the body?"

"Nope."

"So how? You've been poking around at the 102, haven't you?"

"Why not? What are you lighting up a cigarette for? I thought you were going to quit."

"Cut down. No one ever said anything about quitting."

"What are you? Worried I been talking to his royal piece of ass?"

"His who?"

"Miss innocent. You know who I'm talking about."

"Oh. Him. Why would I care about him? You do mean the big arrogant one?"

"Ha. That's funny. That's exactly the way he described you: the little arrogant one. No, wait. He said the little snotty one."

"I don't care what he said."

"Not much you don't." She leaned over the sill. "Boy. It's really wailing out there. I hope Daddy brought Michaelaen indoors." She opened the freezer, cracked the ice cube tray into the sink, and tinkled more ice into her glass. "You know what I think? I think he likes you."

"Tch."

"He was married, you know."

Claire said nothing.

"Apparently, the lady didn't let her right hand know what her left was up to. I mean, she screwed around."

"Zinnie, I don't *care* about Johnny Benedetto. Really! So stop speaking about him."

"Yessir!"

They listened to the rain.

"Tell ya one thing, though. He's a crackerjack detective. All sorts of commendations and sharpshooter medals. And he's handy. He even fixed Furgueson's old bomb of a car for him."

"Here comes your son," Claire picked the curtain up with her toe, "—followed by our soaking father."

In they came, joyfully splattering water onto everything. The Mayor, quite recovered from his run-in with the law, greeted them in his effusive style. His alarming baritone went off at irritating three-second intervals, insisting they join him in the old sit-beg-give-take, tradition being the cornerstone of culture. Off he flew then with his Milk Bone, on a successful tournée of the dining room table legs. Back he gallivanted for a culminating snortle under one of Mary's many scatter rugs. Crunchy scatter rugs.

Mary swept the bone bits up with a bored sigh and dumped them into his toy box. They could talk about the ticket later on. Stan looked tired and she didn't want him worrying about the hundred dollars now.

"We wuz at the junkies!" Michaelaen shouted. "We sold the brass pipes and we got fireplace irons!"

"How enchanting," Mary said. "What's next? A fireplace?"

"Who's minding the store, Pop?"

"Hank's there. I been lettin him open up the last week or so. Get to spend some time with my grandson, right, pardner?"

"Right!"

"I thought you didn't trust Hank."

"Oh, he's all right. He's good with the Spanish customers. That hot tamale music doesn't bother him."

"Nuthin but spics on Jamaica Avenue, anymore," Mary shook her head.

"Hispanics, Mary," he glared at her. "Whatta you wanna do? Teach the kid here to be a racist?"

"You're the one who always says you're gonna sell out because of them!" Zinnie laughed.

"Whatever. I'm just waitin for the Koreans with a bag of cash. When they come in, I'm selling the business. You watch."

"You wouldn't do it, Dad. You say so but you wouldn't."

"Ha. You watch. I'll retire."

"I've been wanting you to retire for five years," Mary said. "That neighborhood *is* going to the devil. But you won't retire. I know you."

"Oh, yes, I will. Or I'll look for a new store up in Kew Gardens. You watch."

"And pay those rents?"

"The Jews are the only ones who can pay rent?"

"That rent? Yeah."

Michaelaen losing interest, put his hand in his blue jeans where it felt good.

"Jesus! Mary," Stan shouted at her, "can't you stop him from doin' that?!"

"Give him one a your cannons, Pop," Zinnie narrowed her eyes. "Let him play with something more to the point."

CHAPTER

4

The rain beat down on Aqueduct and steam rose from the muddy track. Pokey Ryan watched carefully as the boards recorded the latest bets. The lines up to the fluorescent-lit windows dwindled the closer it came to post time. A big jump came onto the board under number five. That was what he was waiting for. Pokey walked calmly out to the stands and whipped out his flashlight. Usually he positioned himself deeper in the portal but today it was so dark out that that wasn't necessary. He gave it five healthy blasts.

Across the track and past the stables Johnny Benedetto shut the window, tossed his binoculars onto the bed, and picked up the phone. He ran a finger down the racing form. Number five. Number five. Here we go: Miss Know It All. He listened to the phone ring at the other end. "Eddie? Johnny. Can I still get in on the fourth race? Yeah? Gimmie Miss Know It All twenty times in the fourth. Got that? Good." He hung up. Candy from a baby. He shook his head softly, put on his shoulder holster, and headed out the door.

"Here we are, your honor." Claire relaxed the clothesline leash even more. Now they stood a good ten feet from each other on the top of the hill. Behind them and below was the still-slippery curve of Park Lane South. In front and below was the underwater green of the glittering woods. The storm had knocked down plenty of branches and left the whole place wild. Prettier than ever, the Mayor thought. A sunlit pandemonium. It wasn't often that he came in these woods. Not since that last run-in with a rowdy pack of wild dogs. An honorable defeat, mind you, but not the sort one would like to repeat in the extreme near future. They wouldn't give him any trouble with Claire about. They feared humans, didn't they? A motley crew. He still could feel those scars. Especially right before a rain. That was why he'd come home so early this morning . . . and missed a good soaking. Good for something, those old wounds. Bad for others. Now they'd keep him on a leash. Infernal bother! However was he going to keep the neighborhood in order if he was kept indoors? Or attached to a human! She had her hulking camera with her, too. How were they going to have a good run with that thing clanging about her neck? Always stopping to take pictures of any tomfoolery!

"Look," Claire came over and knelt down beside him. "I'm going to take you off your stupid clothesline, but I'm going to have to put it back on when we leave the woods, all right? You won't just run off on me, will you? Good."

She unhooked him from his irritating noose and scrubbed his back with her short nails. "C'mon," she laughed. "We're off."

And off they did go—not quite as energetically as either of them had planned, however. Claire would stop for a shot here and there and he would halt for just about any gamey essence. They were an excellent running team, each equally short of breath at frequent, corresponding intervals. The European Jews were out now. And there were other joggers, thrilled to once again have fresh breathing air after the clean wash of rain. Claire didn't like to take the main routes. The others looked so official that she was shy for them to see her not wearing what seemed to be the uniform: some sort of platypuslike tennis shoes and buoyant pastel-colored leotards. She and the Mayor kept to the thicket, colliding good-naturedly with nature as they bolted through. Each of them was lost in thought.

Now, what in glory goodness is that? The Mayor periscoped his dark snout upward, not understanding for the life of him why one of Stan's more radiant symphonies should suddenly come up here and interrupt the birds' song. It was, in fact, the dizzying strains of the "Skater's Waltz." The Mayor looked at Claire, but he couldn't decipher that expression of joy and pain all at once.

Claire was captivated, transported momentarily back to Munich any Wednesday afternoon in the Englische Garten, the oompah-pah band in full swing, the sun in your eyes, and the bright yellow beer. Oh, yes. There were times when you remembered why you'd spent so many years there, after all. She smiled at the Mayor. "I think we've stumbled across the carousel," she said.

The Mayor wasn't having any of it. An organ concert in the woods, indeed.

"No, no, really, it's all right," she told him. "This must be the old carousel they've renovated. I read about it in the local paper. Look, fellow, come here and have a look. It's all magnificent horses. Hand-carved. God. I remember this from when Michael and I were kids. We loved it here. We used to catch guppies over there before they drained the pond."

The Mayor took one look at the whirling cavalry horses and the fancy pastel chargers. That was it. He turned to go.

"Oh, come on. Don't be such a spoil sport. You hear? Now they're playing the 'Merry Widow Waltz.' I can't believe they actually renovated this place. When I left Queens it was a filthy haven for dealers and junkies. Whoever did this did a beautiful job. Jesus, it's pretty. I've never seen such lavenders and subtle pinks and mossy greens like that on a carousel; they're usually so garish. These are unbelievable." Claire shot while she spoke to the Mayor, trying to calm him down with the sound of her voice just long enough for her to get something really good. There weren't many kids, just a smattering of babies and tired parents, but no one could be unaffected by the beauty. The shining faces blurred and she put the camera down.

There was a guy looking at her, an older guy, maybe sixty or so. Maybe younger. It was hard to tell his age. He was either very blond or very white. His eyes were piercing and as pale a blue as Claire had ever seen. They almost weren't there. The man lowered his monkey wrench and came out from the bowels of the machinery into the light. He was older than she'd thought. He continued to watch her. Always sensitive to people's shyness at being photographed, she put her lens cap back on and dangled the camera across her shoulder.

In a thick German accent, he shouted something to another mechanic still working at the center of the gears. Claire didn't catch what he said but the unfriendliness of his tone chilled her. She shivered and turned with the Mayor to go. There were also times when she remembered quite well why she had left Germany.

They hurried along. Claire hadn't realized how far they'd come and she moved quickly, her shoulders brushing the overgrown plants. There was poison oak in here, she remembered, and poison ivy all over the place. The carousel had jarred all sorts of memories.

"Hello, there," someone said and Claire whirled around, frightened. The murder was still fresh in everybody's minds. It was a man. A good-looking man at that. He was tall, slightly older than she, and extremely thin. The Mayor, caught as unawares as she, bared his fine row of teeth (he'd always been criminally vain of those teeth) and Claire had to grab him by the tail before he lurched for the man.

"Sorry," Claire smiled not too apologetically, "he's very protective."

"Good thing he is! This isn't the safest place in the world anymore." The man stared intently into the foliage. He, too, wore those trendy pastel togs.

Claire nodded sympathetically. What was that accent? "Czech?" she asked.

"Pardon?"

"Are you Czech?"

"Ah! No. Close, though. Polish."

"Really!"

"You have a good ear. And you are . . . wait . . . let me guess . . . German?"

"I'm American, but I did live there for years."

"Ah!" He was sweating, wiping his hands on a snow white handkerchief. "And now?"

"Right past Park Lane South. Directly on the wrong side of the tracks."

He laughed and then frowned. "The Jamaica Avenue el?"

"No," she rushed to assure him, reminding herself distressingly of Carmela, "—the other one. The trestle. The Long Island freight."

"Oh, yes. That's still very pretty there. Quaint."

"Mmm. Lots of pigeons, though."

"It's lovely in here now, isn't it? I like it so much better than Central Park. It's really a virgin wood, isn't it?"

"Yes."

"And there are stables," he went on. "The horses are all nags, of course, but it's great fun all the same. Do you ride?"

"Not lately." Even the nags cost twenty bucks an hour.

"Do you jog every day? I've never seen you before."

"You've caught us on our first day out, hasn't he, your honor?"

The Mayor didn't bother to look up. The idiot reeked of patchouli.

"What's your name? May I ask you that?"

"Claire Breslinsky. And yours?"

"Stefan. Stefan Stefanovitch. I'm living just off the park myself." He fell into step with them. "I'm sorry. Do you mind if I walk with you for a bit? I'm all in. Why do you laugh?"

"I'm just thinking of my sister. She'd kill me if she knew I was talking to a perfect stranger in the woods."

"The proverbial protective older sister—"

"No, younger. But she's a police officer."

"And you? I don't expect that you are anything as . . . uh . . . rudimentary as a police officer."

"That's a very condescending way to put it and you obviously don't know a thing about the complexities of the New York Police Department, but, no. I'm a photographer."

Stefan Stefanovitch had broad, narrow lips. They broke into a wide grin. "I knew it! I knew you were an artist, the minute I saw you!"

"Eee, I hate that word. I just bungle away with my camera, really. I don't create as much as point and hope for the best. How about you?"

"Diplomatic corps. In town. Over at the UN."

"That sounds like something to do."

"Not really. It's frightfully boring. Listening to dreary speeches all day long and suffering through endless stuffy cocktail parties at night. Being a photographer sounds like much more fun."

Without looking at him, Claire silently agreed.

"What sort of photography do you go in for?"

"You mean who do I like? Oh, Mary Ellen Mark. Diane Arbus."

"Arbus?" He scratched his head. "Wasn't it she who said, 'Nothing is ever the same as they said it was. It's what I've never seen before that I recognize'?"

Claire whirled around. "Word for word!"

"I saw her work in London, years ago. When I was up at Oxford. Platonism, wouldn't you say?"

"More like metaphysical idealism," she argued, pleased.

"Well. Here's where I turn off."

They both hesitated.

"Nice having met you," she said.

"Yes. Awfully. Will you run tomorrow?"

Claire stopped. "Gee, I don't know. Let's see how my legs feel after today. Maybe I'll be covered with Ben Gay. I'm not particularly sporty."

"Wait, I have an idea. I'm having a mob at my place tomorrow night. Perhaps you'd like to come?"

"Oh, I don't—"

"You could bring your sister," he fumbled through his pocket, "—the policelady. I have nothing to write my address down on but you could find it easily enough. It's the first house on Park Lane South with a tile roof. The only one between Mayfair and Grosvenor that faces the street. You can't miss it. Eight o'clock. Dress however you want."

"I don't know. I—"

"Don't say no!" he insisted, taking her hand in his own slender one and kissing it. He was already off. "See you then!" he cried.

The Mayor looked at Claire. Oh, yuck, was she smiling? Could she *like* that hideous man? Of course, she wouldn't go to his stupid party. Preoccupied, they picked their way through the overgrown roadway entrance and didn't notice the unmarked car in the bush. Johnny Benedetto slumped down in the seat and urgently folded one more stick of Doublemint into his mouth.

CHAPTER 5

Come *on!*" Zinnie hollered down the cellar stairs. "If we're going to this dumb party, let's *go!*"

"All right, all right," Claire muttered to herself. "Be right there," she yelled from the fuzzy red interior of the makeshift darkroom. "Just finishing!" She scanned the last sheet of black and white as it materialized. Oh boy. Beauties. Real beauties. She inspected them with her loop. The foliage of the woods blended with the Yiddish faces and then, pop! you saw them . . . camouflaged but distinct all over each picture: oval, ancient portraits like gnarls in the trees.

"Clay-er!! Come on!" Zinnie's irritated voice bellowed. "It's eight a'fucking clock! Are we going or not?!"

Claire hung the last sheet up on a wire over her head, rinsed her hands, and switched on the light. She'd go over the last ones later. With one last wistful look, she left the darkroom and climbed the stairs. Zinnie was sitting at the top, Carmela was slouched along the wall.

Zinnie pursed her lips. "I told her she couldn't come."

"Of course she can come," Claire smiled, her heart sinking.

"I don't care. I mean, if it's a private party or something just say so and I'll stay home."

Claire looked at the two of them. Zinnie was thoroughly annoyed, the way she always was if Carmela was involved. Carmela's cheeks were two bright patches of insulted apprehension. She was all decked out. The funny thing about Carmela was, as meticulous as she was in her dress, the room she left behind looked as though an army helicopter had flown through. It was always the same: the better she looked, the filthier her room. What state it was in now Claire could only imagine, because Carmela looked terrific.

"Oh, come on," Claire laughed. "If he doesn't want all three of us he can—"

"Ought to be glad to have three extra women," Carmela pushed the screen door open with a burst.

"That's right," Claire didn't hesitate. The minute you made Carmela feel you didn't want her around, she'd stick like glue. It was some perverse insecurity that made her that way—who knew why? Claire had left Freud back in Germany where she hoped he'd do her Teutonic folk some good.

Zinnie, taking stock, decided to let it drop. "Lock the door," she hissed. "Shall I take my car?"

"Oh, let's walk," Carmela said. "Then we can all drink."

Claire stood still. The Mayor watched her with those heartbreaking liquid eyes. Her parents had taken Michaelaen to McDonald's and then on to Crossbay Playland for a treat, so there was no one around to see.

"Oops," Claire said. "He just slipped out."

"Claire!" Carmela crowed. "He'll get another ticket!"

"No, he won't," Zinnie said. "Who are they gonna give it to? Him?"

"And who's going to pay if they follow him home?"

"Shut up. I'd like to see one of them follow him home. They'd be worn out."

"Wait till Mom finds out—"

"Who's gonna tell her, miss goody two tits, you?"

The three of them watched as the Mayor headed off in the direction of Lefferts Boulevard. He looked once over his shoulder, furtively, then skedaddled fast as he could away from them. There was no stopping him now.

* * *

They climbed the hill with the same suspicious optimism with which all women over twenty-five start out for parties. Zinnie was in a good mood. Carmela too, for once. She'd always wanted to get in with the diplomatic set. This was as good a chance as any, even if the opportunity had presented itself through Claire. As for Claire, she was thinking about those pictures she'd left down in the cellar. Something about them . . . like a word on the tip of your tongue . . .

It was pleasant along Park Lane South. The houses changed to villas and the sun was pink above the woods. That meant good weather for tomorrow as well.

"Why didn't you wear my sundress, Claire?" Carmela asked, looking her up and down with disapproving eyes. "Aren't you hot? You know you could have borrowed it."

"I'm fine," Claire smiled, hot. She was glad she hadn't worn the lavender sundress. She almost had. She'd stared at it on its hanger and held its skirt up to her cheek. It had had the same feel to it as a shawl she'd had once, and as she'd stood there in Carmela's closet she'd remembered that shawl whipping around her in the breeze and how she'd walked happily, innocently through the forest outside Rishikesh and how it was so fine that she'd kept right on walking, past the sunlit temple and the perfect mossy fields. She'd relived the shock of seeing the back of her lover's neck as she'd turned from the shelter of the trees, recognizing that neck first, his back to her, his face to the lovely young Indian girl. He'd put out his arm to capture a strand of the girl's windy hair that covered her eyes and he'd anchored it kindly to her small, seashell ear. Claire had walked up to them, smiling brightly, consciously oblivious to their sudden discomfort, pretending (for whom?) that nothing had happened.

And she'd walked away from the lavender dress. She believed in the vibrations of clothes. She had things, beautiful things that suited her, that she would never wear because of something that had happened to her while she'd had it on. Such as a woman in the store not approving of her while she'd tried something on and she, thinking nothing, buying the item anyway. Those feelings were recorded forever in the fiber of the fabric, and Claire would relive that dislike every time she put it on. No. She was glad she hadn't worn that beautiful dress.

They walked and walked.

"Where is this place?" Carmela demanded finally. "My feet are killing me."

"Serves you right for wearing my shoes," said Zinnie.

"Your feet were always bigger than mine! When did your feet get smaller?"

"Probably when you put on all that weight."

"What weight?"

"Let's not talk about weight tonight," pleaded Claire, who had camouflaged her figure very nicely beneath a powder blue Afghani sheath. "Let's have a good time, all right? This is it."

"This?!" Carmela dropped her purse.

"Who is this guy, Claire?" Zinnie gave a low whistle, "—a king?"

"Don't be silly. He's a diplomat. It's not his."

"It wasn't Marcos's either," Carmela checked her nose inside her compact. "What's the matter, Zin? You'd rather have the acreage in the back of the house? You don't like money? You think if money could buy happiness Franco Bolla would have his teeth fixed?"

"I wish I'd worn something else."

"You just miss your gun."

"I've got my gun."

"You look adorable," Claire said.

"I don't."

"You do."

They tripped up the cobblestone path that led to the side of the villa. There were yellow-and-white-striped tents set up along the yard, well hidden from the street by tall privet hedging. Lanterns twinkled, as early as it was, and groups of people stood chatting here and there, sipping what appeared to be champagne.

"I thought Poland was communist," said Zinnie.

"Don't *we* pay for diplomatic housing?" Carmela ruminated on a thoroughly new sort of column. A political column.

"I think so," said Claire.

"If I drink too much," Carmela said, "don't bother to carry me home."

"No, we won't, dear. You stay right here and check out our good tax dollars. Da?"

"They're so damn operatic looking," Zinnie complained. "Oh, hell, Carmela, what are you doing putting on *gloves*?"

At that moment, Stefan spotted Claire. Silkily, he glided across the tilted lawn. "Don't tell me!" he stretched out his dinner-jacketted arm, "—not one policelady, but two!"

"Wadja, tell 'im I'm a cop?" Zinnie glared at Claire.

"No, this one is a writer. This is Carmela and this is Zinnie. I hope you don't mind my bringing the whole family."

"Mind?" Of course Stefan didn't mind. Three beautiful sisters were an asset to any party, weren't they? They all agreed they were. Stefan guided them over to the canopy and settled them each with a glass of champagne.

"He looks like a sun-bleached Count Dracula," Zinnie whispered in her ear.

Carmela fluttered her eyelashes at Stefan. "One thing that women forget nowadays to do," Claire remembered reading in one of Carmela's articles, "is flutter their lashes."

"I've always been dying to see the inside of this house," Carmela was telling Stefan. "Can you believe that I've lived practically around the corner most of my life and I've never been inside! Do you collect anyone in particular?" She steered him away.

Claire felt the wine whiz right to her head. "Count Dracula seems to have found his bat."

"Oh, he'll be back," Zinnie poked her between the shoulder blades. "Men like that want a little hard to get. You don't think he doesn't have women throwing themselves at him all day long? Anyway, who cares? He's no big deal. Debonair. Tall. Witty. Rich. I'm so glad Freddy's not here. He'd fall in love with him."

"Stop worrying about Freddy. He'd want you to have some fun."

"No, he wouldn't."

"All the more reason, then."

"Jesus. Catch that old broad. Are those chandeliers or earrings? Everybody's so *rich*!"

"And boring, I bet."

"Yeah, well. You can't have everything." Zinnie looked about her apprehensively . . . eagerly. As though she'd found herself out on the tip of the high board and wasn't so sure which course to take. She is so pure, thought Claire. No longer innocent, but pure.

There was a band of musicians in tuxedos circuiting the lawn. Claire finished her drink and when the waiter passed she took another.

"Look at this," Zinnie sniggered in her ear, "a croquet mallet."

Sure enough, there were half hoops and mallets sprawled across the lawn on the other side of the house.

"What bliss," said Claire. "Bygone fragments of a more gentle era."

Zinnie pirouetted across the grass and picked up a mallet. She swung it crazily around her head. "Game?"

"C'mon, Zinnie," Claire looked around uncomfortably. "Cut it out."

"Why? Don't you want to play? You've been talking about getting some exercise. Let's see a little action here." She kicked off her shoes and held the splintered mallet in a batter's stance. "Look. There's a ball."

"I can't take you anywhere," Claire griped jokingly. But

she meant it. You never knew what Zinnie would do. She got so desperate and arbitrary sometimes. "I forget how to play," she grinned unhappily.

Zinnie proceeded to line up the hoops. "This can be home base," she dropped her curly blond head and nudged it at the first stepping stone. It was bordered in chamomile.

"You can't use a slate for base," said Claire. "And croquet has no base. I think."

"What happened to the little champagne man? There he is. Yoo-hoo!"

"Zinnie! Stop it!"

"Why?"

"Everybody's looking."

"So? Let them see someone having a laugh, for once." She swung her mallet. The ball traveled through several hoops and landed, perfectly round, at Claire's long toes.

"Nice shot. Only aren't we supposed to each have our own balls?" There was no sense in arguing. It would just make Zinnie worse.

"That's the spirit!"

"Mademoiselle!" A Nigerian fellow in tails who'd been watching, ambled over with another ball. He presented it to Zinnie as one would a precious gift.

"Oh, hello," she said. "Want to play?"

"*Volontiers.*"

"What's he say?" Zinnie frowned.

"He'd love to. What's your name?"

"René."

"Okay, René, you've got second base." She dragged him over to a far-off hoop.

"You're a sick girl, Zinnie. This is croquet."

"Queens rules. You can't beat baseball. Or do you think you can?" Chips of green in her blue-flecked eyes lit up with challenge.

"No, Zinnie. I do not, for the last time, think you can. Now can we stop this?"

But several more officious types, curious and bored, had

wandered over. They let themselves be bullied into position. This was all to the stern disapproval of the servants, but by now what could they do? The Tunesian vice-consul was having a smashing time in charge of third and one wouldn't want to upset him. Nor any of them. What a muddle.

Zinnie had one team arranged on one side and Claire, absorbed now, the other. She continually checked over her shoulder to see what Zinnie was doing. Zinnie was, Claire realized, as natural a leader as she had ever met. If she'd have been a man . . . Claire thought before she caught herself. Why, nowadays, a woman could do anything a man could do. Why was it that even she, who believed this, still had trouble incorporating it into everyday thought? Because it had always been she, in each of her relationships, who'd done the dishes. That's why. No matter how much money she'd made or hefty chores she'd shared. Christ, it was exhausting. The whole man-woman thing could make you ill. And so resentful. She didn't want to be resentful. She took a deep, cleansing breath and tried to return to her previous bemused state. There, that was better.

"This," Zinnie was informing the vice-consul, "is American culture. Just make sure that no one steals your base. See, any player from the other team can come and steal it while you're not looking."

"But this is not a just system!" he cried.

"Yeah, but you get to voice that opinion and live."

"Carry on," the Turkish ambassador poised his mallet.

Claire noticed that Stefan and Carmela were nowhere to be found. Zinnie distributed her evening bag's supply of sugar-free chewing gum. It was, she assured them, prerequisite. All sorts of fancy shoes were off, tossed into one raucus and plebian heap. By now there was nobody left on the other side of the house. The game simmered into a businesslike seriousness and time flew by like magic. Suddenly it was the fourth inning, and what a job it had become to see that devious ball coming. One by one the lanterns all around the property went on and Carmela and Stefan emerged from the glamorous front door. Stefan's face fell. Not Carmela's. She arranged her expression immediately into the appropriate butter-wouldn't-melt-in-your-mouth. Claire's team was up. The Lebanese official's wife was at bat. Her teammates cheered her on with slurred directions—they were all experts now. The lady swung and missed. A titter went up from Zinnie's team. She swung again, this time connecting. The ball raced through several hoops and cracked into the Nigerian fellow's ankle.

"Yow, yow, yow, yow, yow, yow!" He limped hurriedly in a circle.

Everyone trooped over with inebriated concern.

"Hello, stand back, I'm a doctor," said a handsome young blond man and they all moved aside. Zinnie lowered the wounded player onto the ground and she and the doctor took control. Claire backed off. Zinnie liked that young doctor, she could tell. She grinned to herself. Now let's just watch and see if he's married, she warned Zinnie silently. She found her shoes and walked across the lawn. There was a bench behind the tent where she could sit down and study the house. You seldom saw lead-paned windows like that anymore, or mossy stucco with ivy shooting up each corner. Nowadays the locals aluminum-sided any natural surface they could get their hands on. This was really the sort of place you could get used to. Quickly.

The others were wandering back. The wounded man was not badly hurt; Zinnie and the doc had him propped on a chaise lounge and were administering advice. Claire saw Zinnie throw back her head and laugh. Boy, to laugh like that again! Stefan came over and sat down next to her.

"Hello, troublemaker. I take it it was you who got the servants so upset."

Claire gave a noncommittal frown. She wasn't sure whether or not it was going to be advantageous to take the credit. "I hope that man isn't hurt. He was such an excellent shortstop."

"I suppose you see yourself as having saved the party," he remarked, amused.

She felt herself redden.

"You have an interesting family. Your sister Carmela. She's very knowledgeable about art, isn't she?"

"Is she?"

"Yes, indeed." He leaned over and removed a baby grasshopper that'd landed on her arm. She liked the way he did that, with fine feeling, not injuring the little fellow's legs. They watched him spring away. Stefan, charmed at his own kindness, exhaled a wacky, megalomanic chuckle.

Claire wafted in the hurricane of his cologne. Is there no one right for me? she thought. "You have a beautiful place here," she said.

"I'm so glad you like it," he said.

"Pretty hard not to like."

"I suppose not . . . so close to Manhattan," he paused. "And such polite neighbors. So very polite." He gazed into her eyes. Claire turned and watched the other guests. She liked cultivated, hard-drinking people. They were so active. Not like the drug enthusiasts she'd known in New York. Carmela, the prom queen, was hoofing across the dais with an Arabian. They were doing the fox trot. The Nigerian was hobbling now among the other guests. He was very proud of his wound, exhibiting it to anyone who would admire it. Claire looked around for Zinnie. There she was, still down at the chaise lounge, balancing a sandal from one naked toe, listening intently to something the young doctor was saying. Claire's heart went out to her and she felt something catch in her throat. If anybody hurt Zinnie she'd come after him herself—with an ax, if need be.

"Tell me something, Claire?"

"What?"

"Anything. I do so like to hear the sound of your voice."

"I was just thinking how easy it would be to murder someone . . . under the right circumstances."

"Yes, indeed. It's life that's difficult. What about suicide? Do you ever think about that?" He liked the direction of this conversation. He was enjoying it. He reminded Claire of a fox, the way his little white teeth glittered and poised in the air. She wondered what he'd been up to with Carmela. They'd certainly had time to go the full nine rounds. "No, I've given up suicide as a preoccupation. Haven't thought much about it since I was a teenager infatuated with self-pity. Suicide is always fun to think about until someone you love actually up and dies. You realize abruptly how inevitable your own end is. Shall we dance?"

Claire, Zinnie, and Carmela, arms linked, made their way down the hill. They were singing "Will You Still Love Me Tomorrow?" Carmela had lost one of Zinnie's shoes but Zinnie didn't mind. She was filled to the brim with glorious awe for a charming young unmarried doctor who hadn't left her side even after he'd secured her telephone number . . . and that after she'd told him she had a son. Carmela, resigned as she'd been to Stefan's unswerving interest in Claire, had somehow managed to secure more than five separate invitations to God-knows-who-all's near future parties. She was also very drunk. Zinnie had a firecracker voice. "Tonight you're mine, completely. You give your love, so sweetly. So tell me now . . . and I won't ask again. Will you still love me tomorrow?" Zinnie walloped out her solo and then they jaunted through the last chorus. No kidding, they congratulated themselves as they turned the last corner, they really did sound just like the Shirelles. They stopped short. Parked right in front of their door were three blinking police cars.

"Michaelaen!" Zinnie screamed and the three of them flew down the hill. "Michaelaen!" Zinnie fell on the sidewalk and got up before Claire even saw her go down. She was up on the porch and into the house before any of the cops could stop her. When Claire got there she saw Zinnie, her arms around Michaelaen, choking out loud, violent sobs. Her knee and elbow were trailing blood, but she didn't seem to notice that.

Several uniformed policemen were standing in the hallway and there were plainclothesmen all over the place.

"What's going on?" Claire's heart beat wildly, taking rapid account of both parents seemingly safe and sound on the steps. Her father had his arm around her mother. They both looked strange. Was her father's hair that white? They looked like old people.

"We were robbed, Claire."

"What?"

"Yes, robbed."

"We don't know what they got yet."

"Oh my God . . . and I let the Mayor out."

"Oh, I knew that was bright," Carmela slurred from right behind her.

"It might have been," Stan's tone was dead-weight lead. "Whoever wanted in that much might have killed him."

The Mayor heartened at his words. So Stan knew without measure the distance of his loyalty. To go down with the ship . . .

"I just wish we knew what they *took*!" Mary held her elbows and looked around creepily. "That's the thing." She wasn't going to go checking around until those fine officers got through going through every room, including the closets. She was past the point of caring what they thought when they found somebody's galoshes on a dust mop on somebody's folded shirt. I've no reason not to be a nervous wreck she told herself, her face pink as roses.

Claire looked around her at all of the cops. If this had happened to anyone else on the block they never would have sent more than one car. The place was all lit up. Spaces in the house were lit that never had been lit all at one time before. She looked around for the Mayor. There he was, sitting squarely on the porch watching the great to-do with big brown eyes and a broken heart. He'd missed the whole thing. Claire shot bolt upright. "My cameras!" she whispered and ran.

A few moments later she reappeared at the top of the stairs. "They're gone. All my lenses. Everything. They took my cameras." She sat down quickly before she fell down.

Now that they knew that something had been stolen, everyone else felt better. Something substantial had happened, a crime of reason, and they could handle that better than an eerie break-in where a small child lived. Detective Ryan came up to her, his little pad and pencil in hand, his blue seersucker puckered, his shoulder holster wetting the line of his white shirt with perspiration. Claire, in her mind's eye, was following the thief—which was what these cops were supposed to be doing, correct? Out looking for him instead of in here politely taking cider from her accommodating mother, who was, without a shadow of a doubt, enjoying this. She was lit up like a firefly. And the thief most likely comfy in some car on the Van Wyck, heading for the city with a Nikon, a Hasselblat, four lenses, and the rest of the loot.

The Mayor sensed Claire's misery right away. He came up and stepped on her foot as if to say, Here I am. Don't you worry, here I am. Your fella.

Carmela was tickled because her jewels were all there: she carried her velvet box down the stairs as though in a procession. This worried the detectives. They wondered why the hell the thief would make off with some "lousy cameras" when there were jewels plain as day on the bureau?

Lousy cameras? Claire staggered back out to the porch. Most of the cops were gone now ("Long as no one was hoit"). The porch boards creaked beneath her. The air stank of urine. Life was an irrevocable mess. On top of it, what if that Johnny Benedetto showed up? Claire rummaged through her purse and came up with her lip gloss, then angrily put it back without using it. Upstairs she could hear Zinnie tucking Michaelaen into bed. Her father had the detectives in his study. Gee, they couldn't get over those cannons! Mary came up from the cellar brushing her hands on her bowling tournament skirt. The silver was all there, mind you, and the cash, still buried deep in the Brillo box, but . . . I don't know . . . it's always a mess anyway down there, but . . . something's not right . . .

Claire stood up hastily and went back down the stairs. It couldn't be. She snapped on the light and a hole dropped from her stomach. The line full of black and whites—the whole lot of them—were gone. Claire blinked. There were color slides scattered all over the floor. Claire turned gray. Detective Ryan, right behind her, put his hand on her shoulder. "Don't touch nuthin'," he said. "Don't even think about it."

"Somebody hadda been watching the house," the cop was saying. "How else would he know they were all gone? Somebody . . . who knew all about her."

"Oh, come *on,*" Claire said.

Detective Ryan bit his lip. This was a riot. Somebody was actually after this girl and she was telling him to "come on." He felt like slapping her in the face to wake her up.

"Listen," Zinnie told him, "Those were the pictures she was taking up in the woods. Somebody didn't want their picture around, savvy? This was the thing. Whose ever picture that was . . . was the murderer."

Ryan winced. No point in scaring the shit out of her.

"I can't believe it!" Claire was saying. "My best shots. Gone. I think I must have been a thief in another life for this to happen to me again."

"So this happened before?"

"Mmm. In India."

"Oh. That lets that out."

Zinnie stared at her. "God, Claire, at least you're all right. Anybody crazy enough to come into the house has got to be desperate. We could have walked in at any moment. As it was, Daddy just missed whoever it was. He said he heard the back door slam and thought it was one of us."

"Miss Breslinsky, think real hard. I want you to try and remember who was in those shots."

"How am I supposed to know which shots are missing if you won't let me go through the darkroom? Oh, Lord. I feel as though I've been raped."

"Just let the print guys in there and then you can have your turn."

"My turn." Claire nodded her head and sat down. It was going to be a long night.

Next door, Mrs. Dixon peeked out through her clean vinyl blinds.

Captain Furgueson knocked on the screen and walked on in.

"Holy Christmas," Stan marveled. "If it isn't the brass."

Johnny Benedetto, down the block in Pokey Ryan's car, fought off the urge to go into the house. He knew Pokey would take care of everything and wanted to see what was moving around outside. You never knew. So far nothing but neighbors huddling under the street lamp. The usual. And the old lady in the wild makeup. She scurried back and forth across her lawn like a berserk bumper car.

Johnny was spent. He was yawning five times a minute. He pinched himself hard. He took deep breaths. A whole family of coons came down single file from the woods and gingerly picked their nocturnal route past the mailbox. When they saw all the commotion at the Breslinsky house they stopped, turned around, and marched, just as cool as you please, through the backyard next door. He watched them dine on the contents of three garbage cans, get up one by one onto the birdbath, and wash their hands as though they were human. You had to admit that animals were sometimes more understandable. There was nothing more treacherous than a human out for blood. He fell asleep with his mouth wide open and a deaf ear to the rhododendron bushes rustling.

CHAPTER

By Tuesday Claire was seeing truly great shots wherever she looked. That was the way it went, wasn't it? The minute you didn't have your camera, everything looked like the potential cover of *Life* magazine. They finished supper quietly. Everyone was spent from too many avid discussions of the theft, the murder, and, good Lord, the implications. Claire was fed up with being locked indoors—even terror becomes tedious—so she decided to go for a clandestine walk with the Mayor. She had to go out sometime. Her parents' fierce, well-meaning warnings about solitary ventures made sense, but not to live freely was not to live at all. You might just as well have been murdered yourself. It made Claire boil to think that some vermin could stilt her life-style any more than he already had. She had to think. Get out. They wouldn't jog, just go for a normal walk. It wasn't as though she had to wait around the house for a phone call or anything. With one last mournful look at the phone, she left. Johnny Benedetto had no doubt heard about the robbery. Not that he should care. Murder, apparently, was the only subject grand enough for him. Annoyed, she decided to cut across Eighty-fourth to the rim of the woods. The Mayor looked back at her with approval. He'd watch out for them. On a bench right across from White Hill, who should be out watching the sun set but Iris von Lillienfeld. Iris's face was hidden by a broad-brimmed straw hat, but it was her all right. Natasha, her poodle, posed at her feet. Claire hastened her step. She felt, rather than heard, the car engine pull up alongside her.

"Get in the car."

"Exactly what do you mean, 'get in the car'?"

"Just get in. I wanna talk to you."

Claire fingered her New Delhi bangles. "I can hear you very well."

"Get the fuck in the car."

She sat down primly and left the door open. The Mayor jumped in, too.

"Close the door."

She did. He slipped the stick into gear and took off.

"Where are you going?" For one panic-stricken moment she thought Johnny might be the murderer. He had, she supposed, just as much reason as anyone.

"I'm just takin' you someplace. To talk. All right? Just to talk."

"Fine."

The Mayor watched Natasha's pretty face grow small in the rearview mirror. It was superb for her to see him whizzing off like this.

They drove along in silence. Johnny cruised down Cross Bay Boulevard and before you knew it they were heading for Brooklyn on the Belt. Claire looked out the window with studied indifference. It was a beautiful night, calm and hot. Johnny whizzed along, keeping his hands tight on the wheel. Neither of them spoke. The Mayor, afraid of being carsick, had his nose out Claire's window. With his ears flung back away from his head he looked, he felt certain, like a veritable cocker. Claire wasn't sure why nobody was talking, but if that was how he wanted it, it was all right with her. She had one mad moment when she felt like asking him what sign he was, but she quickly overcame it. To their right were the lights of the city and to the left the high cliffs of the Rockaway dump run amuck with great seagull.

He turned off at Sheepshead Bay and slowed the car down in the traffic. Wherever you looked there were Italian cafés. The car nudged along between Cadillacs, everywhere Cadillacs. Coming up were the docks and the day-fishing boats, lined up and banging gently into rubber tire moorings. Groups of people promenaded in front of the cafés—Russians mostly, Johnny was telling her, this being the middle of the week. On weekends this place was jammed. You came out from the city just to watch the boats, eat raw clams, feel the breeze around you like a loose suit. There was something about looking at a boat like that on the water—Johnny couldn't keep the pride out of his voice. They mightn't be his boats but this was his territory now. He was on home ground here, parking the car on the sidewalk, pointing out this joint and that, zipping around the front of the car to open the door for her. She was missing her camera again. Those Russians. Lumbering past the delicate cappuccino tables on thick-stockinged legs landed resolutely on the shores of Brooklyn. Hefty arms propelling second-hand strollers enthroning pudgy Kruschevs. Eighteen to a table, battling even knife-toting waiters for more chairs. Boy, she missed her camera. What on earth was she going to do? She'd never be able to replace them. She'd been too ashamed to tell her family, but she no longer had insurance for them. When the policy had been due for renewal (where had she been, in Ceylon?), Wolfgang had convinced her that they should use that money for something more sensible . . . like a car. Well, he'd smashed the car and where was she now? Looking pretty damn stupid to herself.

Johnny led her past the milling immigrants, past the clatter of stalls set up in a flea market. "You want somethin?" he asked her. "Go ahead. You want a toothbrush? They sell those real fancy jobs from Italy. No? How about a phone? Hey, don't laugh, they're dirt cheap down here."

They crossed the broad boulevard full of flashy cars. The Mayor rubbed against her ankles as they scooted across—Lord, he hated these teeming places with a passion. Self-consciously, Claire stayed a step behind Johnny. She was afraid he'd notice all the pink she had on. She'd put on the pink with the hope in the back of her mind that she would run into him, and now she was afraid he'd see right through her: pink was a complimentary tone for women over thirty. Men were not dumb.

Johnny held the door open for her. It was a little wooden place right on the water, the only one. The rest were all confined to the other side of the boulevard. They walked through a room devoted to tourist accompaniments: carved sea captains from Maine, conch shells from the Bahamas and spaghetti bowls from Napoli. Claire felt him watching her apprehensively. She smiled a little too brightly. It was the first time they'd been that close. Right there in the middle of the shop she took a good whiff of him. She could have stood there for the rest of the night. One more room was the restaurant area, and the next, through a mobile of shells, was a broad dock with netted jars of candles on rough hodgepodge tables. Paper lanterns were clothespinned to the telephone line. The moon was a lopsided egg smack on top of the bay.

"Can't bring no dogs in here, bud," a skinny-assed waiter whooshed past them.

"It's all right, Guido." An old man in a Yankees cap stood up from the table nearest the cash register. "They're with me." He put his arms around Johnny with his eyes and shook his head. "So you finally remembered the way to Brooklyn, eh? Get over here!" He gave Johnny an affectionate clobber, then put him in a headlock. Johnny grinned from ear to ear.

"This old battle-ax is Red Torneo," Johnny laughed. "Red. Claire Breslinsky."

Red gave her an unembarrassed once over. He straightened up. "Now *this,*" he took her hand in his, "*this* is more like it." He led Claire to the seat overlooking the bay and stepped back to admire her one more time. The Mayor took to Red right away. The man smelled of crab meat and beer, one respectable combination. He snuggled right in at

Red's old bare feet. This was the sort of chap who'd pass you half his dinner under the table. The man had class.

Claire was one minute setting up fashion shots along the railing with those twinkling lights across the water, one minute snatching glances at Johnny, admiring the friendship that shone from the two men. Her past was sometimes like a curse. She couldn't do anything without all the art directors in her history nodding approval or shaking their bygone heads in veto. You really had to watch how you whiled away your time, didn't you, because it was always going to be there influencing you. Johnny and Red were catching up on old times. She stared into the black water. How rotten it was that it had to have been a murder to bring him into her life. For the first time, she imagined the murder as it must have happened, the enormity of it, that moment of absolute clarity when that little boy Miguel must have known it was too late, it had gone too far, from bewilderment to fear to pain to certainty. She shuddered. Johnny didn't even look at her. He took off his jacket and laid it on her lap without breaking his conversation with Red. Claire turned her face away so that he wouldn't see her eyes fill up. She never cried and she was shocked at herself. Outside of the tears of her nightmare she'd be stuck to remember the last time. Angrily, she swallowed the tears back inside of her eyes, bending over and letting the ones that were already there drop to the floor while she fished for her bag. She didn't know why she felt she should be ashamed. It just caught her off guard that such a small gesture of concern from Johnny could bring that on. She liked that he watched her without appearing to, though. Physically, she liked everything about him. Right down to that smug fat lower lip. Why did he have to be a cop? Why, in fact, was he a cop? Because she didn't want him to be. The pretty flowers on the table turned to plastic just as they always had been. Life, Swamiji had told her time and time again, is all the way you look at it. What she had to do was simply grab hold of the table and not let her confusion show. What had happened yesterday, she realized, had not helped her state of mind.

She'd been down in the cellar doing laundry. Almost sure she heard the phone, she stuffed the dress she'd been wearing in with the others about the same color and ran upstairs in her underwear. The phone hadn't been ringing, or at least it had quit ringing by the time she'd got there. She wandered listlessly up to the second floor and into the bathroom. Whenever she saw a shut-tight shower curtain she would poke her head in just to see if Janet Leigh was in there. She wasn't. Wondering what on earth to put on, she walked outside and hesitated outside Carmela's bedroom. In all that topsy-turviness Carmela wouldn't miss one pair of pants. She went in and looked around. What a mess. Dust balls as big as your fist tumbleweeded in the draft from the hallway fan. Rumpled clothes were all over the place. Claire held up a potential candidate. No, she laid it gingerly back in place. That was a blouse. There you go. She saw a pair of almost ironed white jeans and picked them up. The front door slammed. Uh-oh, she stood still guiltily. Maybe one of them had forgotten something and would be leaving again right away. There was a shuffling noise on the stairway. She jumped silently into the closet, closed the door, and held her breath. How humiliating to be caught sneaking Carmela's precious clothes! Vicious sibling battles reared their long-forgotten heads. She went rigid with fear.

And it was Carmela all right. There was no mistaking that cackle. But who was she with? Another muffled laugh and she recognized Freddy. Freddy? What was he doing up here?

"I'm telling you she went out," Freddy was saying. "I let it ring thirty times. Anyway, I'm sick to death of her holier-than-thou attitude."

Claire heard something rip and Carmela cry, "No!" She was just about to throw open the closet door and come to Carmela's rescue when the pair dropped to the floor. She could see them through the downward-tilted slats in the door. Freddy thrashed away. Carmela was underneath him. She was down on all fours, drooling convivially onto a kit of electric rollers.

"What do you got that mug on for?" Johnny's voice brought her back to the present. "Like you're off in la-la land."

"Close enough," she said. Red was watching her, too. He held a Spalding ball which he kept shooting from one hand to the other. She'd seen eyes like that once before. On a hundred-and-six-year-old parrot. The waiter came over and whispered something in his ear. He took off with an agility that surprised her. The moment he was gone Johnny picked up his chair and turned it facing her. He sort of loomed over her.

"So what's the story with this Stefanovitch guy?"

"Huh?"

"You know who I mean. The guy with the mansion you've been hanging out with."

"I haven't exactly been hanging out with him. We jogged once for five minutes."

"And went to his jazzy party, right?"

"Well, yes, but—"

"Was he with you for the whole party?"

"Tch."

"I mean did he go off and leave you alone for any amount of time?"

Then it hit Claire what he meant. He wasn't quizzing her about her private life. He was trying to find out if Stefan was . . . if Stefan had . . . oh, really! "It couldn't have been Stefan who stole my cameras. He was at the party the whole time."

"Did you see him the whole time?"

"Well, no. He was the host. He had people to entertain."

"So he was around the whole time."

"Yes. No. He was gone for twenty or thirty minutes at one point. But he was with my sister."

"Mmm. The brassy one."

"She's not brassy."

"Okay, she's not." He lit a cigarette.

Claire battled with herself for five seconds and then lit one herself.

"My sister is very interested in art."

"Uh-huh."

Claire smoked her cigarette. She certainly didn't have to explain anything to him.

"And you?"

Claire looked at him with puzzled eyes.

"You like 'art'?"

She smiled. "Look, Stefan's a very nice man."

"With lots of cash."

"What's wrong with money? Do you have something personal against money? Or are you asking me an actual, direct question?"

Johnny leaned back in his chair till it almost tipped over. He studied the boats.

"And how do you know that I was at that party anyway? Is someone following me? Are you having me watched?"

Johnny leaned across the table and grabbed her wrist. "Darlin', there's no one watching you but me. Got that?"

Claire felt her insides.

Red came back armed with three plates of baked clams and a tunnel of lemon wedges. "Guido!" he shouted. "Bring us some bread. And a couple a beers." He laid his finger alongside his nose. "And then bring us a platter a calamari . . . with plenty a hot sauce!"

On the way home, the Mayor threw up. It wasn't too bad. Claire heard him give a couple of dry heaves on her lap and she yelled for Johnny to pull over, quick. He swerved onto the shoulder, then into the parking lot from Lookout Reach. They stood over him, concerned parents, as he relieved himself of buttered pretzels, shrimps, some *basta chorta,* and quite a few horseradished clams.

"Better out than in," philosophized Johnny as he went to fetch a box of tissues from the car.

"It's all right, your honor," Claire soothed him. "You're better now."

"Atta boy," Johnny encouraged him, "atta boy." He didn't want a repeat performance back in the car. "C'mon. Let's walk him a little bit down to the edge."

They trolleyed across a narrow cement crossway after the dog and took off their shoes. His honor, good as new, went on ahead to scavenge for mussels. The cars behind them in the parking lot weren't empty but you couldn't see anybody in them, either. Claire worried for a moment that it would give Johnny ideas, but he just walked along beside her not saying too much, telling her a little bit about Red and how he'd come into his life and listening when she finally opened up and told him how Michael had died. Then he wanted to know about the men in her life. She told him briefly, in headlines, accentuating her own stupidity, not sparing herself at all.

"And how come you never married either of them?"

"Stupid I am. Dumb I'm not. It was pretty obvious, even to me, that I'd set myself up as the victim in both relationships."

"Yeah. Well. You can't be a survivor until you've been a victim first."

"I guess that's true." After what Zinnie had told her about his wife, she knew exactly what he meant. "That's what happened to you, too, wasn't it? I mean in your marriage?"

"Look, don't go asking questions like that, all right? I don't want to talk about it."

"Well, excuse me! I thought I heard somebody say they just wanted to talk to me. I thought that was the point of this entire venture. Rest assured, I'll never bring it up again. Or anything else for that matter."

"Why do you have to keep going on and on about it? You can't just let things drop? You got to hang on to the negative?"

"Ah. The old pot-calling-the-kettle-black routine."

"So now you're gonna be pissed off."

"It doesn't mean that much to me to piss me off!"

"Good!"

"Fine!" And it was fine. He was just what she *didn't* want. She had no intention of falling for him in the first place. Nor he, apparently, for her. They marched back to the car. Relieved, she opened the door, the Mayor jumped in, she leaned over to hook up her sandal. He grabbed her around the waist from behind. She swung around to belt him and landed with her mouth on his, a drawn out whirl into oblivion so far away and intoxicating that when he let her go, she almost fell. He drove her home as they'd come, without saying a word.

Claire bolted awake in the wee morning hours. She'd been dreaming that someone had found her cameras. It was so real that she was more surprised than depressed when she sat up in bed and realized where she was. She pulled a nightgown over her nakedness, got out of bed, and padded downstairs. All the fans were in high gear, hot air gusts tearing through the house cooling nothing. The Mayor, asleep on the kitchen floor, put up both ears.

"Hi ya. Locked in?"

He loved this girl. You never knew what she was going to do.

"Come on, then. Sit out on the porch with me for a while. I had a dream. Shall I make us some toast? A little cinnamon toast wouldn't hurt, would it? I'm so confused about this cop. A cop. Just what I didn't want. What was it Swamiji used to say? Whatever it is that you fear will come at you as though magnetized. He really knew his stuff, that swami."

The Mayor waited politely while she fidgeted around the kitchen stocking up, then they headed for the porch. Together they sank into the hammock and heaved a sigh. This was really the place to be. They had her up in the attic nowadays. She had a nice cot with a feather quilt in the box window but it wasn't the porch. Now this was terrific. She with her thoughts and he with his rocketing heartburn. The spider on the rail had already rebuilt his web. He must just love this spot. Birds of a feather, she supposed. The rabbits in their cages began to scuffle. Claire covered the Mayor's mouth and his infernal whimperings for more toast. "Who's that?"

The screen door opened and there stood Michaelaen in his bathing trunks. "I *knew* I heard somebody up," he rubbed his eyes with a fist.

Claire laughed. "Hop in."

Michaelaen climbed up to join them. He gave the Mayor an affectionate bite on the ear—a habit of his, not always too comfortable for the Mayor but necessary to their familiar routine. He'd brought his Tootsie Rolls along. This was exciting. A secret club. "I'll trade you one Tootsie for a toast," he bargained.

"One Tootsie for half a toast, pardner. Take it or leave it."

"How bout two Tootsies for a whole toast?!"

"All righty."

They collapsed in giggles. Then he sat up straight and looked furtively around him. His cheeks filled up behind tightened lips.

"What's the matter, Michaelaen?"

"Nuthin'." He was remembering the last deal he'd made. With Miguel. He didn't know what, but something bad had happened to Miguel. Maybe they never should have gone that time with the other kids, in there where they got to see those pictures. Those pictures where the little boys and girls didn't have all their clothes on and they were doing stuff to each other. Only he wasn't sure what. At first it had been fun, like. Only now he was a little bit afraid, because if he told, then Mommy could get shot. Or worse. So sure he wasn't going to tell. And he didn't want nothing bad to happen to Aunt Claire, either.

"Tell me. Come on. You can. I cut down smoking for you, didn't I?"

That was true. She smelled better than ever. Not as good as Mommy, but good. And things were hopping since she'd come to live with them. Claire grabbed his foot and held it tenderly. That was the wrong thing to do. "I was thinking about the raccoon," he lied. Claire was thinking about why she'd never had a child. There had been all sorts of reasons not to. And the part about becoming something dried up, well, that was all that that had been: a reason. Not wanting to have somebody someday look at her and think that. It wasn't as if she would ever feel that way about herself, anyway. She always had been dried up in some ways and fruitful in others. No, that hadn't been it. More often than not it had been the fear of being totally dependent on some man who would then turn on her. Without question, losing interest fell under the category of betrayal. And the men she'd chosen to love always would have strayed without the constant pull of her sexuality. Had she been hating men all along? Ridiculous! Although she could have been using her sexuality to attract the wrong kind of man just because she scorned them so much that she wanted to prove how despicable they were. Had that been another fear that she'd been trying to draw near? Hadn't she searched the world finding unworthy subjects to love so she could always be right? So righteously right. Keeping busy hating the wrong in others so she wouldn't have to hate herself. Claire took one good long look at Michaelaen and she knew that she had been wrong. She'd been wrong all along. A cool, light wind blew across the porch. A Canadian wind. Open Indian spirits come to look. The Mayor pointed his snout to the sky, then yawned, then fell asleep, as did Michaelaen, then Claire. The wind chimes wept above their heads and nobody knew what else would happen next.

CHAPTER

7

Freddy pedaled his bicycle like mad through the woods at dawn. He liked to pick out certain produce for the restaurant himself and you had to get there good and early. He bumped through the pine forest and whizzed onto Park Lane South. There was no not braking down White Hill. White Hill was steep, and every year or so another kid got killed sledding through the stop sign on the bottom. And the tow truckers. There was great competition among them to be the first at any wreck. The first one there got the job. Like modern-day cowboys they galloped through the rural neighborhoods at heart-thumping speeds. Plenty of them had crashed at the foot of White Hill. Plenty. The street had a veritable glitter from all the ground glass of accidents throughout the years. You always wanted to be careful around there. There was a tree down at the bottom, just a bit off the crux. It was the oldest tree in Richmond Hill, a good thirteen feet around the trunk, and that tree, as noticeable as it was, was made invisible by the devastating white of the hill. Nobody knew who'd originally painted the San Francisco–like slope, but whoever it was had done a good job of it. It was still white and it had been for as long as even old Mr. Lours could remember. Freddy pulled over at the tree and put his feet on the ground. He blew his nose and wiped his face. Geez, this was one hell of a tree. Funny he'd never noticed it. You could see the front porch of the Breslinsky house from here. He got back up on the bike and pedaled down. Oh, for God's sake! Claire had Michaelaen outside with her again. This was really the limit. Freddy didn't like Claire. She would get up and leave the room in the middle of one of his stories. And, worse, if she stayed, she rarely bothered to laugh. She wasn't a nice Queens girl. She was hard. Yes, that was it, she was hard. She had this childlike bashfulness that fooled you, when in reality she was nothing more than a tart. A world-class tart. Taking pictures round the world. If that was what she'd been doing, where was her money?

Freddy wheeled his bike over and looked at them. The Mayor opened one eye then closed it right back up again. Ugly old dog. Ought to be put to sleep. He looked at Michaelaen's face collapsed in sleep, so beautiful, so infernally a replica of Zinnie's that if he didn't know Zinnie's character so well he'd wonder if Michaelaen were his. The sound of someone skittering about up on the second floor put him back on his bicycle. Probably Mary getting up. He didn't feel like shooting the breeze with her. Mary did go on and on. Off he went.

It is *Föhn*, was Claire's first thought as she opened her eyes. Sirocco. The high-pressure, delicious wind. Weather that bowled you over with its perfection. The only thing was that people didn't exactly know what they were doing in it and neither did they much care. Michaelaen and the Mayor still slept soundly. Claire remembered Johnny in a rush, before her defenses were up. Maybe he'll call, she thought. Maybe I'll get up and go inside and the phone will ring.

A garbage truck lumbered up the street. The compacter roared and overalled men flung the cans through the air. Claire watched them with interest. Years ago, when Michael had died, they'd found a nest of mice in the cellar. They were Michael's mice, or at least he'd protected them by never telling their parents about them. He'd made Claire swear she'd never tell, either. He didn't want Pop to go knocking them off, he said. Poor little fellas. The mice, as though in silent contract with Michael and his live-and-let-live policy, had gone about their teeny lives unnoticed. Claire remembered very well. But after the accident, the whole time Michael was laid out in Mullaney's Funeral Parlor, the mice had raced crazily through the walls at home. With uncanny terror they'd clattered noisily over the rafters. Stan had set his traps with grief-stricken, dedicated preoccupation. They were only little mice. All mixed up. Of course somebody had had to do something, but Claire remembered how she'd hated her father for his industrious and careful murders. One morning, the morning of the funeral, she had watched from the upstairs window as the garbage men had picked out a wrapped up newspaper from one of the cans that had tipped, and a baby mouse had slid out onto the curb. The garbage man had picked up the thing by its tail and flung it into the chopping blades. She had felt such shame at that moment that she'd wanted to hide. She hadn't wanted anyone to see Michael's mice. Not ever. She hadn't wanted anyone to know any more of his soft and tender weaknesses.

"Why Claire," her mother came up suddenly behind her, "Why sweetheart, don't cry!"

She didn't even know she'd been crying, but there it was, hiccupping and sobbing out of her like a child, finishing the job that had started up last night at Johnny's kindness, taking fuel from her mother's concerned tone. She cried on and on, amazed all the while that these great gulps of water were coming out of her. She was two people then, one watching, one doing, and the watching side marveled at the wholehearted self-pity involved, marveled that Michaelaen didn't wake up from her noise, and recalled the smell of the pine needles from the last time . . . when she'd buried the cat. There had to be some meaning there, but she wasn't sure what. Strangely enough, that had been the start of some hope in her life, being out on her own without that bastard Wolfgang. Now maybe she was feeling hope, too. You didn't cry from despair. You breathed shallow breaths and you tried to feel nothing, but you didn't cry.

"There, there," her mother was saying. "They'll find your cameras, Claire. And if they don't, we'll get you another. Don't worry, Claire. Bonnie Claire."

Bonnie Claire? She looked up and laughed. Her mother hadn't called her that since she was a child. Ah, poor Mom. What had she gone through back then, losing a son? And telling her now with her face all screwed up in compassion that they'd buy her a new camera. As if they had any money for things like that. As if they had any idea how much even half of her equipment would cost.

"I'm all right, Mom. I'll be fine. I guess it's all sort of a strain."

"Sure a strain is what it is. Why don't you come along with me to mass?"

"Now, Mom. I'll be just fine. You know I will."

"I know. But all the same—"

"No 'all the same.' Come on. You've dropped your rosary. You don't want to be late. Look, here comes Mrs. Dixon." And indeed she was, walking across the lawn in right-angle zigzags to avoid the webs. She rolled her sparkling shopping cart behind her. They'd stop off at Key Food straight from church.

"All right, I'm off. I'll say a prayer for you, special. Claire?"

"What?" She wished her mother would go already. She didn't want old Dixon to see her with her eyes all red.

"That John Benedetto drove you home last night, didn't he?"

"Mmm."

Her mother still stood there. "All right. I won't ask questions. Just try not to do that anymore. Go off without a word. I was worried." She hesitated. "See you later then."

Claire waved to Mrs. Dixon and the two women sped away, not even giving so much as a nod to Iris von Lillienfeld who stood in distressed admiration of her blooming, eight-foot-tall hollyhock.

Claire wiped her cheeks and walked across the street. "*Guten tag*," she said.

"Good day," Iris snapped. Her lipstick was awry and an exhausted royal blue Spanish shawl clung limply to her sparrow's shoulders.

"I . . . uh . . . I've noticed you out here several times and I wanted to say hello."

"I guess dat means you gonna say hello now."

"Oh. Yes. Yes, it does."

"Vell?"

"Pardon?"

"Something else? You vant something else?"

"No," Claire decided she could play her game. "I don't want anything else." She headed back across the street. Old codger, she grinned to herself. She knew a thing or two about reeling in a trout.

"Pisces," Mary eyed her husband over the paper. "Try not to worry so much about financial problems."

Stan looked up from his bowl of Sealtest vanilla-fudge. "Tales of the Vienna Woods" bombinated through the kitchen.

"All your worries will soon be over with the moon moving into Virgo."

"It doesn't really say that." Stan returned to his dessert. He gave it one more squirt of Reddi-Wip.

Mary looked hurt. "Sure it does. Pisces. Right here."

"Notice how she doesn't show you the paper, Pop," Zinnie said. She had her mother's number. How many times had Mary tried to get her to stay home from work by pleading any old bad omen under Gemini.

Mary threw the paper furiously into the air, losing the page and all threat of investigation.

"Ma," Carmela said. "You're so naive."

"Influenceable I might be, dear. Naive I never was. Naivety is a gift. Something, I might add, that none of my children were born with. The lot of ya come into the world with crisp frowns of revelation tattooed to your foreheads." She started to sing one of her old Irish songs, old "Molly Malone": "She wheeled a wheelbarrow through streets broad and narrow . . ." Claire looked up, amused. How she had hated her mother singing those songs when she'd been a girl! It used to embarrass her to no end.

The Mayor watched them fondly from the floor. It had been a grand meal. The finest whittle of garlic roast pork and Mary's special spinach baked in white sauce and laced with Gruyère. Ah, you couldn't beat that Mary once she got started in the kitchen. There was no match. No wonder Stan had married her.

Claire was thinking, all right, if he's on nights, he'll just be waking up. Any minute now the phone will ring. He would certainly want to know if she remembered anything new from the missing photographs. Or if Carmela had lost sight of Stefan at the party. Carmela had said no, but then you never knew with Carmela. She might think of an absence as a desertion to her femininity. She certainly sat there looking cool and polished, although Claire knew she wasn't. Her perfect nose had the start of a shine and she kept turning, looking nonchalantly out the window.

Michaelaen jangled Mary's change purse between his knees. There was rock 'n' roll between those coins. All at once he jumped up and shrieked. Freddy was at the back door with a cherry cheesecake. They were always glad to see Freddy. Even Stan, despite himself. You couldn't stay mad at Freddy for very long.

"What news from the front?" Zinnie asked when they'd divided up the cake and settled down to a second dessert. Freddy took his time and licked the fork with a big red tongue. He loved to have the floor. Claire looked away. "It hasn't been easy," he said finally. "I guess you all know by now that I've been interrogated?"

"What?" they all said.

"Yes, indeedy. And not with kid gloves, let me tell you. After they solve the murder, Carmela, you ought to do a story on the underhanded methods of harassing innocent suspects by the police."

"You weren't a suspect?!" Mary's arm went protectively, instinctively around Michaelaen.

"Well, maybe not a suspect," Freddy didn't want to go tipping the wheel of credibility and ruin his story. "Not exactly. But they sure put me through the third degree. They most certainly did. And you'd think they think we've never watched a 'Kojak' in our lives the way they do that old one buddy, one enemy routine." He looked to Zinnie who was studying her sneakers. "They roughed me up. I've had an awful week. First the opening and now this."

"What? This?"

"They've got some flibbertigibbet insect from the stationhouse posing as a bartender. As if the killer is going to walk into *my* place and announce himself. It's just too much. Somebody asked him for a Harvey Wallbanger and he gives the guy a Rob Roy. A Rob *Roy*!"

"An honest mistake," Stan defended the cop.

Freddy ignored him. "And I'm almost positive this undercover dick is on drugs. Cocaine. I'm sure he is."

"Talk about unfounded accusations," Zinnie sneered.

"Well, he's wired on something. You should see him." Freddy gave his cruel and dumb-faced imitation of a space cadet. They couldn't help but laugh.

"Maybe he'll improve with experience," suggested Mary.

"Barely plausible," Freddy shook his head.

"He's probably wasted from working too many hours overtime," Zinnie said. "There's a lot of pressure on the 102 right now."

"I wonder what ever happened to those license plate numbers?" Claire asked suddenly, but no one was interested in that now. Freddy still had lots to tell. He rubbed his hands together.

"Shall I make another pot of coffee?" Mary stood.

"And I've got this *other* bartender," Freddy nodded yes, "who is so good that I'd give him a raise if I wasn't afraid that he'd realize how good he is and take off on me for the city."

Nothing if not honest, thought Claire.

"*Or* the airport. They're paying big bucks down there in inebriated tips. But this kid's a redhead," he rumbled Michaelaen's hair. "Curious tribe. No tribe at all when you think about it. There's one in every large family. Stubborn bunch."

"Yeah, so what about the guy?" Carmela was terse.

"Oh. The redhead. If he left I'd be really in trouble. Unbelievable. He must be ambidextrous. I don't know how he does it."

And I bet he does it with a drop of the eyelids and a purse of the lips, Zinnie hummed inside her head. She gritted her teeth. She knew who that redhead was. His lover, that's who. He couldn't even resist referring to him in front of his son's family. Such was his enthusiasm. Sometimes Freddy was a real canker sore.

"See that's the thing. I don't *need* another bartender right now. He's just taking tips away from the others is all he's doing. He's just in the way. Plus he *looks* so unaesthetic with his big walrus moustache. In this day and age when a Ronald Coleman is the thing—"

"Hoy Jesus," sputtered Stan.

"Well, it gives the place the wrong look. People walk in, they take one look at him, they want a beer instead of beaujolais nouveau."

He prattled on and on. Claire tuned him out at the mention of a redhead. She remembered a redhead. Where had it been? Every thought she had was interrupted by the urgent pressure of the thought of Johnny Benedetto. The Mayor looked at her with panic. To notify her of what was coming. It was either Claire or Stan. Stan would give him a trusty little once around the block, when what he yearned for was a journey. Claire pushed her cherry cheesecake over to her father, stood up, and went for the clothesline. If Johnny called, at least he'd realize she wasn't sitting around waiting for the phone to ring.

"Be careful, Claire," Stan said.

"I must have told you twenty times, Mary," Freddy was saying as he picked through the supper dishes, "don't use the Gruyère with the spinach and the béchamel. Use the Emmentaler."

"What's the difference? It was scrumptious."

"It's *my* recipe," he wiggled his head at her.

Claire shut the door. There was old Iris out on her lawn. She was carving a rainbowing mist with the hose. Claire sneaked up behind her and crossed her arms over her chest.

Iris turned around and glared. "Oh. Pollyanna, is it?"

"What a rude thing to say. I'm grumpy and cantankerous myself. I'm no such thing as a Pollyanna." She heard herself defending her distemper and started to laugh.

"Vot's so funny?"

"Uh . . . Me . . . You . . . I don't know. That coronet on the top of your head."

"Vot?" she patted her coronet. "It takes me a very long time each morning to assemble dis, you know."

"Yes, it does look like it. It's pretty elaborate. But then so are you." That was what she said to her, like that and right from the start, without any ifs, ands, or buts. This was the kind of relationship they were going to have, like two already drunken men in the middle of the night bumping into each other in some old pub . . . they were both right at home from the start in the impudent banter of recognition, two souls lost and found out the hard way. Claire walked over and fingered the foxglove. "*Digitalis purpurea*," she identified its Latin name, showing off.

Iris, not missing a beat, continued: "Fingerhut. Revbielde. . . . Vitches Gloves."

"Fairy Thimbles."

"Dead Men's Bells."

Claire stood there, stumped. "Ah!" she said then. "Bloody Fingers."

Iris laughed, delighted. "Gloves of Our Lady. How do you know about dese tings?"

"I used to read about them. In a place where there was nothing else to read."

"Vere vos dat?"

"In India."

"Ja. I heard dat's vere you ended up."

"You heard about me? From whom?"

Iris snorted. "I got my sources."

"Right. I remember you used to tell fortunes."

"Me? I never did dat. Never. Dey used to tell dat story und I let dem, but I never did."

Iris did, too, used to tell fortunes. She knew because Michael had seen her. He used to watch her like a hawk.

"Tell you vot. You help me carry dat foxglove to a sunnier spot und I'll let you maybe take my picture. Und," she continued her bargain, "I'll giff you cookies."

"Cookies, too, huh?"

"Ja. Und don't act so surprised. I seen you vatching me mit dat camera all hooked up."

So. Iris didn't know what had been stolen. Either that or she was more sly than Claire was inclined to believe.

"All right, you old bandit. Do you have any gloves, at least?"

Iris stood there blankly.

"No gloves. Fine. How about a shovel?"

"Ja. Dat I got." She led Claire into the barnlike garage. Things hung on rusty nails that looked as if they'd crumble if you touched them. It smelled of old, dank everything. "One ting I love," Iris was saying, "is my plants. I talk to dem."

"Yeah?"

"Sure. Vy not? Old voman like me? Gotta talk to something."

She was excited, bent over and digging around in some boxes. Claire thought, that's no future, that's not what you live looking forward to. Being so at the mercy of strangers.

She will die all alone in her house and not a soul will notice till her body rots and smells and the dog starts howling. No one will happen to know where she'll be laid out but every antique dealer and real estate shark will cluck nervously over the place the day after she's gone.

"Come on," Claire took the mighty shovel from the narrow woman, "let's see how quickly I can scruff up yet another pair of my sister's shorts."

Together they approached the magnificent foxglove. Iris von Lillienfeld crooned away, notifying it of its imminent journey. It was no small task. What seemed to be a simple four-foot fixture turned into a person-sized thing with its heavy, gangling roots exposed, and Iris insisted on getting every root up. "Vatch dat one!" she cried. "*Yoy! Vorsichtig!* Careful, careful!"

And Claire was careful. She'd forgotten how nice it was to get your fingers good and filthy dirty with the fragrant, deep-dug earth. You remembered your own mud pies. You forgot that winter ever froze New York and left you with nothing out of doors but brittle twigs and rigid ground. This lush beauty fooled you, let you think it would go on forever. Iris stooped over her, a ravaged cameo worried for her dear foxglove, her single sprouts of whisker very evident and sturdy in the horizontal light.

Together they tugged and they pulled. Still the foxglove wouldn't budge. Claire began to think that maybe it had a mind of its own. Why move the thing to a sunnier spot when it had grown this indomitable where it was? Perhaps it would very simply refuse. No, it couldn't do that. Iris was determined. It could very well up and die, though. No. No, on second thought, Iris would keep it alive just by watching it. She'd talk it back to health if she had to. Now Iris stuck the pitchfork into the hole and wobbled the lower roots. Son of a gun, marveled Claire, she's stronger than I am, the old faker. Iris looked at her quickly, maybe reading her thoughts. "It's chust a matter of balance," she explained. "Like jujitsu." And out came the foxglove.

"I see."

"Und den you can put dose pansies back in the shadow," Iris instructed her, the kindly film star to the Mexican gardener. Claire didn't mind, though. She'd waited for so long to get in touch with the old woman that she kept doggedly on, her nails already split and caked with black. And Iris didn't bother with conversation. She stood alongside quietly, apprehensively watching for signs of any agonized branch.

The Mayor was performing for Natasha, Iris's poodle, who watched condescendingly from the ivy. He covered his complete routine of independent jumps and snout grovels and he did them well, then flopped to the ground with a weary change of heart.

Claire's knees were black now, too. The white shorts she'd borrowed from Zinnie were stained with grass. "Oh, hell," she said when she saw that.

"Dat's all right," Iris prodded her impatiently with the shovel handle, "you'll get your reward in de other vorld."

So Claire continued. There was a whole new other hole to dig to put the flower in. She had a great belief in the "other world." She also knew that foreign diabolical spirits could enter into your body without your even knowing it if you put yourself in a susceptible position. Such as going to Macumba ceremonies and uncrossing your legs when the devil came in. Don't laugh, she told herself even as she started to laugh into the mud. Remember the zombie girl down in Rio? Yes, it was true that that girl had let herself in for it, selling her soul to Fatiema the hag just to hook up with some no-account hot socks from the Gerada de Ipanema. What had she paid her? Forty dollars? Something like that. A couple of laughs. And it had worked. Yes, indeed. That beautiful man had hung around that girl as though his life had depended on it. It had, sort of. She'd had to give him all the money she'd earned in San Paulo. The girl would sit there in the Gerada de Ipanema with her vodka lime and stare at the carnivali world with vacant oozy eyes and wait for him. And he'd beat her, too. That poor girl. She hadn't had much of a life but she'd had him. She'd had what she'd really wanted and gone for . . . easily, simply . . . on a dare, really. But she'd done it. Yes, not everybody believed in it, but Claire knew that you could have anything you wanted in the world. All from black magic with chickens flying in a grungy candlelit "church." You could have what you wanted all right. What they didn't tell you was all that went with it, what a price you had to pay. Claire knew. She'd been the zombie girl.

"I hope," she leaned back on her haunches and pulled her hair into a knot, "that you mean the life after death and not the 'life' of walking death."

Iris took one step backward. Always pale and powdered as good Queen Elizabeth in her final days, Iris went one notch paler still. "Dat's enough!" she whooshed her hand back and forth at Claire. "Dat's goot! You did a fine chob. Dat's enough." She yanked the trowel from Claire and gave her a push on the shoulder. Not a love tap, either. The Mayor, lounging imperiously in the portaluca, sprang to life. His four dainty feet churned with rapid ignition before he could right his portly girth. Once up, he gallivanted across the lawn to his Claire's side. He didn't go so far as to bare his teeth, but his gaze was steadfast animosity. No matter that Lü the cat prowled just underneath the porch. Or that Natasha watched him, not so haughtily now, from the ivy. When push came to shove one stood fast in the face of all terrorism. "It's all right, boy," Claire bent down and unruffled him with soothing strokes. "It's all right." She wasn't the least intimidated, he noted. Let the old biddy do her own gardening, by jingle. Or hire a man, the way everyone else did. When they reached the end of the shrub, Iris did a most surprising thing. She tottered after them in her chorus girl slippers and shouted, out of breath from the strain of the run, "Come back tomorrow around four und I'll giff you a nice fenugreek tea. Yes?"

"Ja wohl," Claire grinned without turning. The long crooked shadow of Iris reached out like a club-footed path in the street.

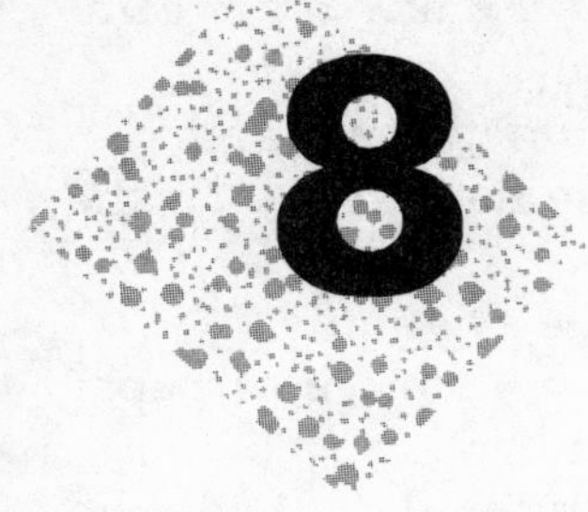

CHAPTER 8

Johnny stood bewildered in the camera shop. The salesman laid a seventh possibility into his hands. "Now this little model has automatic everything. Right down to your lens opening."

Johnny didn't know what a lens opening was but by now he was afraid to ask. "Okay. Now let's see that first one again."

"Which one, sir?"

"The first one you showed me. With the gizmo that made everything look close up."

"That's a lens, sir."

"Yeah, that one."

The salesman went back under the counter. "Here we are, sir."

Johnny studied the unfamiliar apparatus. "Now would you say a professional would use this lens?"

The salesman dabbed his upper lip with a hanky. "With which camera, sir?"

"Oh. With this good one here."

"Oh, no, sir."

"Well, which one would he use it with?"

"A professional would never use that camera."

"I get it. So show me again which camera a professional would use."

"The Nikon, sir."

"The one that means I gotta go for my lungs."

"That's the idea, sir."

"Hmm. And professionals wouldn't use any other camera, huh? Never?"

The salesman flung his left arm into the air and discovered his watch. "Well. Some do use the Canon. Or the Olympus."

"Yeah? So how much is that . . . the Olympus."

The salesman wrote the new price on a piece of paper, already cluttered with outlandish numbers.

Johnny shook his head and muttered. "And the Canon?"

"Together with which lens? With that model you looked at three."

"Okay. Go back to the Olympus."

"That's the one on special."

"Yeah, but it's still good, right?"

"Sir?"

"I mean it's not some fegazey outfit?"

"Fegazey?"

"Yeah." Johnny took a deep breath. "Like fake."

"Certainly not."

"And that comes with the flash and all?"

"I did tell you that, yes."

"Oh. You did?"

"Several times, sir."

Johnny clicked his gum and looked at the guy. "Wrap up the whole thing."

"The OM-2S with accessories, sir?"

"Yeah."

"Will that be gift wrapped, sir?"

"Sure. Go ahead. Wrap it up nice."

The salesman, in his element now, went about the elaborate job of dressing up each package in its own bold yellow paper, precisely slicing off any excess with a ruler and then zooming one blade savagely along the blue string ribbon and voilà! one curly decoration just as saucy as you please. He presented the attractive tower of boxes to Johnny. He stood before the counter patiently; what's more, he was all smiles.

"Will that be all, sir?"

"No. Now you can take the whole thing and shove it up your padooza. I wouldn't buy nothin' from you if you were the last salesman in Queens. Now I'm gonna go down the street and buy the whole kit & kaboodle from the competition, you nasty little piece a garbage."

It was nine o'clock at night and Claire still wasn't at home. She'd gone to pick up her nephew at Freddy's place, so there were two things he could do. He could wait right here in front of her house and have her see him waiting when she came back. Or he could go up to Queens Boulevard and surprise her, risking missing her altogether if she came home a different way. That wouldn't be too good because then her mother would tell her that he'd been there and by the time he caught up with her she'd have had time to arrange her face however she wanted. He couldn't risk that. He had to see her eyes in their moment of recognition, before she disguised them with propriety. This was crucial. He had to see if she was going to be as happy to see him as he was going to be to see her. The present he had for her in the shopping bag was incidental. The icing on the cake. He made a silent bet with himself that she'd refuse it, too. That was the kind of girl she was. Only he was going to make her accept the camera no matter what. He'd see to that. Johnny paced up and down the walk. No matter how hard he tried, he couldn't remember what she looked like. He could get the hair, the mouth, the eyes . . . but he couldn't put them all together. One thing he had in front of his face as though it were painted there was that ass. Johnny cleared his throat. He paced back and forth a few more times. Mrs. Breslinsky stuck her head out the window.

"Sure you wouldn't like to wait in here?"

"Oh, no," he blushed at his thoughts so inappropriate to her mother's vicinity. "I'll just wait awhile out here. Couple a things I gotta ask her." He looked down, puzzled, at his fancy shopping bag. He could hear the crickets.

"I see. Well, if you change your mind."

Johnny waved and smiled. The hell with this. She'd probably take Park Lane South. He hopped in the car. Another thing. If she was coming along Park Lane South she might run into that Stefanovitch bastard. He took the corner without stopping for the sign.

Freddy's place was across the boulevard from the municipal building. He could leave the shopping bag in the car or he could lug it with him—no, he'd walk in empty-handed and take it from there. Of course there was nowhere to park. The hubbub of the street made it impossible. And of course he would be driving Pokey's whale of an Oldsmobile. He'd tuned it up for him and now he couldn't get rid of it. Pokey had discovered the delights of his snappy sports car and wasn't in a hurry to give it up.

He pulled up dead in front of the joint underneath the NO STANDING sign and put Pokey's shield number on the dashboard, rejoicing as he always did that with his responsibilities came privilege, this probably being his favorite one. Not that there were that many anymore. Used to be, a cop was respected for the chances he took. You went in to the fruit and vegetable store, the guy wouldn't let you pay. You got your coffee and doughnuts from the diner, the cashier would wink and you'd zip out the door. And you took care of those places. You risked your life for a couple a lousy hundred bucks in the cash register anytime you went around back when you saw a screwy light on at three in the morning, and those owners, they used to appreciate it. Now? Jeez. Now the same owners made a stink when they saw you cuff up the suspects too tight. It was all rights and privileges for the criminals these days. No doubt about it. The city wasn't changing . . . it already had changed.

He slammed the door shut and walked up the pink marble stairs. Self-consciously he pushed his hair back. He hated joints like this. Women all tensed up and on the make. Men, if you could call them men, with hairdos and nipped-in waists and shellacked eyelashes. A fellow in a chartreuse shirt down to his knees eyeballed him up and down. He could have slapped him. Then, through a forest of good-luck-bannered potted plants he saw the back of her head at the bar. She was tapping her fingers impatiently along an empty bottle of Perrier. At least she wasn't chatting away happily with some creep. (In reality, she was waiting for a moment alone with Freddy. She was going to tell him exactly what she thought of his slimy interlude with Carmela.) The kid, beaming, was being detained by a silver-eye-shadowed flight attendant type who was cooing and oohing all over him. She bent over, breasts exposed, and gave him the celery stick from her bloody mary. Michaelaen clung shyly to his father's hand. Shit. Johnny didn't want to talk to him. He turned on his heel before Claire could see him and went back outside. What if Freddy was going to drive them home and they went out the back way through the parking lot? He went back in. A lawyer type in a dinner jacket approached Claire and he saw the two of them banter back and forth and then laugh out loud. He watched Claire blow an easy stream of smoke in the man's face and deliberately turn her back on him. And that takes care of that, thought Johnny with relief.

Derickson, from the 102 and looking every bit of it, was mopping long-stem glasses behind the bar. The other bartender was either off or on a break. Johnny knew he wouldn't risk blowing Derickson's cover. Derickson was too smart to do anything more than look right through him, but at the same time he didn't feel like letting the whole station house know that his interest in Claire was anything more than professional. Bunch of old fishwives. He went back outside. He noticed that his palms were wet. What am I, delirious? he asked himself. He walked across the boulevard to the big stone statue, a naked statue of a man the old-timers called the Fireman. There he was, this huge muscular Greek, balls ass in the middle of traffic. There was a wooden bench there, mercifully free of bums, and he sat down on it, watching the door all the while. Even if they went out the back way he could still see them from here. And then he saw the Mayor. He must have walked right by him several times, for there he was, tied with his clothesline to the parking meter in front of Freddy's place. Johnny flew across the street. "Hi ya, Mayor," he greeted him affectionately. "You remember me, don't you?"

The Mayor watched him blandly. He'd been following Johnny's indecisive helter-skelter all along. Now there was no doubt in his mind that Johnny was smitten with Claire. Although he'd guessed that from the start, way back in the confusion over the kosher chicken. If there was anyone who had a nose for that sort of thing it was himself. Now what was this? Johnny was untying the clothesline and escorting him across the boulevard. This was a rare opportunity indeed. What exotic strains of frowziness might he encounter here? Truly he did love Natasha, only once you were as old as, let's do face it, he now was, each opportunity that presented itself, handed to you, as it were, was well worth taking. One might never have the chance again. Alone, he would never even consider the risk of crossing a boulevard. Why he'd never been across a boulevard. And now he was. He was just becoming involved in what could very well be the musk of a dane when he felt his clothesline stiffen. He looked about. Across Queens Boulevard he could see Freddy coming down the steps with Claire and Michaelaen. Claire was being very cool toward Freddy. You could see that even from a distance. Michaelaen wasn't keen on leaving at all. He loved that place. As many french fries as he could lay his hands on. All of a sudden Claire threw her arms up into the air. Back and forth she raced. Then around in a circle. Michaelaen, always distinguished, did not panic. He was quite used to the disappearance of the Mayor. He'd grown up within the routine of it. However, he did put his thumb in his mouth and kept it there. Freddy ran inside and came back out. Claire was looking underneath the parked cars. The Mayor thought all right, a game's a game, but this one has gone far enough now. He looked up at Johnny, who was looking idiotically spellbound and crackling his knuckles.

Claire was thinking of the stricken pairs of eyes she would face back at home if she didn't find the Mayor. Frantically, she craned her neck in all directions. Someone could have hit him and he might be lying out there broken and bleeding and with no one to care for him. And all those cars just nonchalantly speeding by. She broke out in a fervent sweat. Freddy put an arm of solace around her shoulder and she flung herself free of him. "Look!" hollered Michaelaen. He pointed towards the newsstand on the corner. There was a pedestrian crossway there and an entrance to the subway. Out from the exit, Tut from his tomb, emerged the Mayor, waddling, pink tongue dangling, and Johnny Benedetto rushing accommodatingly behind.

"Your honor!" Claire fell to the ground.

Johnny squatted beside her. "I just happened to be coming up from the subway," he said out of the corner of his mouth, "and who do I see but the dog here." It wouldn't hurt for her to think destiny had played a hand. She'd like that sort of thing. And so she did. Her eyes, when she looked up at him, were pools of sparkling wonder. This grateful ardor, if it hadn't come from such a cheap trick, would have caused him no small joy. Uncomfortably, he stood back up. Michaelaen claimed his rightful end of the leash and they walked in a tight band back to the restaurant.

"This is wonderful," said Freddy. "If you hadn't come out from the subway at that exact moment. . . ."

Claire shuddered at the torrent of possibilities. Michaelaen watched Johnny with careful admiration. He didn't know quite what to make of Johnny. Both Claire and Freddy spoke derisively about him but he noticed they both buckled to attention the moment he was around.

"Were you going to take the bus or a cab?" Freddy asked him. "I'm just taking Claire and Michaelaen home. I'll drop you all off at once. You don't live far, do you?"

Johnny looked over at Pokey's Oldsmobile. "I'll just hop on the . . ." he was about to say "bus" when he saw a lady parking cop writing out a ticket. If they all left now he could stop the bitch. She could see the detective shield in there. What the hell was the matter with her?

"I wouldn't think of that," Claire said.

"No, really. It goes right by my house. I'd rather." He looked past her at the traffic cop. Claire followed his eyes. All she saw was a taxi full of pretty girls in gauzy dresses disembarking.

"Don't be silly," she said without certainty.

"No, I want to. Really."

Claire tipped her chin to look at him. So that was it. He hadn't liked the kiss she'd loved. He didn't care about her after all. What a silly fool she was! Of course, now he could see how ugly she was with her nose all sweaty. "Well, thank you, then, for saving the dog," she muttered.

"Hey, don't mention it." He let go a manic laugh. The policewoman picked up the windshield wiper and smacked it down on the ticket. The jig was up. Then it hit him. Claire's mother would certainly tell them he'd been there forty minutes ago. There was no reason now not to come clean. "Uh . . . look, I didn't want to say nothin' before. Didn't wanna worry you or nothin', but I got a car right here."

They looked at him, puzzled.

"I been sorta following you," he said to Claire.

"What, still?" Freddy studied Claire with scornful interest. "You think *Claire* is in some sort of danger? I doubt that." He laughed a condescending little laugh. "She's a little bit past the age for a child molester's interest."

"Is that right?" Johnny put his face up against Freddy's. "I guess you got this whole business all figured out."

"I didn't say that." Freddy's sardonic tone faded fast.

"You were just acting like that for no reason, like."

"Yeah, that's it. No reason."

"'Cause if you got any ideas about what's going on around here, we'd be more than happy to listen to anything you have to say down at the stationhouse."

Freddy went pale. He hoped with all his heart that the customers just going in hadn't heard that.

The traffic cop sauntered by. "Whatsa matter," Johnny shouted at her, "you never heard of professional loyalty?"

"Hey, mister, I just do my job."

"That's a cop on duty, sister."

"Yeah, well I got my orders. I ticket anybody, any vehicle sits itself down in my no standing."

"Johnny," Claire said, and as she did she realized she'd never said his name like that before, directly to him.

"What."

"Perhaps you could drive us home. Then Freddy wouldn't have to leave at all. It's getting awfully busy in there." As if to demonstrate her point, a gang of snappily dressed coke types went rollicking up the stairs.

"Hey." Johnny rolled his shoulders. "Can a corn."

"I take it that means you will."

"Yeah."

"Tell your mother," Freddy said to Michaelaen, "that I'll be over tomorrow to see her."

And Carmela, thought Claire, sick to death of him.

"Off you go," Freddy tapped him on his bottom.

Neither Claire nor Johnny spoke until they dropped Michaelaen off. They both smiled pleasantly from the car and waved to Mary as she let the boy and the dog into the house.

"You didn't have to make a fool of him in front of his son," was the first thing out of her mouth.

"He's a piece of shit."

"Maybe so. But that knowledge isn't going to help Michaelaen grow up a happier person."

"Happier than what? Happier than who? You? Me?"

Claire let her breath out slowly. She didn't know what to think anymore. Especially not with him this close to her. "Whatever happened with the license plate numbers?"

"Nothin'. Didn't turn nothin' up."

"Oh." She waited.

He didn't want to tell her about the only old golden Plymouth he did know about, the one that sat in front of the station house for as long as he could remember. Furgueson's. Captain Furgueson's. 5473 BNJ. So she had her numbers right. Only the thought of Furgueson molesting kids was so ridiculous it almost made you want to laugh. The only body Furgueson was known to molest was over twenty-one and top heavy. Which was where he'd been on his way back from the morning of the murder. He didn't want to tell Claire about that, though. Nancy Drew here would have the whole neighborhood informed. Truth and all that crap. And where would that leave Furgueson? Divorced, that was where. And from a very nice old broad. A lady. So why hurt either of them? The famed wall of blue loyalty between cops was not always a bad thing. You had to be loyal in this game. He looked over at Claire's worried, pretty face.

She'd been staring at him. "Were you really following me?" she asked.

"Yes." He looked through the rearview mirror at the shopping bag on the backseat and sighed happily.

"Because you think I might truly be in danger?"

"Truly," he mimicked her.

"Why, though? Anyone who thought I could hurt them would surely be satisfied with the films. I would think. Or hope. I don't mean to say that I'm afraid. At least not unreasonably so. I carry my white light about me so I couldn't possibly come to any real harm."

"Your what?"

"My white light. Around my aura. Stop looking like that. What are you thinking when you look at me like that?"

"What do you care? You've got your aura thing there protecting you."

"Yes, but what are you thinking? I'd just like to know. Or perhaps you disagree with the theory that fear attracts fearful things and peace repels them?"

"I'm thinking you're really stupid, you know that?"

"I wouldn't expect you to understand," she heard herself saying. "While I was over there chanting, you were over here . . . stun-gunning or whatever." She was pleased with the effect this statement had on him. He controlled his rage, however.

"Somebody might think you still know something," he said stubbornly. "Something you been choosing to keep to yourself for the time being."

"I don't know anything. I keep telling you."

"Except maybe you do and you don't know it."

"But I would remember something. I really don't know anything. I keep telling you."

"The killer doesn't know that. And who says he's rational, anyhow?"

"The killer! It's like a film. I can't believe this is happening."

"Neither can the dead kid's parents."

That shut her up for a bit. It was quiet enough for Johnny to realize he was driving them around in circles.

"You wanna go to my house?"

"No," she replied as a matter of form.

"So you wanna go to a motel?"

"Let me out of the car."

"Huh?"

"Just stop the car and let me out."

"What the fuck's wrong with you?"

"With me? I don't even know you and you're talking about going to a motel? I think there's something wrong with you!"

Johnny locked her door from his control panel and kept his finger on the switch. "You're gonna sit there and tell me you don't feel nothin' between us? Is that what you're saying? You really wanna get out?" He let go of the switch. "So get out!" He waited. She waited. "'Cause if that's the way it is, then my mind isn't tickin' too quick. Or what is it? You want me to play the game with you? Come over to your parents' house with flowers? Is that what you want?"

"I don't know what you're talking about."

Johnny made a horrible grimace and grabbed the cement loaf stuck in his jeans. "This! This is what I'm talkin about! Whenever I get within ten feet of you!"

"Ach du liebe scheisse!"

"Ach du liebe this!" he shouted, reaching under her skirt. "Oh Jesus," he groaned. "You're wet." He climbed over the stick shift with the alacrity of a ballet dancer and pushed her seat into a reclining position. Recovering from his surprise attack quickly, she punched him in the chest, then once in the ear with a high choral bang. Still he held devotedly on to her underwear and still she kept her knees locked tight. While their limbs continued to wallop in combat, Claire's mouth had called an independent open truce and the tongue that attached itself to hers fit snugly in there like the perfect juicy glove. He collapsed on top of her in bewildered frustration and she realized where she was: pinned to the emergency brake and suffocating quickly. A blaring horn sounded from someplace.

"What the hell?" Johnny picked up his head. Not having bothered to pull over, they now had six or seven cars backed up impatiently behind them. He grappled to retrieve his hand and lurched back to his seat. Claire looked about frantically and tugged on her skirt.

"You've gone and ripped my knickers," she panted.

"I love you, too," he said and shifted into first.

He made a quick left onto Woodhaven Boulevard. Up in the woods on her right she could barely make out the soft lights of the merry-go-round.

This is it, thought Claire. Nothing on God's earth can stop us now. She settled back in the big plush seat of the vast American car and let him take her wherever he wanted. There was a button on her door. She pushed it and the window opened. The night time came in, the huddled streets blurred past and she still felt the hard, kinetic weight of him on top of her. Good thing I shaved my legs, she thought. A siren passed them, a squad car racing in the opposite direction. He said he loves me, she marveled. He's watching me out of the corner of his eye and he wants me as much as I want him. Another bweep bweep bweep of a radio car cut through the noise of the deafening el train. Johnny did a U-turn on 111th and Jamaica. She saw her reflection in the bakery window, sliding across the seat and flattened against the car door like a passenger on the Roundabout, the carnival ride that whips you around until you're dizzy. "What are you doing?" she cried.

"I'm taking you back home," he said, his mind on something else entirely now. "Something's going on."

He pulled up in front of her mother's house with a screech and practically pushed her out the door. She stood on the curb, looking at him as though he were mad. "Go in the house," he ordered and turned the big car around one two three. "I said go in the house, dammit."

She went into the house.

Johnny followed the noise. In the very same pine forest where they'd found the body of the little boy Miguel, where no one in his right mind would ever think to look for trouble again, some kids up there, young kids getting high in the summer night, had stumbled across the mutilated body of a five-year-old girl.

This time the papers had a field day. Furgueson at the 102nd had everybody working overtime, and that meant everybody. Nobody said boo. They all wanted this guy and they wanted him quick. This was their precinct. It made them nauseous to think of some monster out there just sick enough to try it again. There weren't too many cops who didn't have little ones of their own at home.

By morning, all of New York had had a tour of the Richmond Hill pine forest over three major networks. The squirrels were mad with joy from all the Drake's Cakes and doughnuts the crowds had left all over the place. Reporters got in everybody's way down at the station house and when Furgueson had them thrown out, they interviewed the people on the street. This was no longer one alleged "minority crime." Or something within one family. This was beginning to look like a habit. The dead girl had been a perfectly charming blond innocent with cherry lips and pink hair ribbons—the whole thing. She'd been missing only five hours, last seen on her tricycle in front of the Park Lane South candy store. This was news, big news, and the media was out to milk it for every ounce of hypnotized fear and fascination its viewers were sure to tune in for.

A few of the reporters had themselves televised up in front of the carousel. It was awful to see it on television that way, they all thought. How hard they had worked in the community to bring it back to life. Nothing over the years had brought the people together with such pride and happiness. Nobody didn't love the carousel. And now, to see it used like this. It was a sin. A real sin.

At the Breslinsky's, the newspapers were spread out on the kitchen table. There they sat, recounting with fascinated horror just how close they'd come to being at the candy store yesterday and, who knew, right now it could have been themselves, God forbid, dressing up to go solemnly down to the morgue.

"And I say," Stan insisted, "that it could never happen in a family like ours, where we keep such close tabs on the kid. We would notice the moment someone talked to him."

"Stanley. Sweetheart. It only takes a second. Look how the children run around the block wild as Indians and there's no one to pay them a never you do mind. I mean it can happen to anyone." She shuddered. "You can be as careful as you like, but then there's always that unguarded moment."

"Oh, come on. I saw that Miguel kid around here a hundred times, up and down the block with the other kids. You can't tell me his parents kept tabs on him."

"Daddy, that's easier said than done. How many times have I come home from work and there was Michaelaen, across the street," her voice rose. "Alone. No one around. So you come on."

Claire, her face half buried in her hand atop an elbow on the table, listened to their morbid might-have-beens. Mary made another batch of waffles and laid them caressingly on top of the cold ones. No one would eat those, either, but the effort of it soothed her. She didn't exactly know the parents of the dead girl but she was almost sure she'd seen the mother, the day before Easter it must have been, on line at the butcher.

Stan had a feeling he knew the unfortunate father. He'd come into the store once or twice. For nails. Or linseed oil, he thought it was. He'd know him well enough to nod hello.

Annoyed by this claim, Mary scooped the colder, bottom waffle onto his plate.

"What's this for?"

"It's good. Just because you couldn't make up your mind about it doesn't make it bad."

"I don't want a waffle, Mare!"

"And you who told me to make them!"

Here the Mayor stood and waddled confidently to his empty dish.

"Did I ask for waffles? Did anybody here hear me once ask for waffles?!"

"Gimmie one, Ma. Only gimmie one from the top. I don't want a cold one."

Indeed, it was chilly enough in the kitchen to make you want to warm up. Mary had the air conditioner on maximum. She felt safer in the cold, today of all days, barricaded from the murder lurking outside with the doors locked tight. They huddled together as though from a winter's storm.

Michaelaen came up from the cellar. He put his sneakers on his lap. The first knot was easy. Then you did a loop. That was easy, too. It was that darn second loop that got him. Did it go around the first loop or stay right where it was? The possibilities exploded in the air until he had to close his eyes. Here he would stay until, like any exasperated ostrich, he felt the coast was clear. Something was going on. Everybody was yelling and then whispering. Especially Grandma. You had to be careful when Grandma started whispering. Michaelaen opened his eyes and saw his old friend Miguel's picture right in the paper. Miguel was probably in jail, he thought morosely. There were some things you just knew you weren't supposed to ask about.

Stan turned the page. He didn't want Mary to notice the horoscopes and get started on that. Then the doorbell rang and the dog howled. Michaelaen ran to the front and the Mayor trotted after him. "It's the back," said Zinnie. "It's the back," hollered Mary. They trotted to the back. Carmela got to the door first. It was Johnny Benedetto. He came into the kitchen ducking, big fellow that he was, one corner of his mouth stuck upward. Claire felt herself blush at the sight of him and the sight she knew she must be, rumpled in her father's Yankees T-shirt and a red plaid robe she'd discovered behind the bathroom door. She felt his eyes go right through her, and then he acted as if she wasn't even there.

"It's crazy out there," he said. "I can only stay for a minute."

"Of course, of course," the family nodded in unison. They knew he was working on the murders. They wouldn't bring it up unless he did. They were a family on the "in," a fact that was etched importantly all over their faces. Stan patted him fondly on the back and signaled for coffee. This is wonderful, Mary thought. She had three waffles on his plate before he sat down. A man needed his strength. Good thing she'd had Michaelaen pick those raspberries. She gave the sour cream a fluff up with her spoon and licked it with a smile to demonstrate how mm-mm good it was.

Claire was embarrassed by all of this coddling. Even Michaelaen stood rapt at Johnny's knee. What would he think, they'd never seen a nice young man? She'd never brought a fellow home? Oblivious to her, Johnny wolfed down a deck of waffles and held out his plate for more.

Carmela had to go to work. She went upstairs to the bathroom and Claire was glad to see her go. Carmela looked so chic. Even Zinnie, whom she loved with all her heart, looked far too cute for so early in the morning.

"You sleep all right?" Johnny asked her.

She almost jumped. His eyes were teasing her.

"Not bad." She gave him what she hoped was a look of nonchalance.

"I got somethin' for ya."

What did he mean? Was he going to give her a kiss? Right in front of her parents? There was a street-sharp danger that accompanied him and you never knew quite what he would do.

Johnny was more nervous than she was but his demeanor was deliberately cool. Inside, he swelled with the love he felt for her and the awe he had for her family. A real American family, he thought, his orphaned heart pounding. Just like on television, with no one on drugs or drunk and all of them casually sitting down to home-cooked meals together as if it were the most normal thing in the world. Hell wasn't being one of twelve kids in a tenement flat the way they showed you on "Eyewitness News." Hell was being out on your own every last morning in a different burger joint, greasy spoon, whatever. They were all the same. He'd heard a poem once, in passing, on some jerkie's radio. He didn't remember the whole thing, but part of it had hit him like a hammer: "Nobody playing piano . . . in somebody else's apartment." That was him. That was his life. These people here, they didn't know what they had. He stood up, knocking over the heavy oak chair, then picked it up as though it were some featherweight. Mary didn't even glance at her linoleum. Claire clasped the robe to her chest in a panicky gesture but he turned and went out the door. Then back he came with a shopping bag from Lipschutz Quality Camera Store. He laid the whole thing down on her empty plate, obliterating her from view. "What's this?" she said.

Her family, eyes bit as buttons, nodded her on.

"Go ahead," he urged her. "Open 'em up."

Uncertainly, she tugged at a ribbon.

"Not like that," Zinnie yelled at her. "Rip the mother open!"

"Here's a knife," Mary sang.

Stan, a veteran of too many birthday parties throughout the years, went back with one eye to Jimmy Breslin's column. He hated Breslin. Or so he said. The columnist's heated opinions held his devoted daily fury, though. Some hates were indeed akin to love.

"Here," said Johnny. "Open this one first. This one's the main one. Maybe you're gonna like it. Maybe not." He said this as though it didn't matter to him one way or the other. Claire peeked into the box. It was an Olympus. A good old Olympus, just like the first thirty-five she'd ever shot with. She hadn't had one in her hand for years. Professionals all used Nikons nowadays and she had followed suit, but many a time she'd had a yearning for the downright lightness and practicality of her old manual Olympus. She broke into a smile, such a smile that he knew he'd done the right thing. Whatever he'd done wrong with her so far was wiped out good by this. He knew he shouldn't have jumped on her like that last night and he was sorry. But not too sorry.

"Such an expensive camera," Mary touched it tentatively.

"I had a little luck at the track," he offered humbly.

Claire opened the next package. It was a seventy-five-to-one-fifty zoom. "I can't believe it," she said. "I can't believe you knew just what to get."

Johnny shrugged. "I saw you up in the woods with that kind of lens. At least I hoped it was that kind. I mean if you don't like it or it's wrong you can take it back."

"The lens is wonderful," Claire said.

This news was met by the rest of them with satisfaction. They knew how picky Claire could be. Next she opened the flash. She shook her head with wonder. Johnny sat back down for the rest of his waffles.

For some reason Claire was overcome by a sickening sense of suspicion. Her mother dalloped the last of the sour cream onto Johnny's plate and she watched their eyes meet conspiratorially. It hit her as the signing of the deal. She had no idea why she felt that way, but there it was, strong and real in her, the witness to the signing away of the proverbial truant daughter. She burned with shame. And Johnny. He looked so damn smug. Suddenly she couldn't stand the sight of him.

"I can't accept this," she told him in her gravely voice.

They all stopped talking and looked at her.

"It's much too kind of you. I . . . thank you . . . but I'm sorry. I can't accept it."

"Can't accept what? What are you talkin' about?"

"I can't. It's just too much when I hardly know you. I'm expecting some money shortly . . . a great deal of money . . . and I'll be able to replace my cameras myself, you see."

The Mayor searched his brain. Embroidered and elaborated grains of truth rang truer than fact. But so did lies. He wasn't quite sure what was going on. "It's much too kind of you," she was saying again. "It's just too much. Thank you, but I can't." Claire studied Johnny's face for traces of change. Still he watched her with that mocking, amused, unblinking, infuriating look. No one in the family knew exactly what to do. "Excuse me," murmered Claire and she left the table. It didn't surprise her that they were all whispering. Uh-oh, the Mayor thought, and he followed her out. She was standing, hunched and listening, behind the door.

"Don't worry. Claire's just a dumb girl." Michaelaen, the little traitor, was comforting Johnny. Michaelaen's sense of protective guardianship only extended to the offended at hand.

"Three things my mother told me about life," Stan's voice rang out suddenly. "'Never,' she said, 'eat meat loaf out.' That was the first thing. Two was: 'Never loan money you can't afford to give away.' And the third was, 'Never, but never think you might be smarter than the stupidest woman.'"

CHAPTER

That's it," Claire said out loud. "That's the last of them. They've all gone out."

The Mayor came to attention at once. He hadn't realized she'd been speaking to him. Had he been dozing? He blinked reassuringly at Claire. She was standing at the window. "The yard is full of crows," she said. "I can't understand what the sun is doing shining. I've never known crows to creep around the backyard unless it was to rain." She looked at him and he looked at her. He wished there was something he could do. She was so obviously in a bog. He used to be very good at that sort of thing: lightening people's loads. All he'd had to do was wraggle around undulating his charming little rear and they'd literally melt. That kind of frivolity wouldn't do nowadays. It wasn't seemly for the stout to try to be too cute. Not past a certain age. And then there was that ever-humbling reminder of one's limitations: arthritis. The mind went on and the body just disintegrated. The way of the world, he supposed. Ah, well. One placed too much importance on one's own capabilities. More often than not, what was needed was a simple ear to listen. With Claire this was especially true. Because she'd go on and on whether you were there or not. There were those who would think this odd. He, a democrat, did not.

"I don't know what it is," Claire said, "about that man. He puts me so on the defensive that I don't know what

I'm doing. Or saying. Now I've got myself in a fine mess. I haven't got any load of money coming in. I only said that so they wouldn't feel sorry for me. I can't bear the way they all watch me with such pity. It's disheartening." She was tooling a broad figure eight in the carpet. "And I know they want what's best for me. But him. He thinks he can dare to be familiar with me, and I just won't have it. I won't!" She picked an orange out of the bowl and began to peel it. The smell of it filled up the room. "It's good to have some peace and quiet for a change. Someone who's been alone for as long as I've been . . . let's face it, you need time to yourself. You know, this jogging business seems the right thing to do, it just seems right for other people. Not for me. I won't lose any weight jogging. I'm sure I won't. I'll just build up a healthier appetite and wind up gaining. And on top of that, my breasts will sag." She sank to the floor and proceeded to do sit-ups. She did five. On the sixth she groaned and strained and made a terrible face. "After all," she stopped and looked at him, "I am in love with him. At least I think I am. I know I'm in lust. I've so often confused the two and wound up sorry I had. In the beginning it's always so hard to tell." She stood up, covered with dog hair, and went searching for the telephone book. "What are you looking at?" she said. "This is the twentieth century. Women telephone men all the time. Anyway, I'm not calling him, am I? It can't hurt to have his number in my book. There have been two murders, haven't there? And I am involved somehow, whether I like it or not. Honestly, it's like being caught up in a circle of evil." She stood suddenly still. The Mayor sat up. She looked over her shoulder as though she expected someone to be there. Then she walked into the kitchen, to the table where the newspapers were still spread about. She pored through them, looking for she didn't know what. The *Post* was all sensationalism. The *Times* was cut and dry. She flipped through the *News*. ". . . there were certain similarities in this murder that lead authorities to believe," etcetera, etcetera. Ah, here it was: ". . . the body was found in a circle of pine not ten feet from the scene of last week's crime where the victim, Miguel Velasquez . . ." A circle of pine. Again. She sat down. She could see old Iris out the window in her garden. What on earth was she doing? Digging? What was it Michael used to say about her? "Magic is her middle name." Of course Iris couldn't have killed little children. The idea was preposterous. But somebody had. And whoever that had been, she suspected, had some knowledge of the ceremonial occult.

She was duty bound to share her suspicions with Johnny, wasn't she? Of course, she could be completely wrong. She hoped she was. It wasn't just a cheap excuse to get in touch with him after she'd behaved so badly toward him? An honorable bridge across the childish moat she'd dug? Well, then, what if it was? The end, if she were right, would surely justify the means. She approached the hallway mirror and inspected her face. She didn't really look old. What she needed was a bath. She returned to the kitchen and rifled through the cabinets. Vanilla. She pulled the bottle down from the shelf. What else? Olive oil? No, he would have enough of that. Almond oil. That was nice. Yes, she took that down, then spied the jasmine tea. Perfect. She carried her booty furtively up to the bathroom and brewed herself a bath. The Mayor watched, appalled. What women went through to cover up their natural provocative scents bewildered him. Claire lowered herself into the pale scented water. Ugh, thought the Mayor. He decided then and there to go out for a quick spin and take some fresh air. He left harriedly by way of the newly reinstated doggy door, a nice little hookup Stan had arranged through what used to be the back stairs. He'd be back before she even noticed he was gone.

Now that Claire had made the decision to call Johnny up she had to figure out, besides the business at hand, what she would say. It always started off with her losing her temper. This time she would be very cool. She would trick him. She would tell him the truth. Fine. What was the truth? That she couldn't get him off her mind? That would go right to his head. There was no telling how arrogant that would make him. "Hello?" Claire stood up straight in the tub. "Hello?" Had someone come in? She could have sworn—no, that was absurd, the Mayor was here. He would eat anyone who tried to get in. Or at least bark them to smithereens. She sat back down, relieved, and turned on the hot water tap. Her nerves were good and shot, weren't they. What she really needed was a big dose of bourbon with a ton of chipped ice. Or no ice. But the steam from the gentle water was lulling; she really didn't want to budge. And she was getting just the smallest bit fed up with seeing herself as an alcoholic. Claire blew softly out of her mouth. She could hear the Mayor waddling about in the hallway. Or was that the pine against the house? The sunlight through the milk glass window was so beautiful. Just beautiful. There was a small clock radio plugged in up on the ledge; someone had left it on, but the volume was so low you could barely hear it. She felt the Mayor's comforting presence. "You know," she said to him, "even if my being straight with Johnny did go right to his head, I mean, what of it? Either I want him to know how I feel or I don't. Now, I'm just putting off the inevitable, hoping he'll do my job for me; come back once again so I can tell him no again." It was pretty obvious that she was postponing commitment for the top-ten thrill of the chase. And she, who fancied herself the great seeker of truth, had better face the fact.

The telephone rang with such jarring suddenness that Claire bolted upright and sprang out of the tub before the first ring ended. At that exact moment the radio hit the water, went zzzip and made a dull, guttural crackle where her body had just been.

"Christ," she answered the phone.

"Hello? Zinnie?"

"Hello? Oh Jesus, I just almost got killed. I'm sorry. Who is this? God!"

"Hello? This is Emil . . . you all right there?"

Zinnie's enamored young doctor. "Yes. Yes, Emil, I'm fine. I just had a terrible close call. The radio fell into my tub and," she shuddered with goosebumps, "and I think if you hadn't called at that moment and wakened me out of my reverie, I'd be dead. Do people die from radios in bathtubs?"

"Certainly."

"Well, then you just saved my life."

"Fine," he surprised her by saying. It always astonished her with what nonchalance the medical profession greeted life-and-death drama. "I was hoping to catch Zinnie in," he continued.

"No. No, she's on overtime, I think. I don't know. I get so mixed up with her schedule." She continued to look at the tub. "I think it blew the fuse. The overhead light is out as well."

"That's good. Just make sure it is blown before you take the radio out of the tub."

Claire followed the wire with her eyes. It was plugged into another wire that went out into the hall.

"All right then," said Emil. "Tell her I called. And I hope you're all right."

"I'll write it down." She heard the Mayor running down the hall and wondered where he was off to. "Good-bye," she said, "and thanks." Gingerly, she tried the light switch. It didn't work. She pulled the radio out and let the water out of the tub. How easy it is, she thought to herself. You're here one minute and gone the next. Just like that. She remembered Johnny. The best way to begin, she'd heard it said, was to start. All right. She'd give up procrastination for action. She toweled off hurriedly. Where to begin? Call? She had his address. Why not drive directly to his house? He lived in South Ozone Park, three or four miles away. It was still early in the afternoon. If he wasn't there, she would leave a note. "You'll come with me," she said to the Mayor, who'd just come up the stairs. "Let me just go and look at that circuit breaker first. We'll bring back the camera at the same time." Johnny might even persuade her to keep it, she realized hopefully.

See that? remarked the Mayor to himself. She didn't even miss me. Just as I'd suspected.

Claire's heart leapt at the thought of keeping the camera. She'd be right back in business. She dressed quickly, with a light, happy heart. She dried her hair with Zinnie's dryer and brazenly stole Carmela's car.

Once you got past Liberty Avenue, Lefferts Boulevard was chock full of Indians. This didn't bother Claire. She felt right at home. Purple and pink flower beds grew in whimsical tufts across the little front yards. They'd torn down all the German fir trees, the Indians, so they would have more light. Mighty sunflowers loomed with determined cheerfulness between the garbage pails. There was a wedding going on, the dark, plump bride just coming out of the rented white limousine. She wore a Western wedding gown and her bridesmaids their traditional saris. The young men stood about with shy, expectant, self-important gestures. "It's good luck to see a bride," Claire told the Mayor. He enjoyed a ride in a car, as long as they weren't on their way to the vet.

On Rockaway Boulevard Claire turned right and drove through a visible cloud of gasoline fumes. She God blessed American shampoo with its vivacious redolence. Now they were in the Italian sector: pizza places, gas stations, hubcap specialty lots. She drove along putting rouge on in the rearview mirror. When she decided she looked all right, she made a left at the Aqua Motel and cruised down the row of blocks. She liked to drive. As soon as she could get her hands on some money, she'd buy herself a nice little used car. Here the houses were semiattached brick with geranium pots on perfect cement stoops. There were several grottos to the Virgin and one black-faced jockey, still carrying that years-ago burnt out white lantern. On the right side the houses' backyards faced the racetrack and you looked right across the field to the distant bleachers. The last house on the last block was Johnny's. It was just a plain old house, she reasoned, but even so, her blood pounded through her temples. He probably isn't even home, she sniggered wildly to herself. She checked her purse to make sure she would have pen and paper handy for a note. If she had it, she calmed herself superstitiously, she wouldn't need it. The Mayor leaned against her, panting reassuringly. His breath, she noticed, was atrocious.

Johnny's lawn was parched and uncared for in this quarter of Italian husbandry. Prickled hoses spurted up and down the block. There were grape arbours and tomato plants in every backyard. Johnny seemed to be cultivating a bevy of Coke cans in his. And car skeletons. It looked more like a car cemetery than somebody's home.

She parked the car in his driveway, then backed it out and parked parallel to the curb. No sense being presumptuous. With studied calm, she got out. The Mayor flinched at the low-flying 747 that roared darkly through the still-bright light. That's what you got when you lived near the airport. A timid team, they climbed the steps. She pushed the bell. It chimed out the theme from *The Godfather*. Good Lord, she thought. She waited. She tried the knocker. Still nothing. What did she want with some slobby detective, anyway? she thought, taking in the rumpled pile of laundry in there on the porch floor. She turned to go. It was a good thing he wasn't at home, she realized now. She wouldn't even leave a note. "Look at this." She heard a voice and her heart stood still. He was at the upstairs window, peering out of the screen. She could hardly see him but she knew he was scratching that furry chest.

"Hang on a second," he said and she followed the

Mayor back to the stoop. When he turned the lock and opened the door she forgot for a moment why she'd come. He looked like a film star. No shirt. Just a pair of navy blue sweatpants.

"Come on in." The sudden dark made her temporarily blind. He'd been conked out, he said. This overtime had him all banged up. "Siddown, siddown."

She took in the room as her eyes adjusted to the light. Here was a rollicking carnival of kitsch. Rubber carnations, enshrined in glass, were shamelessly exhibited upon the dusty coffee table, which was made up of artificial marble itself. Psychedelic flower decals from the sixties peppered the wall. And a touch of glamor: plastic logs blazed in the grate with their own make-believe orange flames. Aesthetically, it couldn't have been worse. And yet, the whole thing broke her heart. He didn't know about those things. How could he? Where had he traveled in his life? To Atlantic City? She couldn't not love him for his lack of opportunity. And she admired the way he didn't seem to mind her catching him in a mess. Unless of course he didn't realize it was a mess.

"You got that vest on," he popped open a Coke and passed it to her.

"Yes."

"I mean, you had that on the first time I saw you."

"Yes." He must know that she was after him. She wished she could float away. This looks, thought the Mayor, like it's going to be a long one. He made himself comfortable in the shadow of a plastic tree. "Back then," Claire nodded. "Before the murder."

"Same day."

"Right. Yes, it was, wasn't it?"

"You like Frank?"

"Sorry?"

"Frank. Frank Sinatra." He waved a battered album.

"Oh. No, I uh . . . prefer Billie."

"Billie?"

"Holiday."

"Yeah? What's he, new?"

"No."

"So. You wanna get in the air conditioner with me?"

Claire laughed politely. She straightened her spine. "Actually, I came here to discuss the murders. I had the feeling I ought to tell you what I thought."

"Oh yeah? Is that why you came here? All right. So discuss."

She cleared her throat. "Well. Both murders took place in a circle. A circle. Nobody seems to have made anything of the idea of the circle itself. And I just thought . . . I don't know . . . maybe somebody could look into that aspect of it. You see, nowadays, cultists seem to go in more for the pentagram, but traditionally it was the circle used in all diabolical ceremonies . . . in occult ceremonies." As she spoke she realized that what she had said would certainly implicate Iris von Lillienfeld. Everyone in Richmond Hill knew that Iris was known as a witch. All Claire could see was Iris's poor white face. Oh, she didn't want it to be Iris. Still, it was her duty to tell. "You see," she continued, "babies have always been used in black magic ceremonies as sacrifice . . . often eaten . . . or . . . or parts of their bodies made into unguents or soups . . . to be drunk or used later to cast spells. Please don't look at me so disbelievingly, it's quite true. The principles of evil have always fed on innocence . . . literally. It's recorded word for word in the *Malleus Maleficarum*, in the report to Peter the Judge in Boltington concerning thirteen children devoured in the state of Berne. You can read it for yourself if you don't believe me."

"Sounds like the third shelf at the video rental."

"Yes, doesn't it? Because there are still so many people who are fascinated with that sort of horror. And always will be, I suppose. All that I'm trying to say is this: instead of a murderer working impulsively, chaotically, perhaps what we have here is a thought-out plan of treachery. A person consumed with power . . . satanic power. I mean, if there is a sort of system here, one could conceivably figure out what might happen next."

"I think you oughta have your head examined."

"Oh, for God's sake! I came here to share my feelings with you, to be helpful if I could, and all you can do is try to make me feel strange. I'll be perfectly frank with you, after you left this morning I felt bad. I started smoking one cigarette after the next and then I thought, great, this is just what I'm trying not to do. It seems everything I try not to do, I do just that. To which you will surely reply, stop trying. Which is, by the way, the essence of Buddhistic thought. Anyway, I stopped smoking only to find myself eating everything in sight. I caught myself and so I naturally thought of you—"

"Naturally."

"And I . . . I felt really close to you and I thought I had to come over here and tell you how sorry I was. For the way I behaved. After you went out and got me the camera. So I came and here I am and I don't feel close you at all. I feel as though you're this perfectly horrible person with whom I want nothing to do—"

"'With whom'? Did I hear you say 'with whom'?"

"Please don't make fun of me."

"Oh, I get it. You can come over here and tell me I'm a perfectly horrible person and you don't want to have nothin' to do with me but I shouldn't make fun of you." Claire watched as the determined upper lip she found so attractive curled inward. "I think you think the whole police force never heard of cult murders. And like it's going to take you to tell us about them. You know what your problem is?"

"I'm sure you'll tell me."

"Your problem is that you always gotta be the one in control. The minute you feel anybody else gettin' up there with you on your Buddha pole, you go all to pieces."

"I truly dislike this room. Did you paint it pea green

for your own amusement or was it like this when you got here? Or perhaps it's your idea of a political statement?"

He ignored her. "You're scared shit to give anyone power over you because poor little you could get hurt."

"My, my," Claire sucked the inside of her cheek. "You figured this out all by yourself, I suppose. A genuine fling into the dizzying heights of psychoanalysis."

"Oh, come on. Anybody acts that superior has got to have some sort of complex."

"It might surprise you to know that there's a vast world out there just full of people who function and communicate on levels other than dese, dems, and dose, and they're perfectly happy." Her eyes bulged. "They're not looking down on anybody. They're just trying to live a gentler life."

He burst out laughing. "I'm talking about apples and you're talking about oranges."

"You're the most infuriating person I have ever met."

"But you're crazy about me. You know you are. Otherwise you never would've come here." He settled back comfortably on a wedge of foam rubber.

That was the trouble with living on a cop's salary. Even if you knew what was good, you'd never be able to afford it. It made her so mad she could spit. "You haven't heard a single word I've said!" she shouted at him.

"I heard you. What do you think, I'm sleeping? I only ought to follow my brain instead of my heart. You'd be my prime suspect if I didn't keep making excuses for you inside of my head."

She bolted upright. "Excuse me?"

"You heard me. None of this started happening until you got back to town did it?"

Claire was speechless. She stared, paralyzed, into a framed picture of Johnny Walker Black as if it might tell her something.

He squashed his cigarette into a dirty pie plate and

looked at his watch. "You could have done them both as far as a jury would be concerned."

"But my cameras," she whispered.

He shrugged. "You could have got rid of them yourself. Throw suspicion in another direction. Could easily have been a woman who did it. Not a trace of semen to be found. And sweetheart. While I got your attention, let me tell you something. You're just the type some jury would love to hang. Expatriate. Member of a weird Indian cult—"

"Cult?! that was an ashram . . . of a very respected guru! And the other an extremely high lama!"

"Try telling that one to a jury. You know what the *Post* would make outa you? With a past like you got? Growin' weird magical herbs in your kitchen? Mincemeat, that's what."

"You're out of your mind."

"No, I ain't outa my mind. And I didn't say you did it. Alls I'm sayin is you coulda done it. Wandering around in the middle a the night like you do. Talking to yourself. I've seen you talking to yourself. Wacky broad." He shook his head. "Shit!" He sprang up suddenly. "Hang on a second." He jumped from the couch to the window, picked up a pair of binoculars and studied the racetrack through them. He wrote something down on a piece of paper, smiled, and picked up the phone. While it was ringing he looked at her and winked. "Eddie? Yeah. Johnny. Gimmie Four Leaf Clover thirty times in the fifth. That's all. Yeah. *Statta bene.*" He hung up the phone and rubbed both hands together.

"You have someone at the track passing you signals!"

"That's right."

"That's illegal!"

"So's the grass you got growin in your mother's backyard."

Claire stood up slowly. She walked to the back door and fiddled clumsily with the lock.

"Just flip the top part to the right," he said.

She waited till the Mayor was beside her, then walked into the bright sunlight and looked into the startled eyes of a golden horse. She hadn't even gotten to the part about the near electrocution. The door slammed tight behind her.

CHAPTER 10

Carmela was ready for her, pacing the porch when she got back home. She was livid. "What the hell do you think you're doing with my car? You don't even have a license!"

"Here are the keys. I have such a headache. I'm sorry. I won't take your stupid car anymore."

"That's right, you won't. You've got a lot of nerve." She snatched the keys and went back into the house. Claire went in, too. Mary was sitting at the kitchen table and Zinnie was sprawled across the countertop. The Mayor, for one, was glad to be home before supper.

"My God!" Claire cried. "You've cut your hair!"

Mary looked up, frightened. She snatched apologetically at her neck. "Yes," she whispered. "And your father hasn't seen me yet."

"Mom! Your beautiful hair!"

"Dead on the hairdresser's floor." She folded her hands and placed them in her lap. "I don't know what came over me."

"It's your new look, Ma," Zinnie said. "No big deal."

"Next she'll be going on a diet," Carmela said.

"And that starts with *d* and that rhymes with *p* and that stands for *pool*," said Zinnie.

"All I meant was—"

"Just shut up. Nobody cares what you meant."

"Oh, I've got that straight. That's nothing new to me." Carmela's eyes filled with tears. "Nobody cares about me at all since the mystic marvel here ran out of luck and had to condescend to live with the likes of us!"

The telephone rang and Zinnie picked it up. "It's for you, mystic marvel."

"I don't want to talk to him," Claire shook her head. "And don't anyone use the bathroom radio. It's dead. And so, almost, was I."

"It's that Stefan."

"Oh. Oh, all right. Give it to me. Hello?"

"Good evening." His accent was thicker over the phone. "How are you holding up in this heat wave?"

"Fine. You?"

'So la la. Listen, the reason I'm calling . . . I'm driving into town tonight . . . Soho. Julio Marble is having a show and I thought I'd have a look at his new work. Perhaps buy something for the entrance hall. Would you like to come along?"

"You couldn't have called at a better time," Claire scowled at Carmela. "That's exactly what I'd like to do. Get away from everything for a little bit."

"Pick you up at seven, then."

"All right."

"Ciao."

"And tomorrow," Zinnie was telling her mother, "we'll go up to the mall and get your ears pierced."

Stefan drove along the Long Island Expressway with the top down. Claire's hair whipped unnervingly across her eyes but he was going so fast that she couldn't catch hold of it to anchor it down. Gladys Knight and the Pips blasted from quadriphonic speakers, Stefan yodeling along with staccato clumsiness. You could take the boy's soul out of Bialystok but you couldn't take the Białystok out of his soul. By the time they got to the colorful, raggedy streets of Soho, Claire was ready for a calming drink and a cigarette, the hell with reform. Stefan left the red Porsche open and the top down. If he closed it up, he explained cheerfully, they would simply break the window to get the radio and that would be worse still, what with insurance costs and unreasonably long waits for import replacements.

"That's absurd!" marveled Claire.

"Ah, but true. Just look at the other cars."

Sure enough, two other German makes had signs taped to their windows, letters to potential thieves: "Radio not here" and "No Radio." It was so funny. These people had spent fortunes on exotic cars, and there the automobiles sat, with brown-paper-bag letters Scotch-taped to their windows. What an incredible city! Perhaps one day an inventive thief would break into one of these cars and leave a note himself. "Just checking," it would read.

She followed Stefan into the gallery. The place was packed. There were playboys and models and agents, record producers and suntanned androgynes in from the Hamptons. The mayor and his entourage, Stefan whispered, were sure to come. Where, Claire wondered, would they put them? A crackling recording of Les Brown and His Band of Renown competed with the din. There was the cloying smell of everyone's perfume. "I'll get us some bubbly." Stefan pressed her hand and joggled away through the swarm.

Claire tried to get a look at the paintings. All she could make out were the brown and red peaks of the canvases. Everyone was chattering about how marvelous they were: "eclectic" and "revolutionary" were the words she heard again and again, and so she dutifully wriggled her way over to the main wall. On a canvas as broad as a barn door was what looked like smashed rubbish. She narrowed her eyes and went right up to it. Crushed flowers were glued onto the canvas and covered with muddy spray paint. "You see," the dowager beside her was instructing the undergraduate at her elbow, "what it means is the end of the world. The annihilation of all that is *vivre.*"

"Yes." The young man in his expensive suit nodded, his sudden light dawning. "Yes, I see that. He's expressing his irrevocably disappointed self, isn't he? The conquering power of darkness! Gad, it's marvelous. More than anyone else, he has his finger on the pulse of decadence." They gripped their heaving chest cavities, the both of them, overwhelmed by the wonder before them. Claire was inspired herself, only not by the painting. It was the two of them that got her. Had she brought along that Olympus she could have taken the two of them from the rear, the way they stood there bent, deferential and solicitously awestruck in front of the ill-looking painting, groveling meekly at the foot of some critic's approval.

There you go, she told herself. If you thought about work as much as your bloody pride and righteousness, you'd have a camera right here, wouldn't you? You wouldn't be worried about what a dishonest detective thought of you. You couldn't create art and worry about what people thought. This artist certainly didn't, and look where it got him: a show in trendy Soho.

"Having fun?" Stefan came up behind her. "Don't you love his work?"

Claire didn't know what to say. To voice the obvious cop-out, "Well, it's different," would have been a lie. It was certainly no different than all the other current, atrocious mediocrities. But then, what did she know? "It's very big, isn't it?" she smiled.

Stefan paused. He was disappointed in her. "You don't understand it. I see that."

"Hmm. I guess not."

"What he's trying to say," Stefan explained patiently, "is that there's no point to it all. All the effort. The miracle of birth . . . it just ends up in death. The beauty of creativity . . . goodness itself . . . it becomes polluted by society, . . . it wilts and it rots."

"It certainly does."

"It's very pure, you see. In its essence."

"Oh."

Annoyed with her, he scanned the room. "Uh-oh! Look who's here! Jupiter Dodd! Now the heads will roll."

"Who's he?"

Stefan looked at her, appalled. "Only the biggest art critic on the East Coast, that's all. He's deadly."

"Really? He looks harmless enough."

"Don't let that docile demeanor fool you. He eats up artists and spits them out for the sheer fun of it. Once he even shot one of them."

"Not really."

"Yes. About ten years ago. This young artist was poking fun at him in a Village paper. Doing caricatures and that sort of thing . . . ribbing him. Dodd walked into the city room and shot him, point blank. Oh, there was the devil to pay. He was ruined of course. Had to leave town for five or six years and by then everyone had forgotten him."

"How did he make his comeback, then?"

"Comeback? I'm talking about the artist. Jupiter Dodd was an overnight sensation. The toast of the town. Still is. And he hates women. Utterly. Where are you going?"

"I'm going to have a closer look at him."

"Claire," he sneered. "Darling. One doesn't just walk up to Jupiter Dodd and introduce oneself. You don't talk to him. He talks to you."

"Is that right?" Claire disconnected his hand from her sleeve. She hadn't had the slightest desire to talk to the man, but the way Stefan put it to her irked her to no end. Got her Irish up. She approached the dapper little man and extended her hand. "How do you do." She gave him a direct smile. "Claire Breslinsky."

"Ah," he said, looking past her at someone else and flagging them with his eyes.

"I wanted to introduce myself," she groped. She could feel Stefan watching with vindictive triumph. ". . . because I'm doing a book on . . . um . . . faces. Faces in the art world, and I thought"—she had him now. Good God. Was there no end to people's vanity?—"well, I rightly thought that a face like yours ought to be included. That arch sense of aristocratic sensitivity. You know what I mean. Black and white, I'm afraid." These fancy schmancy types always went for the subtle. She knew what she was doing, too. He was all ears. If there was one thing every snob believed, it was the manifest validity of his own importance. One of the prettier cosmopolitan sluts was dangling herself before Stefan. Annoying, but not fatal. Stefan's eyes were still on her. She had just been ready to find herself contemptible and stop the silly game. Now she felt fired up, in gear for the chase. She was running amuck with it, chattering rapid fire nonsense, but she was enjoying herself.

"Larson in Paris? You don't say," Dodd said. "I thought he was dead."

"Dead? I should say not. He's got the cleverest, glossiest printing setup in Europe." All lies, of course. But it wouldn't hurt to throw in a little butter-up for an old friend. "He's who's backing me. Surprised you haven't heard anything about him lately. Strictly innovative stuff. You know."

"Hmm. Yes. Well of course I had heard. Word gets around but then you never know. And you think it really ought to be just a one side, one face sort of thing? Not left page face, right page full length?"

"Yes, well one could. Only I think that would be too *Life* magazine. What interests me is a damn good face. A flamboyant face but a wise face—oh, shit. I've left my card in my other bag—a face that stands up to scrutiny and says I like me as I am and you can all go to hell."

Jupiter Dodd had his brown leather agenda from Bendel's out now. He wasn't going to let her get away without a phone number. And Stefan. Stefan was going to pay her back for proving him wrong and being a success with Jupiter Dodd. He was going to like her more for it . . . admire her, at least, but he'd have to pay her back. Here it came. He was flirting blatantly now with the girl.

"I'll be in touch," Claire smiled and walked away. Stefan, still peeved, pretended he didn't see her coming.

"Hi," Claire said. "Remember me?"

Stefan looked right past her. It was Jupiter Dodd at her heels. He could hardly believe it.

"One more thing," Dodd drew her close to him with an air of confidentiality. "I've got these bags under my eyes for crying out loud. Since weeks. So if you want to wait a little while before we shoot. Like till after a long weekend. I don't know. What do you think?"

"I think," Claire grinned at Stefan, "that if you were any more interesting looking, I wouldn't be shooting you, I'd be painting you."

"Ha, ha."

"No, really. You look great. And if you're worried, put some Lipton tea bags on your eyes for twenty minutes. All right?" Jesus.

The gallery director scuttled up to Dodd. "Come, Jupiter. Andiamo! You've got to meet Julio Marble. It's his show, after all."

They all stared at Julio Marble. A man, Claire thought, who looked suspiciously serene for one announcing the end of the world.

Dodd took Claire's hand into his own smaller one. "Will you be coming up to Laraine's later?"

Ashamed now of her little scam, Claire recognized him for what he was: a nice, successful, slightly demented but kind man. What was the matter with her? Was that why she'd become a photographer? To be the one in power? In demand? The poor man's Picasso? The guitar player who's indifferent to music but joins the band to get the girls? How stupid she was. If anyone was vain it was she.

"We'd love to come," Stefan thrust his wine glass between them with an authoritative jiggle.

"Oh, good. Don't not come, now," he scolded Claire. *"À bientôt!"*

"À bientôt?!" Stefan mocked her now with new respect. "What did you do to the man? Talking to Jupiter Dodd about his bags! I can't believe it! Put tea bags on them, she tells him! Five minutes in town and Jupiter Dodd asks her to join him at Laraine's. The girl is a marvel." He was showing off for the glamorous girl at his side now but

Claire didn't mind. Point made, she found herself wondering if the Mayor had had his late walk.

After the show they whizzed uptown. Stefan had a penchant for going faster than the speed of light in a town where pedestrians darted out from the curb just for the hell of it.

"Stefan, slow *down*!" she finally yelled.

"Can't talk!" he shifted excitedly. "Driving!"

"Yes," Claire closed her eyes.

"Wheee!" Stefan's gorgeous sidekick giggled from the rumble seat. There was no reason why they shouldn't give her a lift up to Laraîne's if she wanted to come, Stefan had told Claire. No reason indeed. It occurred to Claire that if he was trying to make a hit with her this was not exactly the way to do it. Or was it? Stefan hadn't seemed particularly attractive to her tonight until he'd draped the vile creature on his arm. Was he smarter than she'd thought? And why were women who looked like that inevitably named Nicole?

"Come on, Stefan! You'll get a ticket!"

"Diplomatic immunity!" he hollered back.

They raced up the F.D.R. Drive, then crossed onto the narrow, tree-lined streets of the Upper East Side. Self-preserving yellow taxis sped out of their way. Stefan swerved dangerously to avoid a Chevrolet that had the impudence to drive at a legal speed. He grinned gloriously (he really was good looking with that white-blond hair and steely eyes), as though he'd made it through yet one more dangerous mission. He swung around the block, then double-parked with a screech beside a row of limousines. Chivalrously, he helped his ladies ascend from their carriage.

Claire was sopping wet. She headed directly for the ladies' room to put herself back together. The place looked like any local Irish bar, but all New Yorkers knew that this was the only place where the likes of themselves would ever eat dinner next to an authentic film star. Or run into one on the way to the ladies' room. It was mercifully empty. Claire tore off her blouse and submerged herself as best she could in the sink. She shouldn't have had all that crummy wine. She sat down on the toilet seat and let her head spin. The wall was papered with starlet's heads cut out from magazines, then lacquered to an amber sheen. Imagine Johnny Benedetto thinking her a suspect! True, there had been that one moment there when she'd thought the same of him. She buttoned her blouse thoughtfully. Why on earth had her mother cut off all her beautiful hair? Now she looked like all the other ladies out in Richmond Hill. Permanently waved. Next would be a lavender rinse. She'd always been rather proud of her mother's obstinate disregard for fashion. Her nunlike skin that had never known more than a cheery lipstick to go with a "good" dress. Her sensible shoes. You could grow up as much as you liked but you still wanted your parents to fit some idiotic consistent image you had of them. You wanted them worthy of your own unworthy love. It didn't seem exactly plausible to Claire, sitting there snug in her sanctuary cubicle, that she had ever been around the world at all. That whole business of the last ten years seemed like a color film she'd absentmindedly watched and not quite gotten the point of. It seemed a lot more as though she were still a kid from Queens who'd come over the bridge for a night on the town and here she was, a little bit tanked, still biting her nails in girlish reminiscence. Perhaps it was the beery atmosphere. One thing was sure, though, she wasn't a kid. She saw that quite plainly on the back of her hand. The knuckles were going scrunchy and no nightly application of hand cream would ever change that. She licked them soothingly.

Why did Johnny have to be a crook? Whatever he was doing at the track was illegal, she knew that. He was ripping off the public. Or at least the mob. Wasn't it the mob that ran the track? She could pretty much figure out how it worked. Some mob lackey waited till most of the bets were in and the odds down, then he dropped a substantial wad on a "dark" horse . . . against the odds but "set" to win . . . and this just before the track closed the betting windows. As there were no phones at the track, they were pretty safe in keeping the new development from any off-track betting, thus keeping the odds to themselves and their profit enormous. That would be where Johnny and his partner came in. It was actually quite clever. Did she really care if he was ripping off the mob? Or even if he was ripping off that vague entity: the public? Wasn't Julio Marble doing the same thing? What was it Stefan had said he was getting for just one of those atrocities? Two hundred thousand. Now that was robbery. She wondered what Johnny was doing now? Staking out someone else? And there would be no end to those adventures of his if she were with him. Every time he would walk out the door she'd have to wonder if he'd ever walk back in. She wished she could be more like her mother, who had Zinnie figured for safe in the arms of the Lord, protected by her own guardian angel. Now that was a thought. Claire wondered if she had one. If she had, he would have probably wandered off while she'd been busy researching Hinduism and Buddhism. And now? What was she now, an orthodox agnostic? Or perhaps angels weren't subject to religion. She stood up and unlocked the door. She looked in the mirror. Not too bad, for a heathen. But was she still considered "in the running"? As a matter of fact, she looked pretty damn good. She picked up her blouse and inspected her breasts. There they were, good as gold, good as new. Happy again, she tucked herself in. Not a moment too soon. The door flew open and there was the flawless, lovely face of this year's most recognizable starlet. Pride truly cometh, Claire concluded wryly, before a fall. With a humble heart, she headed back to the table.

Nicole was propped up on Stefan's bony lap, a sight that would have irritated her more had she not recognized that look of hopeful sadism in Stefan's eyes when he knew she saw them like that. The famous Laraine, for whom the place was named, had parked her feline self at the table as well. She was one of those inscrutable, voluminous women whom men like and women do not (or who likes men and doesn't like women—it's always the same). A woman who wore Chanel No. 5 so well that no one knew what in heaven's name she had on. She was lapping up whatever Jupiter Dodd had to say. There were a bunch of others Claire didn't know, everyone successful and city-ish, and one artist Claire had read about in the Sunday magazine section, someone named Verona.

Stefan shook Nicole from his person, stood up, and found the two of them some chairs. He wedged them neatly into place and Claire sat down. Nicole seemed to think she was holding court and she just carried on, informing the party of the physical beauty of Saint-Tropez. There was no one in the group who hadn't spent many a moonlit night there themselves, but what the heck, they let her talk. It was always somehow wonderful to remember the south of France through anyone's eyes. And after bumping into the breathtaking starlet, Claire could hardly be angry with Nicole. It wouldn't be too long before she, too, would be over the hill. That was one thing that happened to all of them. It certainly beat the alternative, not making it over the hill. Claire congratulated herself for her mature, generous attitude and looked around. They were all very busy downing their margaritas. She ordered a Sea Breeze. Sensible vodka with cranberry juice and grapefruit.

Dodd wanted to know all about her past. She could hardly resist giving him a short but glowing verbal résumé. Lord knew there was no one in Queens who'd ever heard of anyone she'd ever worked with. She was beginning to feel like her old self and told him so.

"But not really?" Dodd was saying. "You honestly live in Queens? In *Queens*?"

"Yes. Actually. With my parents."

"No! How refreshing. And how do you manage getting back and fo—"

"Queens isn't so bad," Stefan interrupted, thumping the table impatiently. Now that Jupiter Dodd wanted her attention, he wanted it, too. "It's quite exciting. Especially now. Isn't it, Claire? With all the murders going on."

"Murders?" Dodd perked up.

"We've had a couple of child murders," Claire explained.

"Not those ones on TV!" Nicole clapped her hands.

"Two that we know about," Stefan said. "There could be more that haven't been discovered."

That was true, Claire realized, imagining the woods full of children's graves.

"I read about them," Laraine joined in. "Horrible!"

"Faggot murders," Stefan said. "Right up in the park. Right where I live."

"How could they be gay murders?" Claire stared at him. "One of the two was a little girl."

Stefan raised one eyebrow. "A ploy, my dear. To cast suspicion on somebody else."

Or bisexual, she thought, remembering Freddy with a lurch.

"Gay?" Nicole went back to her shrimp cocktail. Gay people didn't interest her.

"You should see them," Stefan spat. "They cruise around Park Lane South exactly across from my house. Right in the woods there. It's disgusting! They leave their rubbers anywhere on the ground where little children can pick them up. They . . . they . . ." He was all worked up, but he stopped when he saw how Jupiter Dodd was looking at him. "Those children," he leaned in and whispered, "had slices of flesh cut right off them."

Claire felt a chill go right through her. Whoever would do such a thing wouldn't think twice about killing a cop. What if Johnny did figure out who it was? What if the murderer—

"Claire! What's the matter?"

Claire looked down at Stefan. She hadn't even known she'd stood up.

"Oh, they questioned everybody," Stefan continued. "Even me! And probably Claire, too. Did they put you in a lineup, Claire?" he laughed.

"They talked to me, too, yes." She sat back down.

"And you should have seen the cops! One of them had on, I kid you not, a blue and white seersucker leisure suit!"

Why, that's Johnny's partner, thought Claire, remembering the horrendous suit. That's Ryan.

"No!" guffawed Jupiter Dodd.

"And the other one! He was a piece of work. Right out of a television series. Brooklyn accent . . . the entire syndrome. 'Duh,' he said to me, 'Where'd ya get dem pick-chas?' Pick-chas? He was looking at the Erté. Pick-chas!"

Everyone laughed out loud.

"Then," Stefan continued, his eyes gleaming, "—then he started to ask me about my private life. That's when I put a stop to it. I said, 'Detective, if you have any problems with my sex life you can take it up with my lawyer. . . .' And do you know what he said to me? He said, 'Why? Your lawyer got a handle on where you stick it?' Fresh. Now I'd say that's fresh. Flippant. Not to mention crass. Sorry, ladies. He was such a classically ignorant type, though. Priceless!"

Claire wiped her burning face with a napkin. "Stefan, I hate to be boring, but I'm not feeling too well. Would you walk me to a cab? I'd like to go home."

Stefan didn't hesitate for a moment. He was by her side and shelling cash out onto the table in one movement. "Come," he crooned, "I'll have you home in twelve minutes."

"That's what I'm afraid of. Please stay. I don't think I could take another roller coaster ride tonight."

"I promise I won't go a moment over sixty," Stefan grasped her shoulders cheerfully from behind and gave a tidy squeeze.

"It's all this talk of murder," Jupiter clicked his tongue. "She's a sensitive girl, *n'est pas*?"

Laraine concocted an elaborate yawn and Nicole made optimistic eyes at Mr. Verona.

CHAPTER 11

Going over the Queensboro Bridge, Claire turned clear around in her seat to get a good look at the skyline. The sky had turned overcast but the heavens were lit. New York lived and breathed a great mucky glow of its own. She sighed. That's my town from here on in, she realized, pleased. Oh, it would all work out. She felt better now, all snuggled up in the leather upholstery soft as butter. There was something about a posh car. It made you forget all about tomorrow. Rather like late-night television. She looked over at Stefan. He smiled back, concerned. He wasn't so bad, really. Just a hell of a snob. But then so had she been, back in the Munich days. She stroked the nice leather. There was nothing wrong with being a snob. It showed you were discerning. Perhaps Stefan was only so happy-go-lucky on the outside. Maybe he was as wracked by doubts and inconsistencies as she. After all, she hadn't given him much of a chance.

As though reading her change of heart with some devious instinct, he leaned over and placed one hand on the seat beside her knee. He wore a heavy gold ring with a lapis lazuli stone.

"That's an interesting ring," she admired.

Stefan chuckled. "My great-grandfather's ring."

"Is that so?" Claire imagined herself, years down the road, wearing such a ring herself. And Stefan, dignified Stefan, one day passing his own heavy ring down to their son. The only trouble was, the son looked remarkably like a miniature Johnny Benedetto. "Honestly," she said out loud, "sometimes I get so confused. There really is something to be said for the oblivion of drunkenness."

"Only you're not drunk, are you?" he said, meaning something else. Of course, he wasn't stupid. He hadn't got to where he was by being dim-witted.

"You're the type who's always thinking," he eyed her fondly. "That brain never stops."

"Oh, it stops, all right. It just does so at teeming intersections."

"You know what you need?"

"What?"

"A good dose of security. That's what."

"I've got all the security I need. I'm living with my parents, after all."

"I mean real security. Financial. Then you'd be free to pursue your art."

"I could always get a job, Stefan."

"Or marry someone with a lot of money."

Claire switched on the radio. Why was he saying things like this to her? Did he like her that much? Financial security was an attractive commodity. He knew she knew that. Albinoni's adagio for strings came on. One of her dad's favorites. Now her parents didn't have much more than a pot to piss in and yet they had everything. At least, if you looked at it a certain way they did. Her mother always said there was no security in the world. Just look at Mrs. Dixon. Whatever it was, Mary always had a handy point of reference among her friends. That poor woman. She'd looked after her bedridden mother for years until the poor old thing had died. There was no money left after that and she wasn't getting any younger, so when Rudy Dixon came along, nice big house, good job with a fine company . . . she'd accepted his marriage proposal with relief. Finally someone to look after her. Security. And what had happened? Not two years into the marriage, Rudy had had himself a massive stroke and Mrs. Dixon spent the next thirty years looking after helpless Rudy and cleaning that big house herself. No, there were no sure things, no security in the world. Banks did fail. Stocks and bonds collapsed. You were better off taking your chances with someone you loved.

And there was another thing. Claire had lived overseas long enough to know that an American passport was still a desirable commodity. Even for a wealthy Pole with diplomatic immunity. Stefan was attracted to her, she knew that. Even now his hot little breaths were fogging up her sense of well-being.

She knew exactly what sex would be like with Stefan. It'd be slick, expert sex . . . like between the lines of the glossy magazine advice columns. The music would be suitable. Most likely black and newly released. He would moan. His body would be scented with the most expensive men's cologne from Bloomingdales. He would labor away at satisfying her first, tackling her body with all the cultivated calisthenics picked up at the health club. Yes, he would do his level best. When it was over, he'd sink down onto his elbows and gaze at her with triumphant eyes. Maybe even hold up his Waterford champagne glass for a replenishing toast. And she knew that the smell, the essence he would emote then, what with the talcum and the perfume rubbed away, would be thoroughly repugnant to her. She knew it. Just as surely as she knew that she had no idea what it would be like with Johnny. With Johnny all she knew was that she was compelled to him, thirsted for him with an almost infantile yearning, and had lost her mind when he'd held her. From that moment on she had only one insistent memory whenever she got close enough to herself to turn out the world, when she was drying her face with a towel or when her cheek touched the pillow . . . a dark and fragrant mental picture of a still-unopened blood red rose.

"I'd like to go straight home, Stefan."

"I know. We'll just stop off at my place for a quick drink. Help you sleep."

"That's very kind of you, but no thank you."

"Come on, Claire. Don't play coy with me." He was driving faster now, deliberately intimidating her.

She gripped the upholstery with ice-cold hands. The bottom fell out of her stomach as he cut through traffic like a shot from a gun.

"Come on, Stefan," she heard herself say in what seemed an only slightly elevated tone.

"Excited?" He looked like a beautiful little boy having fun. He went still faster.

She burst out laughing. She didn't know what else to do. It worked. Stefan slowed down, took the turn, and pulled up in front of her house. Even his sudden anger seemed to mellow. "All right," he said as they pulled up in front of her house. "Tonight you're off the hook. But tomorrow night"—he gave her an almost malevolent look—"we'll take a drive. Do you like Montauk?"

"Ooo! So far? Exciting!" She smiled at him, her good-bye full of promise, and hopped out of the car.

He grinned at their secret joke and roared away.

She kept that smile on her face until he turned the corner. She walked up to the stoop and sat down. Something was missing. There he was, staring at her through the screen. She let him out and sat down next to him on the top step, as was their custom, put her arm over him and felt his doggy breath on her hand. "That is one guy," she said, "with whom I will never again get in a car. Something strange there. Boy. Never again. Do you know I was actually frightened for a moment? Always laugh in the face of fear, your honor. It's the only way out."

The Mayor put his chin down on her knees. He was awfully glad she was home, safe and sound. Astonishing how much she meant to him after such a short time. She made him feel somewhat vital. Lord knew she needed looking after. They sat there listening to the crickets. A pack of kids were down the road under the trestle. They heard a bottle break and the muffled laughter, then the giddy shuffle as they ran off. The midnight local lumbered in and out, groaning and wheezing and farting. A cop car passed in front of the house, then parked in its every-night spot up on Bessemer for coffee regular and half a dozen Dunkin Donuts.

Iris's kitchen light was still on. Claire was tempted to go over and take a peek through the window until she remembered how late it was. If anybody saw her they'd think she was breaking in. The hell, she decided. "C'mon," she said. "We're going to do a little spying. You do have a girlfriend over there, don't you?"

They strolled with pointed nonchalance across the street. "Go on," Claire egged him through the bushes. "Pretend I'm not here, would you? Gee. Now that you've got the green light, you act like Mr. Prim and do it off the curb."

It wasn't that. The Mayor cocked his head and his ears went up with a quizzical hoist. It was this baffling sense that something was amiss.

"Just mind you don't tear that big web there," she hissed and followed him through down on all fours. Right above her head was Iris's tentative silhouette. And then she was gone. She left the light on though. She'd be back. Claire pitched herself against the Japanese maple to wait for her return. The living room, aside from the monstrous television set, looked like something from a long-gone era. Through the parted velvet drapes she could just make out the unusual antique furniture, Chinese and Louis XV mostly . . . oriental screens and bookcases and figures . . . little figures . . . what in blazes? It looked like a couch full of children. A hot wind blew and the curtain fluttered shut. The Mayor drew close to her feet. It was so damned quiet. He would have preferred to go but wasn't about to leave her flat. She was glad he was there but dared not speak. She had to get a closer look. If she could just get up to that branch, she could look in the breezeway window.

The Mayor looked on skeptically. Clumsy Claire. She'd never make it. White lightning lit up the sky. Of course. Where else would she want to be but up a tree in a lightning storm? Easy does it . . . easy does it . . . she was up with a round roll of thunder.

"Na? So you've come for dat tea after all!"

Iris's voice, and the sudden sight of her eerie, pale-moon face behind and underneath her, jolted Claire right out of the tree.

She wasn't hurt, but rain was pelting down on top of them now in a resolute gully-washer. There was nothing to do but follow Iris into the house. The Mayor stuck like glue. Iris, trailing an invisible chiffon scarf with one hand up in the air, ushered them in through the hall to the parlor. The smell of cat was very thick.

"Sit down, sit down," Iris gushed. "Take off dose sopping shoes." She was all keyed up.

"I shouldn't have come over like this . . . in the middle of the night. I ought to go, really. I—"

But Iris wouldn't hear of it. She was delighted.

"Ve older people don't sleep a lot, you know. Und I don't too much like da television. So violent. No, no, no, you couldn't have come at a better time, to tell you da trute."

"Fine." Claire took one careful step backward and sneezed.

"Und dis is my family," Iris presented the back of the couch.

I can always beat her up, Claire told herself. She's just a frail old woman. Then she saw who was sitting on the couch. It was a family of dolls. Big dolls, little dolls. There was one enormous one that looked like Shirley Temple. Her wig was golden ringlets of real hair. Most of the dolls were obviously valuable German and French bisque, as old, perhaps, as Iris herself. They were all done up in hand-crocheted, vibrant colors, opulently turned out but now softly muted with time and a gray film of dust. They were everywhere: staring out from glass-doored cabinets and countless musty shelves.

"Dese are my dollies." Iris sat down on the hassock and crossed her legs, revealing just a touch of lace-trimmed slip. Black.

"How nice," Claire smiled hard. She edged over toward the window. It was open and she could always jump out. Across the street a car pulled up. Claire's heart thumped. It was a man, rushing around the car with an umbrella. She didn't know him, wait, she did. It was that doctor from Stefan's party and he was opening the passenger door for Zinnie. "Hi!" she waved, pretending they could see her. "My sister and her new boyfriend," she said. She could hear them laughing as they scooted through the rain. They were kissing now, thick as thieves in each other's arms on the porch.

Iris was talking about how beneficial a thunderstorm was, shooting lovely bolts of ozone into the earth . . . like a tonic for the plants.

"I've never seen so many dolls," Claire crept closer. She hated dolls. Always had. She didn't care how rare they were. Dolls had always filled her with anxiety, even as a child. She couldn't see them face down on the floor . . . they had to be upright (imagine being face down like that every day). No, and they had to be adequately covered, too, not naked in a cold garage the way some thoughtless little girls left them. The worst part about dolls was that once you got them dressed and sitting comfortably, they scared the living daylights out of you . . . looking at you the way they did with icy, unblinking eyes. They were diabolical once they got you alone in the dark.

Iris went away to boil water or something, and Claire had time to investigate the shabby finery of the room. It was sad if you looked at it one way, almost Havishamesque. On the other hand, it was the place of a person who'd chosen her poison at one point and stuck to it, dammit. Each nook and doily held some memory, Claire supposed. There was a series of cat portraits, from aging sepiatone to a brilliant, though blurred, color polaroid of Lü. She guessed she'd rather live like this one day should she become old, independently eccentric, instead of tediously predictable like the other old women around the neighborhood, fastidiously correct with their starched curtains and whitewashed stoops. Dry and forgettable. Interchangeable. You wouldn't find any of them inviting anyone in to tea at midnight, would you? No matter how the visitor had arrived.

Claire decided she liked Iris after all. There was a cut glass bowl filled with colorful marbles on the coffee table. They refracted the light from the art deco lamp beside it in a mottle of pastel along the walls. And who but Iris would think to upholster the Biedermeier hassock like that, in indigo with tapioca constellations? One whole side of the room consisted of shelf upon shelf of books. Metaphysics in six different languages. Leather-bound volumes of the philosophers: Leibniz, Kant, Descartes, Spinoza, Bacon, and quite a few by that old chauvinist Nietzsche. Freud and Jung had their own rows. This all spoke in favor of Iris's innocence, as far as Claire was concerned. Nobody with that much psychological knowledge of self would go around killing children. They just wouldn't. Would they? They would not.

Claire took a quick peek out the window just in case. Zinnie and Emil were still there. Sure. Snug as bugs in her hammock. You could look right into the house from here. She could see her father leaning over some weapon or other in his den, even hear his music, Puccini's something or other. Her mother was up in bed doing her crossword puzzle, her bent, fissured form happily oblivious to all but obscure word origins.

Iris came back in carrying a tray overloaded with pastry and cups and saucers.

Claire smiled. "What's this? The Viennese hour?"

"If you like." Iris rotated her shoulders with a mambo back and forth, getting into the swing of her tea party. Iris apparently didn't go in for supermarket goodies. She baked herself. There was a slice of rum-wafting fruitcake. With a thrill of horror Claire spotted the powder-sugared *rugelach*. She resigned herself to tomorrow's fast and helped herself.

"Dat's vot I like to see," Iris sat down happily, "a goot healthy appetite."

"These are hard not to like," Claire took another.

"Milk? Sugar?"

"No, nothing. Just the way it is, thanks."

"A little schnapps? Because you're vet?"

"Schnapps? What about a cordial?"

Iris threw open a cabinet no farther away than her fingertips. It sparkled with imported bottles. "Pear, plum, orange, peach, hazelnut, or apricot."

"Um . . . pear."

"Pear." With an admirably steady hand she opened the bottle and plunked a good slosh into Claire's teacup and then one in her own. Her fingers were gnarled with arthritis but her nails were perfectly manicured. With what painstaking diligence Iris had achieved that was anybody's guess. Her hands alone would make an interesting portrait. She was going to have to come to a decision soon about using the camera. Why did everything have to be so difficult? You never seemed to be able to do the things you really knew you should be doing without compromising. Nothing was for nothing. "Relationships are so complicated," she said out loud, but Iris wasn't interested in pursuing the mundane.

"Vy," she said, "don't you get yourself knocked up?"

"I beg your pardon?"

"You know, pregnant. You've got the age. Und nothing else to do. It vood be a fine ting to see some new life around dat house."

Claire lowered her eyes and swallowed her mouthful. "What does that mean, I haven't anything else to do?"

"Vell, I mean, I see you over dere. Vandering around all night long. Dat's nice to come home und readjust but now you ought to have someone else besides yourself to take care of. Pretty soon it vill be too late. Trees only ripen in season, you know."

"I can't believe this. I can't believe I'm sitting here with you and you're telling me my biological clock is running out. And just with whom should I have this baby? Have you got that figured out, too?"

"Pfuff! Plenty of men around your house. Dat one always vatching in da vindows at night."

"Johnny?"

"I don't know. Dat one alvays hanging around. You two vould make beautiful children."

Claire nibbled on her cookie. "He's a cop."

"So? Dat's a goot chob."

"Is it? Always walking a tightrope between crack smokers with knives and cocaine pushers with guns?"

Iris pursed her lips. "Day got a goot pension if dey get kilt. Und da way I look at it is dis. Like da Arab says"—here she raised her pointer finger into the air—"'It is written by da prophet ven you shall die. From da day to da hour, yea to da very moment.' All dat udder stuff about chance is poppycock."

"Really? I don't see you with any framed pictures of dead husbands."

Iris sipped her tea.

"Oh, God, I'm sorry! I didn't mean to say that. I don't know what came over me. It's just that I feel suddenly so at ease talking to you . . . as though I've known you for a long time. I never would dare to say something like that to anyone unless I felt close to them. I mean . . . you must forgive me. My mouth goes off before the thought even reaches my brain."

"Dat's all right, dat's all right," Iris waved away her apology. "I like you because you do say vot's on your mind . . . not because you vatch your vords. No, that doesn't bother me. But, as you must know, sometimes we carry da strongest memories around with us in our hearts, not in picture frames."

Claire nodded sadly, remembering Michael. All the loneliness she'd gained with his death could never outweigh the joy of having had him once. Not for a moment.

"I used to have pictures," Iris mused aloud. "But den came such upheaval in Europe. I took pictures myself, once, with a camera. Ach. I was so proud of dose pictures. I even framed dem myself. You can't take dat sort of important ting vith you ven you're getting out of da country."

Now, isn't that odd, thought Claire. Weren't there some sort of pictures . . . pictures without frames . . . why, of course. It had been with Michael, a million years ago. They had to have been children. They'd gotten hold of some pictures, dirty pictures. One of those pictures had made such an impression on her that she couldn't imagine how she had blocked it out. It was a magazine picture, one of those cheap, detective sort of sexy things. There was a man. He was wearing a raincoat and holding a gun. No, then he wasn't a detective, he was just holding out that gun and pointing it at a woman, she was sitting on the bed in her fancy underwear and there was a caption, cut out with letters from comic books and taped into sentences and it said, wait a minute, it said: "Take off your stockings and pull down your panties."

Iris cleared her throat. "Dere is," she said, "a lot to be said for loss itself. It makes you appreciate vot you have. Every bit of it."

The two women looked at each other with mute misunderstanding. Claire remembered her manners. She sat up briskly. "All those pictures you don't have anymore, were they of someone special?"

"Special? At dat time, ja. Dey vere special den. Only now dey are nothing but memories. Now my pictures are the sounds of crowded trams going up the Prinzregentenplatz . . . full of people long, long dead."

Claire shivered. The rain outside was loud and the dust on the window sills had turned to muddy grime. She realized that with the darkness of her loneliness exposed to light, Iris's mystery had disappeared and now she had Claire on her side. They could arrest Iris but no one would ever convince her that she had killed those children. She found herself staring at a pack of worn out tarot cards on the table. The police weren't going to like the looks of those. It wouldn't hurt to get rid of them. The cat jumped onto Iris's lap and rubbed his head on her breast.

"That's an interesting name for a cat. Lü."

"Dat's Chinese. It means the Wanderer."

"You know, Iris, if I were you, I'd put those tarot cards away."

"Pschew. I don't use dem anymore."

"You don't believe in them anymore?"

"Oh, dey work. Don't think even for a little moment dat you can't ask da cards. Dat dey von't tell you exactly vot it is you vant to know. Dat's sure. I don't use dem now anymore because I happen to believe in prayer better. The direct approach. Me? I go right to da top. God himself. I don't bother with dose little saints, either. Und I don't bother with da cards because even dough dey'll tell you vot it is you vant to know, dere's no good reason for you to know it. Not in my book. Anything gonna happen, gonna happen. Vat for should ve know da future? Take da fun out of it."

"Yes, but what about preventive foresight?"

"Dat's vot God gave us intuition for. You rely too much on all these ersatz methods: astrology, palmistry, tarot . . . you lose your telepathic gift. Your own individual nose, as it vere."

"Yeah, I can see that."

"Und anyhow," Iris slapped the air, "I get sick and tired of reading everybody's cards."

Claire laughed.

"Hmm. You tink dat's funny. It's not so funny ven dey won't let you in peace. Ven dey come from all over the place und interrupt your privacy und even your breakfast to find out if da husband is cheating on dem. Who cares? Once you find out you can do it . . . it becomes a real hell of a bore, let me tell you dat!" She sank back in her chair, done in by her own vehemence.

"Come on," Claire said, "I'll help you carry these things to the kitchen. It's late."

"Ja," Iris got up carefully. "I'm not gonna argue vit you. Und you know vot else?"

"What's that?"

"If I put da tarot cards away . . . if I hide dem . . . und the police come, it vill look vorse for me if dey find dem hidden dan if I chust let dem sit dere in da open."

So she knew. She'd figured out already that there was going to be a witch hunt. She was even ready for it. The awful thing was that it was Claire herself who'd supplied Johnny with the idea. She patted Iris on her meager arm and carried the tray to the kitchen. It was a harshly lit room, absurdly brisk and clean compared to the casual squalor of the others. The walls were tiled white, much like a hospital operating room except for the relief of one navy blue stripe around the top.

"My liebling room," Iris's eyes glittered. "I am in here baking all the morning."

"No kidding? Every morning?"

"Chust about. Da kids come, you know. I don't mind dem. Never. So I like to keep da cookie jars full. Dey all have der favorites. Michaelaen likes dat kind you like, the *rugelach.*"

"Michaelaen comes here?"

"Sure. All da time. Vell, sometimes."

"Oh. I didn't know." Neither, she bet, did Zinnie.

"Chust like Michael used to," Iris said pointedly, searching Claire's blue eyes.

Claire leaned against the old porcelain sink. "Do you know what horror is? Not the sureness of death. It's the uncertainty of life that's the horror. Not knowing for sure what to do. I always wish there was some way to tell."

"Ach," Iris dumped the tea cups into a pool of suds. "Dere is no 'sure.' You take a chance. You follow your heart. You know dat."

"That's just it. I never do know. How do you know what the heart is trying to say?"

"You have to listen mit it!" Iris yelled at her. "You vant sure, you listen mit brain. Brain is right-left, black-vite. Heart is like a subvay train. You get off any stop you vant to get home. Quick one . . . march right home. Udder one . . . maybe takes more time, more valking, but is a more charming route. More trees und flowers along da vay. Dat's choice. Your choice. Anyvay, eventually, you gonna get back home. How is up to you." Then Iris hitched up her skirt and started to hum "You gotta have heart."

"You're a regular comedian. I feel as though everything's falling apart all around me . . . whatever I do goes wrong, whatever I reach for turns sour."

"Oh, come, come, come. Noting is dat bad."

"Maybe not. It's just that nothing goes right."

"I know von ting. Ven ting's are going along smoothly, you can be very sure dat you're not getting anyvhere. Listen to me vell, girl, because dis is as true as true gets. Ven you're getting a lot of flack, ven everyting you do meets with resistance, den you know dat you are getting close to da source."

"The source."

"Ja."

When Iris walked her out through the foyer, she handed her an umbrella. It was made of paper and sprayed with shellack. When she opened it, it crackled.

"No sense getting vet," Iris said, "even if it is chust across da street."

"Okay," Claire took it gratefully. "This way I'll have to come back to return it."

"I'd like dat. As long as you don't come too often."

They smiled at each other. "Damn," said Claire, "now where's the Mayor gone?"

At the sound of his name, the Mayor bolted from the depths of the pantry. Natasha, Iris's poodle, followed him out. She was looking very smug. Iris made a disgusted sound in the back of her throat. "Dat dog. He's gonna make my Natasha mit puppies. Oh, vell. Gotta have someting to do, eh? At least animals, ven dey're old and useless, dey can still go out to stud."

Old and useless? The Mayor flinched visibly. What a rotten thing to say.

Iris, clutching her elbows at the door, seemed to feel the need to temper her words as well. "I remember ven he vas a pup," she reminisced. "Vay before even Michaelaen vas born. Dit you know he used to catch rats?"

"Yes, my father always talks about it."

"Strange ting for a dog. Almost unheard of. Und once he caught a thief going into Gussie Drobbin's house. Caught him by da foot und voodn't let go!"

"Yes, I heard about that, too. My mother wrote me about it. That was when they changed his name from Blacky to the Mayor, wasn't it?"

Ah, yes, the Mayor remembered, consoled. And not a bad monicker Blacky had been. Dash, it'd had. A touch of the old mischief. Of course, merit warranted dignity. And one never could go back . . .

"Goot-bye! Goot-bye! Und not to forget dat handsome young fellow. Imagine vat it vould feel in da arms mit a nice little redheaded baby to hold!" She continued to wave as they made their way across the puddled street.

Claire rushed inside. Zinnie was off the porch by now and the house was dark. A nice little redheaded baby, eh? Claire snorted to herself. She hadn't been red for the last twenty years. But bless her for remembering. The old fox. She looked at the Mayor. "Listen to me. We're not even on speaking terms and this is the second time tonight I'm imagining having his baby. I must be off my trolley."

He yawned at her feebly and they went right up to bed.

Across the street old Iris mopped the table with one edge of her kimono. She dusted her way lovingly around the figurines and ruby glass. She stopped when she noticed the cards. Claire had handled them thoroughly, then put them down absentmindedly into three piles. Iris raised her chin in wise disinterest, then turned around abruptly and snatched up the first. It was the moon. Ah, the mistress of the night. Underlying fears wriggling to the surface of a still pool in the body of a crayfish. A wolf and a dog barking. The home of the dead. Illusion. Iris shivered. She raised the second pile. The hanged man. The unconscious again. A sacrifice to be made. Some fearful journey through the underworld of Hades. Iris sat down carefully. She raised the third and last small pile. The wheel of fortune. So. The old order changeth.

Claire was just drifting off when the light went on.

"Sst! You asleep?"

"What?"

"You up?"

"Mmm. Turn that light out."

Carmela put it out and turned another, less offensive, light on. She sat down on the edge of the bed, right at home, and unscrewed her earrings. Claire felt herself stiffen with exhausted rebellion but smiled encouragingly just the same. There was something prepossessing about Carmela, and impressively desperate. You might be riddled by her disturbance but you were also privileged. A realization, Claire supposed, that had something to do with the fact that Carmela was the assured, if batty, first born. She dragged herself up onto one elbow. Whatever it was that Carmela wanted, it would take her a while to get to it. She'd take you for a stroll along her own peculiar brand of garden path and then come out with it as she was just about to leave, an afterthought.

"I've wrecked my car," she announced.

Claire's eyes went round.

"I did. It's all smashed up. On that big curve on Park Lane South."

"Are you all right?!"

"I'm fine. Freddy went through the windshield."

"Oh my God."

"I mean, he's okay. He's got a big cut on his ear. Like it

practically came off." She raised her eyes to heaven. "But they sewed it back on."

"Oh my God."

"Yeah."

"What hospital?"

"He's out. They let him out. They sewed him up and we left. He just dropped me off in a cab."

"Are you sure you're all right?"

"Me? It was so strange. It all happened so fast. The car went clunk and I thought . . . I remember thinking it wasn't too bad, and then there was this terrible sound of shattering glass, and I looked over and there was Freddy heaped up on the dashboard with his neck all funny and I thought . . . I was sure he was dead. He was so still. And then he put his head up and looked at me and he's dripping blood . . . spurting blood, and all I could think was it's a good thing it's on the other side because I didn't want the blood on me. What a thought! I mean what a way to think!"

"So then? What happened then?"

"I backed up the car, we were on Tracey's lawn, right through the sticker bushes—thank God I didn't hit the house—and the car still went, sort of, and we limped up to Saint John's to the emergency room and they took care of him. They were great. Freddy was great. He told them he went through his apartment window."

"But where's your car?"

"Well, then I started to drive us home, but then the thing that was sticking out under the car was dragging like crazy so I figured I'd better park it while I had the chance, and we walked down to the Roy Rogers and caught a cab. Aren't you going to ask me what I was doing with Freddy?"

Claire's head was spinning. She hadn't been able to get Freddy alone to confront him and had then concluded that it was none of her business anyway. She wasn't so sure she wanted to hear it now. "All right," she sighed, "what were you doing with him?"

Carmela twisted her ring. She had a two carat diamond from Arnold that she refused to take off. "I'm seeing him."

Claire fumbled on the nightstand for a cigarette.

"You don't seem very surprised."

"It's Zinnie who's going to be surprised."

"She's not going to find out."

"Carmela. You've got a head-sized hole in the windshield and Freddy the torn up head that fits in it. She's not stupid, you know."

"Freddy's going to have the car towed to his garage in the morning."

"And what's he going to say about his head?!"

"I don't know. He's going to make up some story. I'm not supposed to know. I'm not supposed to have seen him."

"Cozy. Very cozy."

"Claire. They're not married anymore."

"Oh, right. That changes everything. I suppose that's why you're being so clandestine about it. Because it's perfectly all right. Suppose Zinnie started dating Arnold. I suppose that wouldn't bother you a bit?"

"Zinnie sceeves Arnold. She thinks he smells like a corpse."

"That has nothing to do with it."

"You have nothing to do with it, either."

This was good. "You woke me up to tell me this?"

"Tch. What a mess. It's all a mess. I never should have started up with him."

"You're damn right you shouldn't have. And what about AIDS? Just where do you think he's been since he's out of the closet?"

"Claire. There are such things as prophylactics."

"Oh. And you're sure that that's enough? I mean is it worth it? You and Mom were telling Zinnie you didn't want him around Michaelaen, for God's sake."

"I know, I know, I know."

"I mean, it's your business what you're up to, but you can't be pleased with yourself. You can't."

Carmela snorted. "I haven't been pleased with myself since I was in school."

"Because you were challenged there. You only got mixed up in this nonsense because you're bored. Why don't you quit that stupid job and sit down, I mean like really sit down, and write something good. You know you've got to sooner or later. You know it's in you. Don't you owe anything to the talent you were blessed with?"

"No."

"Don't be a jerk."

"Oh, Claire. You talk like a high school guidance counselor."

"So? What's wrong with that?"

"What about you? You could get a job in some terrific studio in the city and work hard and eventually open your own. And what do you do? You wander around here like some refugee from the third world who's too proud to go on welfare."

"That's just what I don't want. A job in the city. A job in a studio. Any studio. That would be the same as your job at the magazine. Being soothingly polite to arrogant clients who you'd just as soon smash in the teeth. I know how those people are and I don't want to turn into one of them. They act so big. They act so . . . so . . . cool. You just want to put them in a black and white film from the fifties and turn off the sound. I'd rather sell cookies in a shop. And keep my photography the way I like it: pure."

"Nothing's pure."

"Yes, some things are. Saving yourself for someone you love is pure."

"I don't know why I bother to talk to you. You're screwing your brains out with that Polack and that . . . that pig cop."

Claire flushed. "Michael was one of those 'pig cops.'

And I haven't slept with either of them, for your information."

"Oh, come on."

"I haven't."

"Well, then you're more of a dope than I figured."

"Thank you."

"You're welcome. I'd love to be there in the morning when the Traceys wake up and see their sticker bushes gone."

They both laughed, Carmela harder than Claire, whose heart had gone light and then lead at the mention of Johnny. Her first instinct was joy, but her reason told her bluntly it would never work out. She remembered what Iris had said, and she hugged her knees with grim hope. Carmela's hearty convulsion was just trailing off in a high, windy note of amusement. She focused her rather bloodshot eyes back on Claire. "Oh, I get it," she said. "You're in love. But with which one?"

"Which do you think?"

"The poor one."

"Bingo."

"Figures. You always were the one to bring home the mutts."

"He's not destitute, Carmela. He has a house. A horrible house, but a house. He's not some cokie, he's—"

"That's all horseshit. What you mean is that he makes your juices run."

"You're so poetic. I always liked that about you."

"Hey. A spade's a spade. So what's the plan?"

"Sit back and wait. Either he'll come after me or he won't."

"You wanna borrow something ravishing to sit back and wait in? Like my strapless jewel green?"

Somewhere in the depths of Claire's mind, preoccupied with the image of Johnny coming across her suddenly in the dazzling green dress, an alarm went off. But Carmela was taking her hand. "Listen, kid," she said kindly, "if I were you, I wouldn't sit around and wait for anyone. I'd go after him with big guns."

"I thought I did. We just wound up wanting to wring each other's neck." She didn't mention his accusations.

"Look. If you want someone, you have to forget your standards and act like a flight attendant. He'll come around. Dress up. Wear heels. Dip."

Claire burst out laughing.

"I mean it." She stood. "You wanna get laid, you have to put aside your values for a couple of minutes."

"But I don't—"

"Bullshit. You do. We all do. As a matter of fact, if you're not interested in the Polack, I'll take him. That is if you really don't mind."

"Carmela, there's something strange about Stefan. I don't trust him. He could be the killer, for all we know."

"Who's talking about trusting him? I'd like to take him for all I can get."

"I'm not kidding."

"Neither am I. I like the type who are up to no good. Mischief. You just don't want me living in that mansion up on Park Lane South."

"Carmela, believe me, I know exactly how you feel. I had quite a few of the same thoughts once or twice myself tonight. But that's not what we're talking about here. We're talking about finding a way to live with ourselves. I mean, look at us. Here we are at three in the morning; I'm still drunk and you're blitzed from God knows what—"

"So I snorted a little . . ."

"Yeah. You only ever snort a little. That's why you weigh about forty pounds."

"Oh, shut up. Just shut up, because I know what kind of sermon's coming. And you just wish you had my slender thighs."

"Thighs, yes, scrawny neck, no."

"You had to get that out, didn't you? Make you feel better?"

Claire listened to her heart pounding in her ears. Why on earth did she let Carmela get to her like this? Nobody had ever irked her this way overseas. Was this what she'd run away from? The people who pushed all her buttons? Turned her into a child? She sank back, exhausted, onto her pillow. Carmela moved over to the doorway and looked sadly at Claire. Cruelty had a way of bringing out the best in her. "Anyway," she said. "I hope it works out with your dick-a-della. I really do."

"Thanks."

Carmela hesitated one more time. "Oh," she said, "by the way. If you could pick up my car tomorrow I'd really appreciate it. Um . . . as you have nothing else to do. With your camera stolen and all, you won't be doing much shooting, right?"

Claire smiled wryly. "Sure. I've got nothing else to do. And tigers never change their stripes."

"What's that face for?"

"I just wish you would once walk up those rickety stairs to see me without wanting something. Just to come up once for no reason at all but to, I don't know, talk or something. The way you make it out to look before you get to what you really want. Or at least just say what it is you want first. You don't have to make an ass of me."

Carmela narrowed her eyes. "I don't know what you think you're doing. The only reason you came home and bothered with us is because you were washed up over there. We didn't see hide nor hair of you when you were a big success in Germany. You didn't even show up for Christmas! Never. You just lived your selfish life and went your selfish way . . . and did you ever think that maybe you were missed? That you were needed? You think you were the only one who suffered losing Michael? You think you loved him maybe more than we did? Do you? Because I can remember nights when I would come up these 'rickety stairs,' as you so picturesquely put it, just to get away from the sound of Mom crying at night. And did you ever hear a grown man cry over there in your travels, in your quest to see the wide, real world? Because I can remember nights that Dad would put on his Beethoven tape and think we couldn't hear him. Or do you think the mourning went away when you left? After the excitement of the funeral parlor died away and all the relatives were gone and nobody from the precinct came around anymore, it was just us, without him. Who the hell do you think cleaned out his sock drawer? You? His dear twin sister? So who are you going to call the user? Me?"

Claire let the one tear roll down her cheek without wiping it. "You're right. And it is because I've been a failure in so many ways that I wound up back here, still looking inward, like a teenager does, trying to know myself and all that. I don't deny that I'm a failure. The only thing is that I've been a success in ways you think I've been a failure and a failure in what you take for granted I've succeeded in. I was such a waste while I was making all that money. I was so nothing, so nowhere. I couldn't sleep unless I had the light on and a couple of joints under my belt. I used to get these great travel jobs, traveling to these incredible places, and all I could see were the printed results I'd get out of it . . . what was going to look great in the dais. I didn't see the Sugarloaf in Rio, I saw an impressive backdrop for the clothes I was shooting. Oh, Carmela! I didn't see anything, I was so driven. So paranoid. I let myself fall in love with a vicious, megalomanic, woman-hating bastard just to satisfy my rotten self-image. And I was right. I was a total shit. I only started to come to myself, to love myself, when I was so broken down and lonely that even I had to feel sorry for me. The best I was was at my worst, with nothing. I just gave up, surrendered . . . and went out on my own. And it was only then that I found the courage to want to come home. So I am using you. I certainly am. But finally for the right reasons."

Carmela was putting her hair in a braid. "'And it was then that I found the courage . . .' How moving. I suppose I'm supposed to feel sorry for you now, too. It must have been awful making all that money without having to take the subway for it. It must have really bent your artistic pride. This might be new to you but, you know, a lot of people never even *get* the chance to be a hack at their art. They wait tables."

"Those are actors, Carmela."

"So they shoot weddings."

"Now what do you want? Me to feel guilty for being successful at what I hated anyway? I've got enough things I feel comfortable being guilty for. That's not one of them. Let me ask you something. Why the hell do you have such an attitude? Did I do something to you? What is it?"

"Oh, I don't know." She sat back down on the bed.

The Mayor groaned. This night was going on forever. Would they never stop jabbering? He rolled over and broke calamitous wind.

They both held their heads in submissive meditation while the thunderous moment passed.

"I always play the bitch with you," Carmela said. "I admit it. You always did bring out the worst in me. But I'm only sending out mixed signals. It's really not so bad that you're home. I mean, it could be worse."

They sat watching each other fondly, warily. The rain battered down above their heads.

"I've got to sleep," said Claire.

"And you won't forget my car?"

"No."

"Good night, then."

"Yeah. Night."

Michaelaen sat up in his bed. What was that? It was raining so hard. He was in his own bed but those shadows made all kinds of funny shapes on the wall. You could never be sure. His heart beat swiftly in his narrow chest. They were supposed to go out for their meeting. There was going to be magic and everything. He slipped out of bed and went up to the window. Boy. It was really coming down. And he felt a little sniffly. No one was going out on a night like this. But he didn't want Mommy to get in trouble. He didn't want anyone to hurt Mommy. What was today? Was it Wednesday? He couldn't remember. If it was Wednesday Mommy was off nights. She'd be home. But if he went all the way down to her room and it wasn't Wednesday, no one would be there. Michaelaen gulped. It was better to take along his old blankie. You never knew if it might get cold. Or drafty. Or something. He found it, right where it always was, tucked underneath his toy chest. How he hated to go down this hallway. It was best to more or less skedaddle through. He raced with his rear end tucked up tight behind him and never looking right or left, just squint so you couldn't see too much and close your ears and hunch up, like.

Zinnie woke up quickly, a blink of an eye and she went from full sleep to full consciousness. This was a talent of cops and conscientious mothers, and of course she was both. Michaelaen slept alongside her most of the time when she wasn't on nights, the hell with what those psychs said in the books—what did they know, anyway? She'd arrested her share of them. Sure, they'd always gotten off, but you knew what you were dealing with. Professional loonies, half of them. She'd let her son sleep beside her as long as he needed her warmth. She smiled at the sweet-smelling body cradling into her arms. Oh Lord. This is what kept her from going over the edge. The things she saw at work! The people! If you could call them that. The things some of them did to their own kids. It made you want to be sick. It almost made you want to quit the whole deal and move out to the Island or up past Westchester. But not quite. Those people, their kids were just as hopped up as the kids in the neighborhoods. And the job, whatever it might be, it had its points. There was a feeling of camaraderie you weren't going to find somewhere else. Like that time one of their own took a bullet and they closed every street and intersection and even the bridge on the way to Saint Luke's. Fast. She'd had the entrance to the bridge and she'd stood there alone in the night in her uniform—that was back when she'd still been in uniform—and all of a sudden like a shot out of nowhere comes this speeding ambulance, over the bridge with no moment of hesitation, one of their own they were going to get taken care of, and save him they did, not a moment too soon they'd said later. And it made you feel good. Especially when the ambulance had been flying by and there you were holding back any interference. The little lights twinkling on the bridge there, and you knew that all the way there, there would be someone else to take over, like a chain. It was horrible. But it was beautiful, too. It had its own kind of grace. And you were part of it. It could give you a chill up your spine. She pulled Michaelaen closer still and buried her face in his tufty hair. His smell was all his own and she reveled in it. Like clover and gum. Water-pistol water from the plug. She closed her eyes. The Mayor, satisfied that all was well and everyone in their proper place, walked contentedly back down the hall.

CHAPTER 12

Mary sat in her chair and looked down at the floor. That was the next thing. A really good scrubbing for that linoleum. Not today, though. And she wasn't going to ask one of the kids. If they couldn't think of it on their own, they could live with it the way it was. That was one thing she just wouldn't do. She remembered her own mother sitting at the same table, probably the very same chair, saying nothing, looking out the window while her husband ranted and raved at the kids. His fine Irish tongue run to drivel with drink and the florid injustices that went with it. He would aim it at the children, at her brothers and sisters and herself. Sure, weren't they the only ones who didn't know better than to take it? Do this, Mary. Go on off, now and do that, Mary. Isn't that tea up yet, girl? Oh, she could still hear him as clear as a bell. Well she wasn't going to have her children remembering their parents for that sort of nilly. Row upon row of upright tulips in the garden, all straight in rows, and never a child allowed near enough to God forbid enjoy them. No. Mary took a noisy, bitter slurp of her coffee. It might be noisy, chaotic memories her kids would have, but they would be gentle and permissive. Yes, that would always be the better way. She'd decided that as a young girl and she wouldn't change that.

Stan came in and sat down. "You wanna sit here all day or you wanna come with me?"

"I was just thinking . . . remembering. How rigid my

own dad was. How we never really knew him. We were afraid of him if anything. 'Dad's comin'!' we used to hiss at each other. Like, the monster's comin' . . . or something. You'd think he would have wanted us to love him, wouldn't you?"

"'Cause if you want to stay here, I can go drop off the Lotto and come back and get you."

"A man as intelligent as he was . . . you'd think he would have known better. Phh. Artist! Artist in false pride is what he was. With seven children and too good to take honest labor of any kind! And my own poor mother swallowin' the bile and goin', with her head held high, mind, to his own mother just to get money to pay the bloody milkman . . . it was . . . it was disgustin'!"

"Mary. Come with me now and stop sittin here thinking. The next'll be the memories of snow and your mother and when she died and before you can say Jack Robinson you'll be wanting me to take you over to the cemetery and on the way stop off at the florist."

"It's Claire I've been thinking about, really. When she was small there wasn't any of this soul-searching stuff. She was a normal, happy little girl, wasn't she? A real Ann of Green Gables. She wasn't the one you would think would get mixed up in all this mumbo jumbo. And it wasn't Michael's death that got her started, either. No, it was something else. Like when she started hanging around down in Greenwich Village after school. Rolling up her uniform above her knees and hitching to the city to go listen to drop-out musicians. That was when she started with all this metaphysical bunk. Remember the palmistry? All those books out of the library! The Manhattan library, too. And now them coming looking for her pictures in the cellar. I knew that darkroom was a bad idea."

"Now what's one thing got to do with the other?"

"Maybe I should have been more stern. I shouldn't have been so trusting."

"You wanted me to remind you about the meat."

"Oh, yikes, that's right! I've got that top round I have to get out of the freezer. You do that for me, will you, dear? And I'll put some lipstick on. The garage freezer."

"Mary?"

"What?"

"What's Claire going to do about that camera Johnny Benedetto gave her?"

"Stanley Breslinsky. That's her own decision now, isn't it? And I won't have you influencing her, one way or the other." Mary rubbed the corners of her mouth with a Kleenex and grinned into her grubby compact.

Stan shifted his weight from one leg to the other. He could just make out the tops of her garters under her skirt. It was the big soft cotton skirt with the pineapples on it.

"And," she dotted each cheek with a smudge from her lipstick and savagely patted, "you'd better start thinkin' about what you're going to do about the old camera . . . whether you'll be givin' it to Claire or not."

"That again."

"Yes, that again. What're you savin' it for? To leave her after you're dead and gone?"

"To be sure. She won't be getting much else."

"Stop jokin' around, Stan. Now, I mean it." There was a quarter of a cup left of her coffee and she finished it off with a healthy last draft. "She could use it now. She couldn't be in more of a crisis. She'll wind up takin' this fellow's camera just to get back in the race."

"He's the best man any of them's brought home yet."

"I know. But you don't know, really. You never can tell. Wasn't it you urging Zinnie to marry Fred? It was. I know Claire has ethics. Too many, maybe. But if life forces her hand, there's no tellin' what could happen. She might go with him just to justify accepting the gift, like."

"She'd be right to do it."

"That's just the point, Stan. It's not to be your decision. It's hers. And if she has her own camera she won't need anything from him. She'll be free to judge him for love's sake."

Stan looked at his nails stubbornly. "If I pushed Zinnie at all, it didn't turn out so badly. You got Michaelaen didn't you?"

"Got Michaelaen! Like he was some raffle prize and me with the right ticket! Sure I'd give him up in a flash if he could have a normal life with a mom and a dad just like every other child, I would! You're hot stuff, you are. Well, maybe not. Not in a flash. Oh, will you give the dog some of your bread and butter?"

"I'm not eating any."

"Well, you're standing right alongside of it! Just give it to him, will you? He's driving me crazy."

"He shouldn't have butter."

"Neither should you."

"Especially not in this heat. I ought to bring him along to the vet's one of these days. He's long due. You like that, wouldn't you, boy? A nice trip to the fine doctor?"

Like fish, thought the Mayor.

Mary stood up decisively and smoothed her skirt. "So when are you going to give Claire that old camera of yours? I mean, if you want to."

Stan was spreading butter back and forth, back and forth. It couldn't get any softer. The Mayor sat patiently down on the cool linoleum.

"Michaelaen still upstairs?" Mary, her germ planted, changed the subject.

"He's shaving. I gave him a shaver with no razor and he's up there scraping shaving foam off his face."

They both were quiet then. They could hear the rabbits outside shuffling in their cages. Stan lit up his pipe.

"I know you're thinking hard," said Mary. "If you don't stop puffing you'll disappear. And you know it's not the smoker who necessarily gets the emphysema. It's the one sitting across the table."

Stan, momentarily invisible inside his cloud of smoke, was dreaming of his latest project, a miniature carousel. Not quite the work of art up in the park, perhaps. Let's face it, he was no brilliant woodcarver like Muller, who created the original merry-go-round, but he did have his own small flair for things. He could have it finished for Christmas if he hurried. He looked over at his wife. Whenever Mary looked this pretty, Stan worried, it usually meant that her blood pressure was up. "I'll go on and get that meat," he said.

Mary and the Mayor watched him with equal expressions of irritation. First he had to choose his tape and attach his earphones. To someone as nimble and quick as Mary, this could take an inordinate amount of time. This morning she chose not to notice. She raised her eyebrows and kept them raised and turned her back. Chopin. Chopin meant the rain would go on and on. Tch. She'd have to go back upstairs and change her shoes. The Mayor sadly noted the first high strains of Chopin as a continuation to his long-standing bout with arthritis. It never failed. He was really starting to take a dislike to this particular composer. This weather took the starch right out of you. Then again, it was always better to know in advance, wasn't it? You didn't want to find yourself too far from home when it started to rain. One thing he could never figure out, though, was whether Stan played Chopin because it was going to rain or if it rained because Stan played Chopin.

Claire slept late. As long as it rained she was deep in the eyes of blue Morpheus, and the minute it stopped so did she. One eye was crumpled shut, the other telescoped the dim attic, not yet sure just where she was. It rested on the note propped on her dresser, bold and yellow, scrawled in Carmela's dynamic script. "Here's the address," it read, "you can pick it up after eleven."

Right. The car. Oh, hell. It felt pretty late. There went all hope of a ride. Where was this garage, anyway? She got out of bed and scrutinized the note. Kew Gardens. Up on Queens Boulevard. That would be the Q37 bus. She looked in the mirror. Why did the corners of her mouth hang down like that? Final, inevitable gravity, that was why. So this was it, eh? Or had the alcohol done it? The lot had done it. She might as well accept it. No mirror round the world had ever treated her so bluntly. All right, fine, she'd jog up there. There was no shame in aging. Or she'd walk. Yes, walking would be far more sensible. She could just see herself having a heart attack if she overdid it. An aspirin wasn't a bad idea, either. Her face would go on her just when she needed it. Just when she was falling in—oh, rubbish! She wasn't falling in anything. More likely she just wished she was in love to justify accepting the camera. Well, she wasn't going to let her panic go turning her into a prostitute, for God's sake. If she had been going to prostitute herself she could have done it long ago and over a lot more than a frigging camera. She blew her nose. She had to do something about her hair. She twirled one strand around her finger and held it up to the milky light. Old Iris still remembered her as a redhead. At least someone did. But really, if you held it a certain way it did still have sort of a glint. Sort of. Hmm. Maybe a rinse? Tch. American television! It made you want to be glamorous. She must stop watching it.

The geranium on the sill caught her interest. She loved them like this, with no real flowers to speak of but the blossoms ready to open. The color was wonderful then, very rich and true. All of it yet to come. Of course, it was possible that Iris hadn't been referring to her own hair at all . . . couldn't she have meant someone else? Someone else watching the house? A redheaded murderer? Why not? Claire regarded herself in the mirror and lit a cigarette. Christ. That fellow over at Holy Child, the one who'd been outside when they'd brought out the white casket, he'd had red hair. Even Freddy's lover, that bartender, was a redhead. What would he be doing snooping around here? Jealous of Zinnie? Good Lord. And that kid in front of the church, couldn't he have been the one to go after her cameras? Wouldn't he have reason to think she'd taken his picture? He'd certainly walked right into her frame. Only he had no way of knowing that she hadn't taken any shots. That would explain why he couldn't find the picture of himself . . . because there'd never been one. Oh, she should call someone. She must do that right away. Really, it was astonishing that they'd left her all alone here! If this were a film, the murderer would be under the porch already. Or in the closet. He might very well be in the closet. Or she. Claire felt the droplets of sweat breaking out on her scalp. Perhaps she really was over the deep end, as Johnny had suggested. Maybe she was the murderer herself? A true schizophrenic. Like *The Three Faces of Eve*! She sucked in her breath. She must be mad. What she needed was an English muffin. Cautiously, she left the room. There, on the landing, stretched puppy style with arms and legs flat out alongside himself, the Mayor stuck out his pink tongue in glad tidings. He had only just come out here in hopes of a draft.

"Well, hello there, cookie," her breathing relaxed. "Good to see you."

Down the stairs they shuffled, as close as they could get without tripping over each other. "On the other hand," Claire continued her train of thought out loud, "just because he had red hair doesn't make him a murderer. And just because he happened to be at church that time could have been mere coincidence." The redhead Iris referred to could have been an old woman's poor vision. Or suspicion thrown on someone else on purpose. Really, it was a nightmare. Halfway down, the doorbell chimed. "Now who," demanded Claire, "Is that?"

The Mayor bellowed roundly and tripped his reassuring, if no longer graceful, mazurka. The six alerted spiders on the mildewed walls adjusted their positions, and there was, just as she'd feared, nobody at the door.

Electrified, she stood stock still. There was no sound besides the Mayor's wheezing pant. The back door! She had to get to it before whoever was out there did. With breakneck speed she hurled herself across the hallway, through the kitchen, grabbing a knife from the gourmet countertop block of six along the way and onto the door she flew. It was locked. She stood there, her spine pressed against the wood, her kitchen knife one calla lily in her whitened hand. The Mayor watched with patent leather eyes. She was having, he presumed, what was known as a nervous breakdown.

"Hullo!" came a voice from the driveway through the creepers. "Anybody home?"

It was Mrs. Dixon.

"Hi," Claire answered back as cheerfully as she could.

"You all right in there?"

"Yes! Yes, fine. Just having breakfast." Even in her dither she knew enough not to add a "care to join me." The woman, once in, would never leave. She didn't mind feeling silly as much as she minded being bored out of her mind.

"Your mom asked me to look in on you," Mrs. Dixon explained. "They've got their bowling meet today, you know. The big one."

"Ah!"

"The end of summer tournament."

"Right. How could I have forgotten?"

"And you know your mom. She didn't like to go off and leave you, what with all the shenanigans going on . . ."

"Gee, you shouldn't have bothered. I'm fine."

Mrs. Dixon looked hurt.

"I really do appreciate your stopping off, though."

Mrs. Dixon shielded her eyes from the sun. "Perhaps you're not alone?"

Nosy old biddy, thought Claire. "Well, I do have the Mayor here. Ha, ha." They laughed together through the screen.

"Well then. I'll be on my way . . ."

"I'm just leaving, too," Claire assured her.

"Good-bye."

"Good-bye."

Claire watched her sturdy frame in sturdy summer shoes retreat through the yard and past the rabbits. "Five minutes with a woman like that," Claire said to the Mayor, "reinforces one's belief in making hay while the sun shines."

The Mayor grinned.

"Now listen. I'm going to take my shower and get going up to Kew Gardens or Forest Hills or wherever this garage is. I know you're going to be annoyed at me but you can't come with me this time. Now don't look at me like that. Someone's got to stay and watch the house."

Certainly, thought the Mayor. But he could do it just as well from across the street at Natasha's.

"You remember what happened last time," she poked him in his tender, portly ribs. "Oh, come on. Don't look like that. I'll be back this afternoon."

But four-thirty found her sitting slumped and even somewhat content over some fabulous white coffee and a peach-kiwi tart. She was up in the Gardens, right across the square from the Forest Hills Inn. It was as green and lush as only old money could make it. Ivy climbed white trellises and mauve stucco walls encased old lead paned windows. The cobblestone road encircled a caretaker's island. On one side were the steep yellow steps of the Long Island Railroad Station and on the other the sleepy Tudor shops. You really thought you were in Nymphenbürg or Bogenhausen.

Claire gazed morosely into her empty cup. The last time she'd had a cappuccino had been with Johnny, down in Sheepshead Bay. "What is it you're looking for?" he'd asked her. Kindly he'd said it, but directly, grazing her fingertips with his own the minute Red had left the table. He'd caught her off guard. "Plenty," she'd said just for something to say. "Oh," he'd sighed. "You see, with me it's different. I don't want too much. Just a boring, old-fashioned life if I can swing it. Like a family," he'd sniffed casually. "But then I don't have the kind of opportunities in life like you've got."

"No," she'd grinned back at him, tit for tat, "I guess

you don't." What a pompous ass she'd been. He'd been trying to be straight with her and all she could give him was a snippy answer like that. How much time she'd wasted worrying that he was just a cop when she should have been wondering if she were good enough for him. And now it was probably too late. "Quite honestly, your majesty," she addressed her higher power, "if you give me another chance here, I'll do my best to live up to it." She thought of the pile of laundry on Johnny's porch floor. "On the other hand," she added, "if you're saving me for something else, well, you certainly know best." Claire eyed her watch suspiciously. She'd parked the car over on Austin Street, the only place *to* park around here, and she'd been happy to find that, even if it was a meter. If they caught you parking in here, not only would they tow you, but they'd plaster your car windows with impossible-to-remove rebukes. Claire took a bite of the buttery-crusted tart. This was so good that she was going to have to have another. The rain-drenched vines hanging down the arcade shimmered prettily with sunlight and the start of a breeze. When she got herself a camera she was going to come back and photograph those houses along there toward the tennis club. Where the little red Porsche was coming down the lane. Good Heavens! That was Stefan! "Hello! Yoo-hoo! Hello!" she stood up tall and flagged him down. He didn't see her at first, but he had to come around the island to turn and then he did see her, guffawed right away, pulled the car right up to the café (gliding right through the red light) and hopped out without opening a door. He was wearing (what else?) his tennis whites.

"Now this is a pleasure," he shook her hand warmly and kissed her cheek. "May I join you?"

"Yes, of course. I was just sitting here dreaming."

"It is a delightful spot. Especially in this *chaleur*!"

Claire scurried her ice-cream chair over to make room for him. Vanished were the eerie feelings she'd had about him in the dark. He was so clean, the way the rich so often were. Right out of the locker room shower. A dental cleaning and gum massage every seven weeks. Ensembles that wouldn't dare pill. For one enraptured moment Claire saw herself waking up in a sunlit room in Stefan's house. She was swaddled in cashmere. A breakfast tray was on her lap. An Ida Lupino telephone jingled.

"Claire?"

"Huh?"

"I just asked you if you'd like another tart."

"Oh. Me? I couldn't! One of those is plenty. You go ahead."

When the waiter left with Stefan's order, Stefan whisked a dove gray suede packet onto the table. Out came a spotless mirror rimmed in jade and a cloisonné box. With all the finesse of a surgeon he poured out a perfect little mountain and divvied it up into several neat rows. Then he handed her a sterling silver straw. She shook her head no. He sniffed two lines up with wild, professional snorts and winked at her as he returned the paraphernalia to its purse.

"Don't look so disappointed," he said. "It doesn't become you."

"It's my dreams that don't become me, Stefan. And now that I think about it, they do tend to be becoming too much like perfume commercials. I keep telling myself I have to stop watching television but I just go on watching it. Maybe this will teach me. There are worse things than laundry after all."

"I don't get it. You're just too quick for me."

"I doubt that. You're way ahead of everyone." She sighed. "It's me. I still expect other people to step in and change my life."

"If you'd give me half a chance . . ."

"I mean like with a magic wand or . . . or . . ."

"Or what?"

"Stefan? Don't turn around now but do you see that guy over—no, don't turn around, I said!"

"Well, where then?"

"Just hang on. Because I think he's going over to the railroad steps. And then you won't have to turn."

"The one with the red hair? With the crossword puzzle book?"

"That's him. That's the one. Is he following me, do you think?"

"A bit young for you, wouldn't you say?"

"I'm serious, Stefan. I keep running into him."

"Well, you keep running into me, too. And I can assure you, you're not following me."

"Y'know Stefan, you're so frigging glib. You're really starting to make me sick. You act like I have no right to think someone might be following me. As though nothing horrible had happened to me. I mean, someone might want me dead. Actually dead and all you do—"

"I know where I know him from! Here let me light that for you. He's the bartender at Freddy's."

"You're joking."

"No. And I ought to know. I've tipped him enough."

"This is really weird. He's the same guy I saw outside the church at the funeral of the first victim."

"Are you sure?"

"I looked right at him through my lens. I remember like it was yesterday because he started to come toward me and I thought he was a relative of the dead kid and was going to ask me not to take any more pictures. Because he couldn't have known that I hadn't taken any to begin with. . . ."

Enthralled with each other's news, they turned together to look directly at their subject. He was sprawled on the steps, eyes closed, his upturned face inhaling the late yellow sun. Any American tourist collapsed upon the Spanish Steps in Rome. His crossword puzzle book lay open on his lap.

"And you want to know the best part of all?"

"What?"

"He's Freddy's boyfriend."

"Freddy's gay?!"

"Well, bi. He's also my brother-in-law. Or was."

"Now let me get this straight . . ."

"No, Stefan, it's all too complicated right now. Call the police."

"The what? The police? Why? Because someone you saw in two different places turns out to be the same person?"

Claire gnawed at her thumb cuticle. "Of course, you're right. Maybe I'm losing my marbles. Maybe Richmond Hill was the wrong idea for me altogether. Except that Iris mentioned a redhead spying on me. Well, she didn't say that exactly, but that's what she meant. I'm sure of it. Jesus. You try and get your life together and you do everything you can to do the right thing and then there are so many things that can go wrong. Not can. Do. That just *do* go wrong, you know? I know I shouldn't be thinking of life that way but there you go, I was born a pessimist. And an optimist. Back and forth, back and forth, my worlds play off each other. And always back to a guaranteed certainty that whatever can go wrong, will. A Murphy's lawyer, as it were. And then my childlike, superstitious, olley olley oxen free, if furtive, belief that if I keep that elephant trunk facing the doorway there . . . or if I pray from Grandma Maheggany's funeral parlor holy picture . . . or if the clouds up there are mackerel . . . then today will go well. You see what I mean?"

"Now Claire. Calm down."

"Oh, you don't get what I mean at all, do you? You and I might as well live on different planets. It's not just Park Lane South that separates our worlds. And another thing. Have you noticed that there isn't one single spider's web up here? Or anywhere near Metropolitan? But they're all over my neighborhood. Why?"

"Spiders?"

"I'll tell you why. Because there's something sinister approaching my family. I can feel it."

"I think you need a drink."

"You mean you think *you* need a drink."

He watched her warily. She was teetering toward the edge. He was wondering how he could remove himself without risking a scene. Fortunately, Claire seemed to be getting ready to go herself. She pulled a ten dollar bill out, slipped it under her saucer, and snapped her wallet shut.

"That should take care of it," she said.

"Please, let me invite you," he said, magnanimous with relief.

"Thank you, no."

"Well, then take back five. A cup of coffee and a tart are not ten dollars."

"I've had two tarts and two coffees," Claire sniffed with dignity.

"Ah," said Stefan, not knowing what else to say.

"My meter," Claire stood.

"Marvelous running into you," he gave her his most radiant smile and she wiggled her fingers at him.

Creep, thought Claire.

Bitch, thought Stefan.

The redhead across the way scissored his lips between two fingers and wondered, What's a four-letter word for *contradict*?

By the time she got home the breeze had turned to wind and the Mayor lay in the middle of it out on the lawn. This is the beginning of the end, is what he thought. It won't get any more summery after this. It will only get less. Before you could run around the johnny pump autumn would be close enough to bite you. That was the thing about summer. It started up slow, taking its fine time getting established, and then once it was there and you just figured out how to cope with it, it would hurry along all willy-nilly right before your very eyes. Rather, he pondered, like life.

Claire commandeered the boat of a car into the drive and pulled it up alongside the house, the way she'd seen Carmela do it. She got a little too close though, and had to disembark on the passenger side. Sliding over, she felt something sticky under her fingers. "Yuck!" she said out loud. It was Freddy's blood. She spit on her hanky then changed her mind and went into the glove compartment to find some tissues. They were crumpled but she used them, scrubbing with short, disgusted strokes. When she raised the vinyl backrest a crack to get the rest clean, she noticed something in there glitter. Sure enough, it was some sort of gadget—no, it was a cufflink. A cufflink in the shape of a roulette wheel! The Erie Lackawanna freight train roared through the neighborhood, obliterating everything but the green, green leaves on the trees.

Claire sank to the ground beside the Mayor. Her fingers, he noticed when she touched him, were clammy and trembling. "What does it mean?" she asked him, burying her face in his fur. "What on earth does it mean?" She didn't want to go on into the house just yet. She had to think. It meant, she supposed, one of two things: Carmela or Freddy. Carmela was out. She might not be in her right mind but she was not crazy. At least not that crazy. Was she? Good Lord, of course not. Claire remembered Carmela as a very little girl. She would wheel Michael and herself around the neighborhood in their broken-down stroller. She'd hated them fiercely but she'd kept a good eye on them. It could never have been Carmela. Freddy. Claire put her head in her hands and rubbed her eyes around and around. Who knew what he was capable of. She was going to have to tell Zinnie about this. The Mayor barked. She opened her eyes. There was Johnny Benedetto looking at her from his car. He was pulled up on the wrong side of the road, one fine dark arm crooked handsomely out the window.

"Hi."

"Hi."

"Still hanging out with your rich friend?"

"Oh, boy. I'm not in the mood for this."

Johnny made a sour, disgruntled face and pretended he was feeling his chin for stubble. He wasn't always, she noticed, the handsomest of dons. It didn't make her like him less, it made her like him more. At least he wasn't continually intimidating. He could be occasionally vulnerable.

"I like you a lot better," she said. "You're more my type."

"Oh, yeah?"

With that one shot of honesty he seemed to return to his complacent, obnoxious self.

"And now I'm very sorry I told you that," she told him, annoyed.

"Yeah, well, that's you all the way: give an inch and take back a yard."

"Am I? Am I really like that?"

"I don't know. Are you? What do you do, piece together who you are with your lover's odd remarks?"

"Jesus, I don't know." She patted the Mayor's head. "Are you my lover?"

"I'd like to be."

She looked up at him. "I've got to tell you something."

"Tell."

"I found this stuck in Carmela's car seat." She handed it to him. "And don't go thinking it must be Carmela, because I happen to know that it couldn't be. So forget about it. But she's been seeing—"

"Fred Schmidt."

"Yes. How did you know?"

"Those two have been painting the town. And they're pretty stupid if they think they're being sneaky. Then they've got that cabbage following them around everywhere they go. He sticks out like a sore thumb, with that red hair."

Claire stared at him. "Who?"

"The jealous boyfriend."

"Carmela has another boyfriend?"

"No. Freddy does. The one who's always hanging around here. Looking in the windows in the middle of the night. At first I thought he was spying on Zinnie. Then I figured out it was Carmela he had a case on. The jealous bartender. You must have seen him."

"Now I know who Iris von Lillienfeld was talking about."

Out the window came old "Sally Go Round the Roses." That meant Zinnie was home. All the more reason not to go in.

"You know I've got to take this over to the station house, don't you?"

"Sure."

"You want to come?"

"No." Not only didn't she want to, but the wet grass had turned her backside into a dark, round embarrassment. "I'm going to change. Do you want to come back and eat here?"

He grabbed her wrist and turned it over to look at her palm. "There's this house up on Eighty-fourth Avenue for sale. I don't know. You're not thinking of leaving town or anything, are you?"

"Am I supposed to answer as a suspect or a potential girlfriend?"

"It's got a front porch with screens. And a fireplace."

"Johnny, anything on Eighty-fourth is going to be outrageously expensive," she heard herself conspire.

"Yeah, but this is a real wreck. Pretty, though. That's why I thought of you, like." He coughed gruffly. "It needs a lot of work on the inside. But I figured you'd like an old kitchen from the forties."

It was, as a matter of fact, the only sort of kitchen she did like.

"And the outside looks kind of like a Swiss chalet. I mean it could. It has a real low overhang. And I'm pretty good with my hands. Really."

They searched each other's eyes excitedly.

"It's on a nice little piece of property, too. If I got a good price for my house. And I might. It's right on the track."

She couldn't believe she was standing there discussing

buying a house in Richmond Hill with Johnny Benedetto. Nor had she forgotten his nearness to the track. "Johnny," she laughed. "Aren't we jumping the gun a little here?"

"No. We're drawn to each other. That's not going to change." He let go of her hand. "Just keep it in mind."

She shook her head with an adult flourish.

"You and I," he looked her up and down, "we haven't even gotten started."

"Johnny, we don't even know if we really like each other, do we?"

"Claire. You and I, we know we like each other. Really."

Stan, at the window, pulling Mary's favorite red leaf around in the lettuce dryer, saw the two of them out there with their heads together. Now or never, he decided, and he went outside.

"And something else you might like to know about," she was telling him. "That redheaded kid who works the bar at Freddy's? He thought I photographed him outside the church after the first funeral. And I have reason to believe that he's been spying in my window. Someone told me they saw him. I think."

At least, they haven't gotten to the lovey-dovey stage, thought Stan. Mary would kill me if Claire took his camera before I told her about mine.

"Is that right?" Johnny seemed interested.

"I mean, I don't have it in for that kid or anything. Really. I would only like my cameras back if he had anything to do with taking them. I wouldn't press charges. I just want my stuff back."

"Unless it's needed for evidence," said Stan, immediately getting the gist of the conversation. "In which case you won't see any of it for a long, long time. Hi, Johnny."

"How's the boy, Stan?"

"Good. Good. Which brings me to the reason I came out here. Claire, do you remember my old camera?"

"No," she said, wishing he would go away.

"Don't let's start arresting people here before we have

anything on them," Johnny joked, raising his hands above his head.

"No, of course not. It's just that—"

"The Contax," Stan said happily. "You remember. From Zeiss Ikon. The one I brought home from Germany. With the 1.5 lens speed."

Claire frowned. "The only reason I mention him is because I saw him again today and Stefan told me—"

"Oh, so you are still hanging—"

"No, I am not. A 1.5 lens speed?" She turned to Stan. "Gee. I don't remem—"

"Of course you don't, because you were just a kid when I was using it. Mom just happened to mention that you might get a kick out of it. It's just wrapped up in the attic doing nothing."

"What's a 1.5 lens speed?" Johnny wanted to know.

"It's incredible," Claire's eyes shone. "It's almost equivalent to a human eye . . . it lets you take a picture in candlelight. Without a flash."

"And they don't make them like that anymore," Stan bragged. "Incidentally, it has the largest base range finder for accuracy distance measuring. And of course a built in light meter." He watched Claire's mouth begin to water. "The thing cost a thousand dollars in the forties. So you can imagine what it must be worth now."

"A kitchen and a camera from the forties," Johnny's hesitant smile lit up. "What else do you want in one day?"

"Yeah. Gee. What is this?"

Stan looked back and forth at them. Some sort of private joke.

Johnny sensed his discomfort (so did Claire, but she was hoping it would give him a hint) and he brought them back to Stan's camera. "So what did you do?" Johnny laughed, "take it off some dead Nazi?"

"In case you didn't know," Stan caught him up short, "military law dictated that all cameras, guns, and binoculars be turned in, at risk of being shot. We were ordered to put all of these magnificent guns and cameras in piles on the street and run over them with a half-track. Oh, geez, it was heartbreaking."

"So my father relieved the army of some of that diabolical task and sent a couple of them home," Claire said.

"Well. You wouldn't want to see them destroyed. So you see, this camera"—Stan was just getting warmed up—"can handle speeds up to twelve fiftieths of a second."

The Mayor rolled over onto his back and let the cool wet seep into his bones.

"Or, in layman's terms, one thousand two hundred fiftieths."

"I'm glad you clarified that," Johnny winked at Claire.

Claire smiled at him vaguely. She was far away, remembering another time and place. It was years ago. She'd taken a house on the island of Jamaica, in Negril. A magnificent little house, with a thatched roof and a small porch not twenty feet from the turquoise sea. Wolfgang had made a bevy of friends up at Rick's (where they all used to run into each other and watch the big orange sun plop into the ocean without fail each evening). She'd gone swimming every day. Lots of people would drop by and Wolfgang (an excellent cook) would concoct enormous meals. A lovely round woman named Emily, very shiny and black, had come with the house and done all of the cleaning up. "All your friends," she would marvel to Claire, "are so sophisticated and chic. My, my."

And then one day a new couple had arrived. They stayed in the house beside Claire's—alongside, not on the water. Their names, Claire remembered very well: Anthony and Theresa. They were on their honeymoon. Anthony, Emily had informed them while she swept the kitchen floor, drove a truck back at home where they came from. A small town, at that, on the south shore of Long Island. And he had a tattoo on his arm. "The south shore," Wolfgang had said, stirring his meringue suspiciously. "Isn't that the wrong shore?"

No one had bothered very much with the honeymooners. And, if truth be told, neither had they bothered much with anyone. They were neither sophisticated nor chic. Claire used to hear them laughing very late at night. She would turn in her bed and look at the beautiful iridescent green chameleon that lived on her wall and she would listen to them. They really were sort of vulgar. Claire would wake up later and later each day, somehow unrefreshed, and fall into the light blue water, where she would stay.

Finally the couple was leaving. Anthony, to everyone's amusement, had rented a boat to come and pick them up and take them near the airport so that they wouldn't have to drive halfway around the island in some dusty taxi. They had to wade out a good ways into the water to get into the boat. Claire had gone out with Emily to watch them go. They were very excited. There were gifts galore for family back on Long Island. Cheap, touristy gifts, but that was the idea, Theresa had defended them when one fell into the water and Anthony made fun of her distress. At last everything was on the boat. Out went Anthony with a last-moment-in-paradise dive. Theresa gathered her lavender dress around her (she was a big young girl) and out she walked, very slowly, erectly, forever holding this moment in her memory. Something caught in Claire's sophisticated heart. "My, my, my," Emily observed. "Now there goes a happy girl. A happy girl."

Claire had never forgotten either of them. And all of those fancy friends they'd spent their time with there were gone, forgotten and invisible.

"Claire?"

"Yes?"

"Don't mention this to anyone," Johnny said, tapping his shirt pocket, referring to the cufflink.

"No, I know. I won't. And Johnny? Come back safely."

Michaelaen trollied round and round his room. The waddle truck he sat on was for small boys but sometimes he would get back up on it for old times' sake. He could think and look at the television at the same time. "Mister Rogers" was on, and even though he'd let them all know he didn't watch him anymore, he did, and he even liked him a lot. Especially when they did the land of make believe. Michaelaen unwrapped his peanut butter cup and popped it into his mouth. There it would melt ever so slowly until it was the best taste in the world and then he'd chew his brains out. Mommy didn't go for that at all. She'd make her eyebrows wiggle down and then she always told what a good thing it was that the job had a dental plan, but she didn't say it like it was a good thing. Worriedly, he eyed the closet where his secret box was. He knew the marble was still in there because he remembered when he put it in there how it had looked. It had looked nice. He had to bring it back though, or maybe someone else would get in trouble, like Miguel. Poor Miguel. They'd sent him far, far, far away. He'd promised Miguel he'd put the marble back and he was going to only . . . and Grandma always said if you didn't do the right thing it would come back at you. So he was going to put it back. If he could just remember where the cufflink was. He scratched his head. He'd better check once more. He might have overlooked it when he'd gone in there to stash the pecan shorties. But no, he didn't think so. It would be much better to have them both when he went back, so he wouldn't have to go back there twice. Just the thought of going back at all made Michaelaen's whole head swim. Uh-oh . . . it could have fallen out of his pocket the same as his quarter had done that time.

First Michaelaen pretended that it didn't matter so much and he kept going in a circle around his room. Only he knew one thing. He didn't want anyone to get in trouble because of him. So he better not tell anyone. Maybe he could tell Johnny. He chewed the skin just healing around his tender thumbnail. But if he told, he could get Mommy killed. His breaths came short and quick and on his tongue he met that eggy, awful taste of blood.

* * *

In the kitchen it was busy and still. Claire sat at the table and chopped garlic and piñoli nuts into basil leaves and olive oil. The air was full with the fragrance and her taste-buds were almost anesthetized with the clovelike snap of the basil. She felt herself charmingly domestic and she hummed "Au Claire de la Lune." It was, she noted, imperative to have a western window like this in the kitchen. She even liked her mother's ginger red geraniums at the moment, all lit up like a *Ladies' Home Journal*. Of course, she would have done it a bit differently, with dwarf hollyhocks, perhaps, or even blooming king aloe and New Mexican cacti. She sliced a lemon in half and caught the bursting juice with the rim of the bowl. There were limitless possibilities. Although she wasn't sure if that house had a western window in the rear. Already she was scheming, she reprimanded herself. Of course she knew exactly which house it was he'd meant. It was the old Patton house. She'd passed it many times on her walks with the Mayor. She'd even looked at it, now and then, for its simple prettiness. She hadn't known that old Miss Patton, an old-world sort of still-wore-a-hat-to-tea old lady, had died. She was the kind of woman who'd leave a good spirit in the house, a Katherine Hepburn sort of a woman, both elegant and salty. And the house, if she remembered correctly, had nice, big, square rooms. She found herself mentally decorating the bedroom in dim yellow chintz. And then imagining Johnny, cold legs from night duty, climbing on top of her under the quilt, raising her nightgown and warming his hands underneath her soft hips . . . She caught her breath and cleared her throat and threw another clove of garlic in. Not to mention the twin dogwood in front of the house. Pure billowy white in the springtime and red as maple ivy in the fall.

The telephone jolted her out of her reverie. "Hello," she said while she smiled at the dog. He really looked like he could use a snack. She tossed him an entire Vienna finger—usually she reserved half for herself, but just now she could only be tenderhearted.

"Yes, hello. Is this the studio of Claire Breslinsky?"

"That's one way to look at it. Who's this?"

"This is Jupiter Dodd's office. Will you connect me with Ms. Breslinsky please?"

Claire pulled her foot down off the chair beside her. "This is she."

"Hold the line, please." The telephone crackled, Spyro Gyra carried on over light FM on hold, and then Jupiter Dodd himself broke in. "Claire!"

"Hi. Gee. What a surprise."

"Nice to hear your charming voice. Have your ears been ringing?"

"Sorry?"

"I've been talking about you to some friends. Have your ears been ringing?"

"Aunt Claire?"

"Actually, no."

"Aunt Claire?"

"Just a second, honey. I'm on the phone. I'm sorry, my nephew was talking to me. So you've been bad-mouthing me all over town, eh?"

"Ha, ha."

Michaelaen tugged on her shorts.

She opened her eyes to their widest circumference and clenched her teeth back and forth at him. Then she shooed him away with a brisk, determined backhand.

". . . so if you haven't already started work on the book," Dodd was saying as Michaelaen's hunched little back retreated out the door, "we were discussing using you to catalogue the gallery's American Women show."

"Which gallery?" Claire poked her nose through the blind and watched him meander out into the street. Iris stood out on her lawn raking seed.

"The Volkert."

Even she had heard of that one. But without all of her equipment . . . "I'm awfully sorry, Jupiter, but you see—"

"Of course, we'll pay your day rate."

"Yes, but . . . did you say day rate?"

"We don't pay more than day rate for catalogue. Nobody does."

"What sort of stuff is it?" She could always start off with her dad's Contax. Rent anything else she'd need. Day rate might not put a dent in a down payment for a house but it would go a long way toward buying chintz over on Grand Street and recovering Salvation Army furniture.

"Mostly modernistic. Objective symbolism. You know, message stuff. That Grillo has such a colossal conscience."

"That's okay. I even like that kind of thing. I admire significance." At least, she confided to herself, a job like this wouldn't compromise her treasured integrity. "To tell you the truth," she told him, "I'd jump at the chance."

"Hmm. I'm afraid there are a couple pop op things, if that offends you."

"Well, it does. But I'd overlook it for the chance to shoot the Grillos. She's very good. I might shoot them at the beach."

"The beach?"

"Yeah."

"Why not. I guess."

Michaelaen let himself out the back door and watched his ball bounce down the steps. Oh. The moon was already over in the sky and the sun was still out at the same time. That would mean something. Miss von Lillienfeld would know what. He walked carefully across the yard and said hello softly to the rabbits. The sprinkler was on, going easy does it back and forth with a squeak every time and he stood right beside it, waiting with his clenched-hard jaw until the inevitable arc of wet would crush him suddenly with icy cold. He knew that this time if he got caught, he'd really get in trouble. This time there wouldn't be Miguel or anyone to make the whole thing fun. No more taking silly pictures anymore, either. He whistled a little bit and looked around. Aunt Carmela came down from the bus stop and went in the house and then the coast was clear. Michaelaen took the screen off Mrs. Dixon's cellar window, climbed inside, and pulled the screen back up into place.

They hung up after ten more minutes of making plans. Claire rubbed her hands together energetically and looked around for the dog. She was going to give him a slobbering kiss. But he must have gone out. Anyway, he wasn't in the kitchen. Oops. She must go out and get Michaelaen. He really wasn't supposed to be out on his own.

"Michaelaen!"

"He's scouring the lawn for money."

"Carmela. Did you drop a cufflink in Freddy's car?"

"Lower your voice, if you don't mind."

"Just did you?"

"No."

"Good. Because I found it in your car—"

"Oh, my car! What a riot. I can't believe you got it back already."

"You're welcome. And I gave it to Johnny and he took it down to the station house."

"Took what down to where?"

"Carmela. This roulette wheel cufflink that I found in your car happens to be a clue. Maybe."

"Oh, I can't bear it. A clue. Who are you now, Miss Marple?"

Claire felt her pulse quicken. She could have strangled her. Instead, she told her about her new job. It did the trick, all right. Carmela smiled unconvincingly and turned scarlet.

"So, what is it, for a month or so?"

"Yeah, you know. As long as it takes me to cover each one. Maybe a couple of months." Screw her. She was fed up with always treading carefully around Carmela's ego. And it wasn't as though the pussyfooting helped any. She was as arrogant as ever, if not worse. "And by the way, if you're still interested in Stefan, I believe he's a free agent."

"You mean it's over with you two?"

"Most definitely."

"Meaning you're back on with Benedetto."

"Not necessarily. But yes." She grinned foolishly.

"Honey bunny, you are so stupid."

"I know."

"He'll be bringing home his beer-drinking cronies and they'll all sit around and talk dick talk and you'll be left with the wives listening to what miniseries they're watching that week."

"Maybe I'll start watching . . . oh, dear, no I won't. Hell. You can still love someone and be different from them. At least, I think not to try is horrible. Not to at least give it a chance."

"You'll wind up pregnant."

"So what? What the heck other sort of way should I want to be, seeing as how I'm in love with him?"

"And you'll get fat . . ."

"So I'll get fat. Christ! At my age there's no better reason to get fat. At least I'll be a real person with my own life. You know, you have all these great friends in town who adore you and they all love to have you around, and yeah, sure, of course, you're beautiful and amusing and who wouldn't want you around, but they all go home at night to their own places, their own homes. They close the door and there they are, together with their own lives. And where do you go? I mean, don't you ever want to find someone you can build something with? Instead of . . . of . . . of clandestinely screwing around with your sister's ex-husband?"

And of course, Zinnie stood just at that moment in the doorway with an ashen face.

"Thank you," Carmela narrowed her eyes and leered at Claire as one would expect a snake to leer. "Thank you very much miss better-than-everyone-else and God forbid you might forget to preach it to them because you've just ruined not one but two afternoons."

Mary and Stan steamrolled through the doorway, pushing Zinnie aside, thrusting plastic bags full of groceries at all of them. Claire got busy right away and then so did Carmela. They buried themselves in cabinets and put away soup cans and dog biscuits and sponges and Jello. Mary just kept handing them things and they just kept on putting away. Stan saw his chance and left and Mary stood there grumbling with her cereal boxes. "Well, Zinnie," she said, "are you going to just stand there like a lump on a log or are you going to pitch in and help?"

"I was just thinking," Zinnie drawled, "about the time we all went to visit Carmela and Arnold in their new home in Bayside—"

"Put that ice cream in the freezer before it melts," Mary said to Claire. "Now what's the Mayor barking at?"

"And just as we were leaving—boy, it's funny because I can remember it like it was yesterday—just as we were leaving and I was the last one out and it was so dark on that porch and Daddy was honking to hurry up and I went to kiss Arnold good-bye, did you know he stuck his whole tongue down my throat?"

Right then the kitchen went still and they all looked at Zinnie. "I mean, I was just a teenager—" she started to say, but she didn't finish, because Mary's hand shot out from across the room and whacked her smack across the face.

"And another thing!" Mary's strong voice roared at the three of them. "If the three of ye go after each other like cats, like blessed enemies, for pity's sake, where will you be when your father and I are gone? What will you do, stand paces apart above my casket? I ask you."

"Ma—"

"Don't interrupt me, I'll be through when I'm through. What did we go and have the lot of you for, if it was only to argue and bicker and hate yourselves till you're green in the faces and wrinkled with lines running this way from jealousy and that way from envy. And all these years I thought when you'd be grown you'd start to care for each other and I would be able to take a backseat and relax, only no, no, it sure won't be like that for a while!"

There the three women stood, their heads hung in adult supplication. Nothing had changed. She would mention her casket and they would all fall to pieces and promise to be good wee lassies once again. Until next time.

"Mary?"

"What is it, Stan? Can't you go back out and bring the dog in? He's driving me mad."

"Is Michaelaen in here?"

"Sure I thought he's with you!"

"He's out on the lawn, Dad."

"He's not."

"Yes, I saw him."

"Well, he isn't there now."

"Glory be."

They went out quickly, each of them taking off in separate directions. Michaelaen wasn't under the porch. He wasn't in the garage. He wasn't in anyone's car, a favorite place of his to be, just sitting in someone's car pretending he was going somewhere. He was, it became terrifyingly clear, missing.

Zinnie stood in the middle of the lawn and shouted his name, again and again, again and again. Her teeth began to chatter.

"Oh God, it's all my fault," Claire came outside after rechecking the house. "It's all my fault."

"Shut up," Carmela told her. "And shut the dog up."

Johnny arrived with Pokey Ryan in an unmarked car, for Stan had called the 102 immediately. They screeched to a halt and went right over to Zinnie. Johnny put his arm around her and cupped her head in his hand. "Now there's no reason to be alarmed . . . we've got no reason to think anything's wrong. But . . . you know . . . we just want to be sure. We want to get some help here, okay?"

Zinnie, holding her fist, shook her head yes. She didn't call his name hoarsely anymore, just every minute or so someone else would and the pain would greet her again, quickly and deeply, another knife in her gut. She couldn't think and she couldn't pray. She only whispered over and over, "God. Please. God. Anything. God. Please."

"Uh oh!" Michaelaen worried. They were all outside. He could hear them. They were looking for him. The darn old Mayor was going to make them find him. It was dark down here. He didn't like it anymore. Maybe he would just leave the things down here on that old shelf and go. But now he heard something else. It was Mrs. Dixon coming down the cellar stairs. He was more afraid of her than all the others put together. Once she'd even hurt Miguel. And then she'd given him money and stuff and taken all those pictures. He didn't think he wanted any stuff from her. He'd just hide for a minute and then when she went upstairs he'd go right home. Of course! He knew a good spot. That old refrigerator with the legs on it. It even had a nice light on inside. He climbed inside and shut the door.

"Somebody shut that fucking dog up," Johnny cried.

"It isn't the sound of the dog," Mary murmured. "It's that other, strange wild sound that's coming from the von Lillienfeld house. What is that sound, then? It is a banshee wailing, to be sure."

"Stop that superstitious nonsense," Stan yelled at her, frightened. "It's the cat. Von Lillienfeld's cat. That Siamese."

"So now we know what but we still don't know why," Ryan shuddered. Whatever it was, he didn't like it.

"That's the sound of the banshee, I tell you."

"So stay here if you want to, but I'm going over there to see what's going on." Stan headed across the street and the lot of them followed. Claire stood where she was. She would have to calm the Mayor down. What was he doing over there on Dixon's lawn, anyway? Between the cat wailing and the dog barking, she thought she'd go insane. She could turn the hose on him. You'd think he was trying to tell them something, the way he just wouldn't let up. She went to follow the hose to the nozzle but it ended out back on the sprinkler. What the hell, he was closer to Dixon's hose anyway. Claire went behind Mrs. Dixon's garbage cans to turn on her hose. There was one can lopsided on a rock, and as she leaned across it she knocked the lid off. As she went to put it back she caught sight of something down deep in the can. Some magazine or something on cheap paper, a star on a red background and a child on a horse. The star was a pentagram, it occurred to her as she turned on the hose. And the child on the horse had no clothes on. She turned the hose back off. The Mayor looked at her. She looked, alarmed, back at the Mayor. With one last, painful snort, he dropped down onto the grass and was finally quiet.

It was quite a while ago—weeks—when this whole thing had started. She and the Mayor had been sleeping on the porch. The garbagemen had made their way down the block and the noise had awakened her. A golden Plymouth had rattled down the block. And Mrs. Dixon had slammed the lid down on the can and hurried back into the house. Mrs. Dixon. What had she been so in a hurry about? Wasn't that the same day of the first gory murder? Hadn't she had a strange feeling then? A premonition of some sort? Or had she simply been a witness to somebody getting rid of something they would rather no one saw? A pervert did not a murderer make. And then she noticed the screen right next to her, a little crooked. A little off. A little crooked for a house whose screens were all in straight as little soldiers. It was utterly ridiculous to think of Mrs. boring old Dixon involved in anything underhanded. She was her mother's friend. Well, if not her friend, at least her dear old neighbor. With never a thought of suspicion. She and Mom walked to church together, after all. Since years. Years and years. They hadn't always. Something had started it. What had happened years ago? Something with Michael? Hadn't something happened to Michael that he'd never told her about? He was frightened of Mrs. Dixon. Yes, she knew that now. That's why he wasn't afraid to cut through Iris von Lillienfeld's yard the way the rest of them were. Because the yard next to his own held some secret more terrifying. All his false bravado had been fear. And Mrs. Dixon and good-hearted Mom had taken to walking together to church. Suddenly she remembered where she'd seen that strange captioned picture: in Michael's bottom drawer. Had Mrs. Dixon given Michael dirty pictures? Claire looked up at the big, fine house. She looked and looked. The garage door was open. Mrs. Dixon still kept Rudy's cars in there. Old cars, they were. From back in the days when all the cars they made were black. Claire could hardly remember Rudy Dixon, how he was before he'd had his stroke and turned into a whiskered, uriney thing to be left by the window in the front parlor. He'd been sort of bald and flashy back then. Yes, very flashy.

Claire remembered herself as a small girl, out here in the driveway, just like this. Mr. Dixon was pulling out of the garage and he'd stopped to say how do. She'd hated him because he called her Red. "Hi ya, Red," he'd said. "How do?" His beefy wrist was as still as an animal on the Pontiac door and his cufflinks, roulette wheels, had glittered like gold.

Claire returned to the present with a wheezing gasp.

"Johnny?" She shielded her eyes from the sun. "Johnny, can you come here a second? I don't know. This is stupid. But there's this screen loose here in a spot where Michaelaen could possibly have gotten into—"

"Who lives here?"

"Mrs. Dixon. You met her. My mother's friend."

Johnny remembered Mrs. Dixon. Hadn't Ryan even asked him who the hell she was? So many of those ConTact sheets they'd taken from Claire's darkroom had her kisser planted all over them. She was always getting in the way. Even the shots up in the woods were peppered with Mrs. Dixon.

"Who else lives here?" Johnny asked Claire.

"Else? Nobody else. She lives here alone."

"Here? In this place?"

They looked up at the big well-kept house. It was so big that it suddenly seemed strange to Claire as well. "It's just that I found something here in her garbage pail and I remember her husband, years ago, having a cufflink like the one I found in Carmela's car and . . . Jesus, Johnny, if she has Michaelaen—"

"All right. Calm down. Where's your mother?"

"They went over to Iris's house because her Siamese . . . Johnny, they all think Iris has something to do with this but I don't believe—"

He peered down into the can and gave a low whistle.

"You run over and get your mother so we can get through the front door and I'll try and jimmy my way in this way. You tell them something else. Tell them"—he smashed his foot through the window—"that the kids broke her window and they want to get their ball. Or see the damages. Just get inside. And get Ryan over here. Tell him what's happening."

"Johnny, if she hurt Michaelaen—"

"Hurry up. Go. Hurry up."

Claire ran across the street. In her mind's eye she saw Mrs. Dixon's plain, pale face. The sound of wind chimes and that face looking up at her from the alley. Those eyes had said something else besides what she had told her, that she'd come to check up on her. She'd looked at her with fear. Because she knew Claire knew without knowing.

Mary pounded on the big brown door. Then she rang the bell. She didn't know what they thought they wanted her to do over here. What would her Michaelaen be doing over here? Why, if they thought Mrs. Dixon had anything to do with . . . why the very idea—like walking backward through her memory . . . so very many years ago . . . she'd come across her Michael in the garage and Mrs. Dixon in there with him. But, of course, nothing had happened. Nothing, Michael had told her. Nothing had happened and he was crying from the fear of the dark. Or had she told him that so he would think it? She knocked harder on the grand oak door.

"Mary," Stan called, "we're going in here whether she opens or not. Just get out of the way and Ryan and I—"

But right then the door opened, a squad car pulled up, Miss von Lillienfeld came outside on her lawn and Mrs. Dixon, seeing them all, pee-ed right down the front of her nice rayon dress.

"Christmas," said Stan.

"Coming through," Ryan came up the steps.

"Michaelaen!" Zinnie cried again hoarsely.

"Michaelaen!" they all called, and they went in and went through the house and kept calling. Only Michaelaen was far far away from them now, and even the hum of the fridge from that moment of opening had stopped. Even the hurry up cold had just stopped.

Claire came down the stairs after Johnny. He was back at the furnace, all sooty, glad not to have found Michaelaen there.

"Come on," he said. "He's not down here. I checked all over."

"Where's my son?!" Zinnie's voice carried through the whole house. "Where's my baby?!"

It was finally over. Mrs. Dixon grasped hold of the back of her husband's cane chair and she knew it was finally over. If only that fool Claire had stayed away. But no. She'd had to return looking just like that little brat Michael who'd started the whole thing. It was all his fault. And now hers. Twins! They were both from the devil, that was where. Stirring things up. Making her remember. Why was Mary Breslinsky looking at her like that? So aghast.

Didn't she know this had nothing to do with her? This was separate.

So why did they keep up this shouting? What did they want? What did Mrs. Breslinsky's girl Zinnie still want from her? Didn't she know it was over? Hadn't she shown them the cameras? She'd never touched Michaelaen. Their precious Michaelaen. They should only know what a little pig he was. What cunning little pigs they all were. Innocent children! Ha! Innocent nothing. Hadn't her own father taught her all that. A hollow-sounding laugh ripped like gas from her throat.

"Come on, Claire." Johnny's voice sounded hollow in the cold, dismal cellar.

She turned with him to go, then looked for no reason back over her shoulder and noticed the trickle of water that ran from the refrigerator. She remembered the sprinkler. Only what would be worse, if he was there or if he wasn't? "Johnny? Johnny, the refrigerator."

She held her breath and watched the light bulb naked on a chain.

His head was on the wall of the sour refrigerator and his face, all pearly and closed, the color of drowned abalone. His hands and feet were blue.

"Helllllp," Claire called with no sound, like a dream where you're trying to run and go nowhere. But Johnny pulled him out, pushed her out of the way, and was running up the stairs and out onto the lawn.

"Get me some help here," Johnny shouted to everyone.

"My baby! Let me see my baby!" Zinnie shrieked, only Johnny wouldn't let her. He was down giving him mouth to mouth.

"Is he dead?" Carmela cried out.

"Hail Mary full of grace . . ." Mary prayed.

They were all coming out on their lawns. Everybody was out and they watched without talking. You could hear the short gasps Johnny made into his mouth, you could feel him breathe for him and the hope that waited, praying, inside every heart.

There was nothing.

Johnny lay down straight on top of him, smothering him, warming him, breathing for him. Making him live, goddammit, with all of the fury and faith he had in him. Come on. Come on. Live.

With an arc of his back like a lover's reply, Michaelaen jerked with one spasm and vomited wildly.

"Yeah," Johnny said to him. "Yeah."

And the ambulance came, the paramedics ran over, and Johnny stood up, covered with vomit and furnace soot, and Claire looked at him standing there and thought she would die of this great love that held her.

They brought Mrs. Dixon out with no trouble. They led her down the steps slowly, almost softly, her very best red ruby earrings clasped firmly to her fat, doughy lobes. The neighbors stood about. Mrs. Dixon worried someone would steal her shopping cart off the porch and one of the officers pulled it inside.

"It's hard to believe," someone said.

Iris von Lillienfeld leaned on her fence. It was true. Monsters never looked like monsters. They were always ordinary people. That's how they got away with evil as long as they did. Iris was suddenly beat. She could use, on this night, a stiff drink.

The Mayor, in the shadow, watched it all. He dare not close his eyes now. He wanted to see, be it hell or high water, which way he was going. And he was going. This had all been too much for his old soldier's bones. Surely, though, it had been worth it. To go out in a bright flame of glory. For he was going. It had all been too much. A hero's death. Yes, what better way. Perhaps a little sooner than he'd expected . . . but for the worthiest of causes. He moved himself and shifted his insides until the great pain lessened. One comfort: he would live on in his offspring.

That was something. Quite something. He thought of Natasha underneath the screened porch. She would look for him. Sadly. And Stan. How his dear friend Stan would miss him. He wouldn't want to go on for much longer like this at any rate. And he'd had a fine life. A long life. Up and down these old roads and the sidewalks raised up at the seams from good roots. Strong roots. Well. This night without him would be fine over old Richmond Hill. Very black and right dotty with stars. Ah, see that. Here came Claire looking for him. She cocked her head as she came over closer. "Oh, no," she whispered softly and she fell to his side and stroked his brave warrior's fur.

They watched together as the hollering ambulance drove the others away and then the quiet rose up with the moon until all of it seemed only terrible. Claire held him close to her then and she started to sing, any song come to mind, just the cheer of her mettle against any fear of faint heart.

He still realized the house . . . and the scents of the family within, growing farther and farther away now. "She wheeled a wheelbarrow," she sang, "through streets broad and narrow. Singing cockles and mussels. Alive alive-o."

And over the street in the pale sturgeon's moon, with the grace of his ancestor's, stood Lü the Wanderer, the old Siamese. He stretched and he walked through the web that had been there. "Singing cockles and mussels," Claire sang. "Alive alive-o," she sang to his bright open eyes.